"How old is Stacey, Leah?"

Boyd's voice was deceptively soft.

Leah didn't answer. She didn't have to.

He remained silent for a moment, watching the child playing in the lake.

"Who is Stacey's father?" he finally asked.

A cold pit opened in her stomach. "It doesn't matter."

His eyes speared hers. *"It doesn't matter?"*

She didn't blink. "No, it doesn't. I gave birth to her, I've raised her and I've loved her. She's my child."

His jaw clamped angrily. "Did you love him?"

Her shoulders slumped. She could only shake her head. How could she tell him that, in her heart, she'd always been faithful to *him*?

"Then why?" Boyd's eyes reflected agony and anger, bitterness and betrayal.

Dear Reader,

Welcome to the Silhouette **Special Edition** experience! With your search for consistently satisfying reading in mind, every month the authors and editors of Silhouette **Special Edition** aim to offer you a stimulating blend of deep emotions and high romance.

The name Silhouette **Special Edition** and the distinctive arch on the cover represent a commitment—a commitment to bring you six sensitive, substantial novels each month. In the pages of a Silhouette **Special Edition**, compelling true-to-life characters face riveting emotional issues—and come out winners. Both celebrated authors and newcomers to the series strive for depth and dimension, vividness and warmth, in writing these stories of living and loving in today's world.

The result, we hope, is romance you can believe in. Deeply emotional, richly romantic, infinitely rewarding—that's the Silhouette **Special Edition** experience. Come share it with us—six times a month!

From all the authors and editors of Silhouette **Special Edition**,

Best wishes,

Leslie Kazanjian,
Senior Editor

DIANA WHITNEY
Yesterday's Child

Silhouette Special Edition

Published by Silhouette Books New York

America's Publisher of Contemporary Romance

To Pat Teal,
with many thanks
for your support and encouragement

SILHOUETTE BOOKS
300 East 42nd St., New York, N.Y. 10017

Copyright © 1989 by Diana Hinz

ISBN: 0-373-09559-7

First Silhouette Books printing November 1989

All the characters in this book are fictitious. Any
resemblance to actual persons, living or dead, is
purely coincidental.

®: Trademark used under license and
registered in the United States Patent and
Trademark Office and in other countries.

Printed in the U.S.A.

Books by Diana Whitney

Silhouette Special Edition

Cast a Tall Shadow #508
Yesterday's Child #559

Silhouette Romance

O'Brian's Daughter #673

DIANA WHITNEY

says she loves "fat babies and warm puppies, mountain streams and Southern California sunshine, camping, hiking and gold prospecting. Not to mention strong, romantic heroes!" She married her own real-life hero fifteen years ago. With his encouragement, she left her longtime career as a municipal finance director and pursued the dream that had haunted her since childhood—writing. To Diana, writing is a joy, the ultimate satisfaction. Reading, too, is her passion, from spine-tingling thrillers to sweeping sagas, but nothing can compare with the magic and wonder of romance.

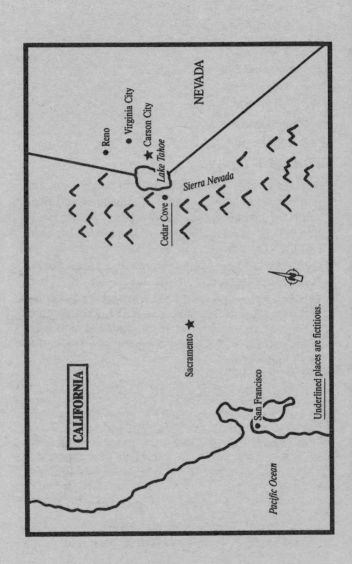

CALIFORNIA

NEVADA

• Reno

• Virginia City

★ Carson City

Lake Tahoe

Cedar Cove •

Sierra Nevada

Sacramento ★

• San Francisco

Pacific Ocean

Underlined places are fictitious.

Chapter One

This wasn't the worst day of Leah Wainwright's life, but it certainly ranked among the top three.

Through a black net veil, Leah watched the Lake Tahoe fog spiraling like steamy fingers, encircling the forest in a damp, gray grip. Its eerie pall shrouded the mourners, creating a mood appropriate for the sad occasion that had brought Leah back to Cedar Cove, the cloistered community of her childhood.

As the minister's voice droned on, Leah numbly closed her eyes, mentally visualizing her father's face. So many years had passed; so much grief. Her memories were vague, blurred by a passing decade and shadowed with pain.

Leah remembered having been in awe of her father as a child, almost frightened of the huge man who appeared like an apparition late at night and disappeared with the light of day. Louis Wainwright had been isolated and distant, yet unquestionably the master of the wife and child who hardly knew him.

Still, she could recall good times—flashbacks of a lanky, stern-faced man offering an ice-cream cone. Her father's eyes had gleamed with pleasure as he'd bestowed the rare treat, and for that small moment, Leah had felt cherished. Sadly, such moments had been too few and far between.

Beneath Leah's feet, the grass was coated with the clammy chill of morning dampness. She was cold—cold to the bone. A whisper brushed the air, a voice she recognized as her own: "I'm so sorry, Papa."

With a discreet sniff, Leah dabbed her wet eyelashes and turned toward the rigid woman beside her. "Are you all right, Mother?"

Cybil Wainwright nodded stiffly and tightened her gloved grip on a crumpled linen handkerchief. Over the years, Cybil had been desolated by her family's alienation but clung tenaciously to the futile belief that eventually past wounds would heal, old scars would fade. Now, hope was gone.

Her mother had aged, Leah realized, and the heavy drape of black linen made her seem thinner, even more fragile than she actually was. Cybil's hair, once a glossy black mane, was peppered with gray and pulled into a tight bun. Her face was lined by pain, her eyes filmed with confusion. She seemed broken, emptied by the years of neglect and grief.

Grief that Leah had caused.

"Mommy?" The tiny voice broke into Leah's thoughts as the small hand she held squeezed a request for comfort. "You look so sad."

Pulling her daughter closer, Leah gave her the solace she herself sought. "It's always sad to say goodbye," Leah said softly, automatically stroking the child's silky hair.

Stacey's lips quivered. "Do you think my grandpa would have liked me?"

"I'm certain he would have loved you, darling." Leah choked out the words as her chest constricted painfully. To Stacey, Louis Wainwright was merely an image from faded photographs, spoken of in the hushed tones of strained and muted voices. Leah pushed away the seeping guilt, the secret sadness. Her daughter was the light of her life, and had Louis Wainwright not been such a rigid, unyielding man, she could have been the light of his life, as well.

But that was in the past—a past that was beyond Leah's control.

Stacey shifted uncomfortably, then poked at a furry dandelion bloom with the toe of her shoe. "Everybody is looking at us."

For the first time, Leah glanced at the group gathered at the gravesite, recognizing most as longtime residents of Cedar Cove. Although her father had had many acquaintances, he'd had few friends; and those who'd come to pay their respects seemed more curious than somber.

Two of the mourners, however, seemed genuinely grieved. One was Lottie Varner, an earthy woman who was Cybil's closest friend. Then a squat, bald man caught Leah's attention and although she didn't recognize him, he was quite obviously distraught. Tears slid from tiny eyes to apple-red cheeks, and a bushy, copper mustache clung to his contorted mouth like a prickly horseshoe.

As Leah's gaze swept the remaining group, she realized that her daughter had been right. Everyone *was* looking at them—staring, actually, with inquiring eyes and intrusive glances.

Obviously, ten years hadn't dulled their memories.

Leah fought a desperate urge to turn and run. This was just too difficult. She should never have brought Stacey back to Cedar Cove.

But somehow Leah managed to swallow the momentary panic. Protectively tightening her arms around her daughter, she raised her chin, staring beyond the throng, returning their speculative looks with feigned indifference.

Then Leah saw him.

"Mommy, you're squeezing me," Stacey complained.

Unblinkingly, Leah's gaze locked on a broad-shouldered man standing tall and alone. He met her stunned stare with guarded eyes and Leah felt the blood drain from her face. The last person she'd wanted to see in Cedar Cove was Boyd Cauldwell; but perhaps it had been inevitable. Deep down, Leah had known that Boyd would eventually seek confirmation of what he must already suspect.

As Boyd's gaze dropped to the child at her side, Leah defiantly lifted her head. In spite of her false bravado, a lump formed in her throat, a choking ache for what might have been.

Boyd had changed over the years. The collegiate zeal Leah remembered had faded and his amber eyes, once bright with youthful idealism, were now veiled, cautious and wary. His thick mahogany hair used to be in a constant state of unruliness, as unrestrained and rakish as Boyd himself had been. But that devil-may-care appearance had been tamed, scissored just as his formerly mutinous mane in a rich red-brown hue was marred by a silver slash spilling across his forehead.

That metallic-colored spray combined with deep creases etching his cheeks to make him appear older than thirty-one, but neither diminished his solid good looks or masculine appeal. In fact, Boyd was even more attractive than Leah had remembered—if such a thing were possible.

But Leah knew that she, too, had changed. Ten years before, a child had left Cedar Cove. It was a woman who had returned.

And Boyd was judging that woman, searing Leah with the unblinking intensity of his gaze. Leah felt her skin heat under his blunt appraisal. She saw deep sadness in his eyes and was surprised at the force of her own aching response to his pain. Leah realized he was visualizing the girl that she once had been; the girl who had loved him.

And the girl who had betrayed him.

As Boyd watched Leah, he wondered why on earth he was subjecting himself to this torture. Oh, he'd mentally argued that he would be expected to pay respects to one of Cedar Cove's longtime residents. At weddings, funerals or baptisms, the Cauldwell family—financially prominent and politically astute—was always represented. The fact that Leah would be at this particular event had had no influence on his decision to attend—of course it hadn't.

And Tahoe deer sprouted wings instead of antlers.

In truth, Boyd had simply wanted—needed—to see Leah again. But he hadn't expected his chest to constrict at the very sight of her. He hadn't expected his mouth to turn dry or his knees to go weak. And never, in his most poignant fantasies, had Boyd expected that his seventeen-year-old childhood sweetheart would have metamorphosed into this raven-haired beauty.

Boyd's thoughts were in turmoil over whether or not Leah had changed—and if so, how much. When it came to Leah, Boyd's thoughts rarely made sense. Her impact on him was still mind-boggling, and Boyd decided that studying Leah in segments might give a more dispassionate view.

Narrowing his gaze, he first noticed how much thinner she'd become, with her sleek figure accentuated by a slim skirt and fitted jacket. Her hair was different, too. She used to wear it long and flowing, but now it was pulled into a sophisticated coil and anchored beneath a veil of black net.

Hushed voices buzzed, the crowd shuffled, and Boyd realized that the service had ended. As the mourners dispersed, some stopped briefly, offering sympathy to Leah and Cybil. Like iron drawn to a magnet, Boyd followed them, his gaze locked on Leah's clear aqua eyes.

"Thank you for coming, Boyd."

The sound of Cybil's voice startled him. Reluctantly looking away from the woman at her side, Boyd took Cybil's hand. "I'm so very sorry," he said. "Louis will be missed."

"Thank you." Cybil managed a thin smile. "Everything has been so...so sudden."

"It was a tragic accident." Seeing a fresh film of tears in Cybil's eyes, Boyd released his grip, allowing her to blot the gathering moisture. He stood awkwardly, realizing that the expected amenities had been completed and he should leave. But Leah was so close, and as her sweet, familiar scent caressed him, Boyd was reluctant to break the fragile link with her.

"If there's anything I can do..." Boyd winced at offering the standard words of condolence.

To his surprise, Cybil nodded somberly. "As a matter of fact, Louis didn't have a lawyer. At least, I don't think he did." She shrugged apologetically. "He didn't confide in me on business matters. I don't want to be a burden, but I'm not sure what should be done."

"I'd be happy to help."

Cybil's expression softened and she turned toward her daughter. "Isn't that a relief, dear?"

"Yes," Leah whispered. And at the sound of her voice, Boyd felt a familiar prickling sensation skitter down his spine.

Boyd permitted himself to look at Leah again. His heart pounded once, then seemed to stop momentarily. How he'd dreamed of her all these years! Leah, with midnight hair and morning eyes still as blue as a clear mountain sky.

He found his voice. "It's good to see you again, Leah."

"You look well, Boyd."

They stood stiffly, warily, measuring the mutual effects of passing years: soul mates of the past reduced to mundane formality. Boyd felt a sense of loss as acute as the day she'd left him.

A small movement caught Boyd's eye. Leah followed his gaze and her shoulders stiffened slightly. "This is my daughter, Stacey."

Curious eyes, as blue as her mother's, regarded Boyd. The hair was lighter, the nose more snub but there was no doubt that this was Leah's child. But the wide, thin mouth and blunt, cleft chin were features that could only have been inherited from . . . the man who had fathered her.

The forceful reminder tore through him. Boyd stared at the little girl as though she were an alien life-form, before Leah's voice yanked him from the unpleasant reverie.

"This is Mr. Cauldwell, honey. He . . . he's an old friend."

"Hello, Stacey," Boyd said, managing a thin smile. "I'm pleased to meet you."

Stacey snuggled against Leah, demurely dropping her gaze, then peeking up at Boyd with a shy, dimpled grin. The familiar gesture sliced through him like a well-honed ax. In Stacey's guileless expression, Boyd recognized a child of the past: the child Leah had once been.

Boyd felt Leah watching him carefully—too carefully. Was it regret he saw in her expression? Perhaps she, too, was remembering times when they'd held each other for hours, unable to bear the thought of separating. For years, Boyd and Leah had laughed together and cried together. They had shared the awakening passion of youth and had been completely devoted to each other.

Or so Boyd had believed. . . .

Images flashed through his brain, crisp and clear as though it had happened yesterday.

"I love you," Leah had sobbed against his chest. "I'll wait for you always."

"I love you, too, honey." Boyd's voice had cracked with emotion. "I'll be back at Christmas break and we'll have two whole weeks together."

Leah had wiped at her wet face. "That's months away. I can't bear it."

"It's hard for me too, but by next year, you'll have a diploma, I'll have a bachelor's degree and we'll have a marriage license." He had caressed her damp face and felt as though he might just explode with the force of emotion. "You'll be my wife, Leah. We'll have the rest of our lives together."

Then he'd kissed her sweetly and she'd molded herself to his body until passion flared into molten fury. Even as Leah whimpered in protest, Boyd had managed to tear his mouth from her honeyed lips. "Only a year, baby," he'd whispered raggedly. "When we make love, it'll be as husband and wife. Then we'll love each other always."

Offering a brave smile, Leah had murmured, "Always means forever."

Pulling his mind from the past, Boyd watched Leah turn away, supporting her mother and towing her daughter toward a waiting car.

It was strange how things turned out, he mused sadly. When he'd gone to college that fateful autumn, he'd been certain that no two people in the world had ever been so in love.

Then something had gone wrong—horribly wrong—and Boyd had returned to Cedar Cove amid sympathetic glances and whispered rumors. But Leah had left. Sweet, innocent Leah had deceived and abandoned him. Boyd now realized that all the rumors had been true.

"The proof" was holding Leah's hand.

The old frame house hadn't changed in ten years. Pulling into the driveway, Leah turned off the ignition and scanned the familiar vista. Beyond the house, the lake still shone like a giant sapphire encircled by the jade-green forest, and the crisp, sweet scent of pine and cedar brushed the air. A branch rustled in the breeze and Leah heard the raspy shriek of a distant jay.

South of the house, Leah's old tire swing hung quietly, years of neglect evidenced by the fraying rope and brown pine needles caked around its core.

Nothing had changed. Everything had changed.

Leah vaguely felt the back seat shudder and heard the slam of a car door, as though from a great distance. She pulled her mind from the fog of memories and was aware that Cybil was still in the passenger seat, watching quietly.

"Mommy? Are you and Grandma coming?"

Leah blinked and saw Stacey standing on the wide, covered porch. "Yes, darling, we're coming," Leah answered, opening the car door as confirmation. She felt a gentle pressure as Cybil touched her arm.

"This is difficult for you," Cybil said quietly.

Leah smiled and patted her mother's hand. "It's difficult for all of us."

"You know what I mean, dear."

Yes. Leah knew exactly what Cybil meant. Stepping around the car, Leah opened her mother's door and helped her up the porch steps. Taking Cybil's key, Leah unlocked the door just as Stacey squealed and pointed toward a fallen log. A fat squirrel skittered across the rotting bark, then sat on its haunches with its tail splayed like a fuzzy gray fan.

Stacey was ecstatic. "Can I feed him, Mommy? Please?"

Smiling, Leah stroked her daughter's cheek before twisting the doorknob. "Change your clothes first, then we'll see what we can find."

As the child bounded up the stairs of the Wainwright home, Cybil went into the living room and dropped wearily onto the faded sofa. As though the effort were too much, Cybil extracted an immense hatpin from her tightly knotted hair, then dragged off the heavy veiled bonnet and set it on her lap.

Leah was instantly concerned. "Are you all right, Mother? You look positively exhausted."

"Hmm? Oh, of course, dear. I'm fine." Cybil managed a thin smile, then her eyes glazed and her lips pursed in concentration.

Leah recognized the symptoms. Cybil had never been one to openly discuss her feelings, so Leah had learned at an early age to interpret more subtle clues: the tightly drawn mouth, the small brow crease and Cybil's quiet, preoccupied manner all suggested that something was troubling her deeply.

Of course, her mother would be troubled. Cybil had just lost her husband of thirty years, and although Leah knew her parents' relationship had never been ideal, she realized that Cybil must be experiencing a tremendous sense of loss.

Leah sat on the sofa and squeezed Cybil's hand. "Please, Mother. Let me help you."

"You've already helped just by being here."

"There must be more I can do." Cybil's gaze darted to the floor and Leah knew that there *was* something else—something Cybil hesitated to ask. Suddenly Leah had a thought: "Is it the store?"

Surprised, Cybil looked up, rotating her palms helplessly.

"What are your plans for Wainwright Hardware?" Leah asked.

"I don't really have any. I know so little about your father's business." Cybil sighed. "Don't concern yourself, dear. I'll talk to Simon tomorrow."

"Simon?"

"Yes, Simon Sprague. You met him this morning."

Leah thought back. "Was he the stout man with the shiny scalp and busy red mustache?"

Cybil nodded. "Simon came to Cedar Cove about seven years ago. His wife had recently passed on and he was looking for a new start."

"Papa hired him to work at the store?"

"Yes. He's been a good friend to Louis—and to me. I'm sure he'll keep the store running until I decide what to do. It's just that . . ." Cybil's voice trailed off and she dropped her hands limply into her lap.

"What is it, Mother?"

"Well, it's just that I wouldn't know where to begin. Inventories, ledgers, bank accounts—everything is so complicated." She slid Leah a glance. "I could call Boyd, I suppose, but he's a lawyer, not an accountant."

Leah finally understood. "I'd be glad to analyze the books for you."

Obviously relieved, Cybil closed her eyes and sagged against the sofa.

Leah removed the bulky bonnet from Cybil's lap. "Why don't you go upstairs and rest for a while?" Leah suggested, placing the hat in the coat closet.

Shaking her head, Cybil replied, "I can rest right here." Reverberating thuds echoed from the stairs and Cybil's eyes lit as Stacey, tucking a plaid blouse into her jeans, skipped into the living room. "Besides, it's been too long between visits, and I don't want to miss a moment." Cybil patted the cushion and Stacey cheerfully accepted her grandmother's invitation, bouncing onto the sofa. "My, you've grown!"

Stacey beamed. "Everyone says I look much older than nine."

Cybil's eyebrow lifted. "And that pleases you, child?"

"Oh, yes. I want to be all grown-up, like Mommy."

Leah felt a pang. "Childhood is much too short, darling. Someday you'll wake up and it'll all be over." There was a sadness to her voice. Leah saw her daughter's inquisitive expression and forced a lighter tone. "This should be a wonderful time for you, Stacey. Enjoy being a little girl."

Stacey straightened indignantly. "I'm *not* a little girl. I'm almost a teenager."

"Ah, yes. Adolescence—the scourge of parenthood." Leah rolled her eyes. "I can hardly wait."

"Oh, Mommy, you're funny," Stacey said, giggling, then turned toward Cybil. "Can I have a cookie, Grandma? And one for the squirrel?"

"Of course, dear. They're in the bumblebee jar on the counter."

"Oh, boy!" Springing from the sofa, Stacey ran across the room and disappeared into the kitchen.

Cybil smiled sadly. "She's such a beautiful child, Leah. So bright and happy. I only wish Louis..." The sentence dissipated. Wishes were useless; the past was irrevocable.

Leah brushed shaky fingers across her brow and turned away. She didn't want to discuss it. The kitchen door squeaked, then slammed, and Leah seized the opportunity to change the subject. "Stacey's going to turn those squirrels into cookie addicts. After we go back to Sacramento, you'll be surrounded by obese rodents in the throes of chocolate-chip withdrawal."

Cybil lifted an eyebrow. "How long will that be? Before you have to leave, that is?"

"I'll stay as long as you need me."

"But your job? How can they go so long without a bookkeeper?"

"I have two weeks' vacation coming and the people I work for are wonderful. If I need more time, I'm sure I can get it."

Cybil knotted her hands in her lap. "Thank you," she whispered. "Having you and Stacey here means so much to me. To hear my grandchild's footsteps on the stairs, to know that you are really here, in this house...it's almost like you never left."

"I know." Leah sat beside Cybil and hugged her mother's thin shoulders. "But it's not as though you haven't watched Stacey grow up. She loves you so dearly and absolutely counted the days each year, waiting for your visit."

Cybil smiled wistfully. "I counted the days, too. Your father was upset that I disobeyed him, but I went anyway. And after a while, he seemed to accept it."

The conversation was strained. Although Leah and Cybil had remained close through the years, they had scrupulously avoided discussing the issues that had ripped the Wainwright family apart. With Louis's death, forbidden subjects were being laid open, and the process unnerved Leah.

Even so, the question flowed out before Leah could stop herself. "Did he ever...ask about us?"

Cybil glanced up warily, then stared down at her own knees. "Not in so many words."

The confirmation hurt. Standing quickly, Leah swallowed, then tested her voice as she walked briskly toward the kitchen. "How does a hot cup of tea sound? I'll put the kettle on—"

"Boyd never married, you know."

Leah stiffened.

Cybil's voice quivered and cracked. "You've always been there for me, Leah. Even when you were a girl, it was almost as if you were the mother, worrying about me and listening to my problems." She made a small choking sound as tears clogged her throat. "And then, when *you* needed *me*, I let you down."

Clutching the doorframe for support, Leah said, "It wasn't your fault, Mother. I never blamed you."

"You should have. The Lord knows how often I've regretted not standing up to Louis, how often I've cried because I let him send you away." Cybil was pale and the skin seemed to shrink against the bones of her face. "Things were never right between Louis and me after that. I couldn't seem to forgive him, even though I knew that he was going through his own kind of hell."

It was more than Leah could stand. "Don't," she whispered. "Please don't say any more."

"He convinced me it would be best for you to raise your child somewhere else. At first, I think he honestly believed that, but eventually I knew something else was tearing at him—guilt, maybe. I don't really know. I always felt that Louis was keeping something from me, and that the secret was chewing him up inside." Closing her eyes, Cybil took a deep breath. "Still, I was cowardly and selfish not to have fought for you, Leah. I never realized how much you had sacrificed until I saw how Boyd looked at you this morning . . . and how you looked at him."

Leah closed her eyes. "You're misreading the situation, Mother. He came to offer sympathy, to pay his respects—nothing more."

Ignoring the limp denial, Cybil was lost in the impact of her own words. "All those years, and you never spoke of Boyd. But today, I saw the pain in his eyes and in yours, as if it had only happened yesterday. I should have realized—'' Biting off the words, Cybil focused on Leah and whispered, "I'm so sorry."

Leah silently cursed that her heart had been so visible. Had everyone recognized her pain, her regret? Had Boyd? Shaking her head, Leah could only say "It's over."

"No, child," Cybil said. "It's not over between you and Boyd. It's never been over. Even when he came after you, I was too wrapped up in my own grief to notice how devastated he was at losing you."

Air rushed from Leah's lungs. "He...did what?"

"It was about a week after you went to Aunt Jo's. Someone had called him at the university, I suppose. I'm not exactly sure how he found out you'd left Cedar Cove." Automatically Cybil flicked away the words, which indicated she felt that how Boyd had learned was unimportant. "He beat on the door until Louis threatened to call the police, than he camped on the front porch for two nights, saying he wouldn't leave until he knew where you'd gone. I never saw a man so distraught. Suddenly he went away, and we heard later that he'd gone back to school. It seems strange, now that I think about it."

"The letter," Leah mumbled.

Cybil looked up, confused.

"I sent Boyd a letter from Aunt Jo's."

"Did you tell him...what happened?"

"No." Leah fought intrusive tears. "I wrote that I was too young to settle down and that I wanted to meet new people, see new places."

Cybil's lips tightened and Leah sensed her disapproval. "I see."

"I couldn't tell him the truth, Mother." Leah hated the pleading tone of her voice but seemed helpless to control it. "You must understand why he couldn't know."

Sighing, Cybil rubbed her eyelids. "Of course I understand, dear. But after all these years, don't you think he deserves to know?"

Leah stared. "You've got to be joking. It would kill Boyd if he knew...everything."

"Perhaps you're underestimating him. You're not children any more. You've both changed."

Ignoring the sudden throbbing in her chest, Leah blinked away the image of Boyd's face. The man she'd seen this morning, the man who had eyed her with speculative caution and spoken polite platitudes, wasn't the boy she remembered.

Yes, Boyd Cauldwell had changed, but Leah's reaction to him had not. He still touched her deeply, stirred those dormant yearnings. Only Boyd could evoke the sweet, deep ache that was tormenting her now, as it had tormented her so many years ago.

Cybil was speaking again and Leah tried to focus on her mother's words. "... running the campaign."

"I, ah, I'm sorry. What campaign?"

"For a seat on the County Board of Supervisors."

"Oh." Leah was disappointed, but not surprised. Cedar Cove residents had always assumed that Boyd would enter politics, following in the footsteps of his powerful father, Senator Fletcher Cauldwell. Leah, however, had always hoped that he would follow his own dreams of defending society's weak and indigent. Apparently the senator had won—again.

Leah managed a pleasant tone. "Boyd will be a fine representative. I know he'll do a wonderful job."

Cybil cocked her head, watching Leah's reaction. "Boyd isn't the candidate, Leah. Craig is. Boyd is managing his brother's campaign."

Leah's skin went cold. Craig Cauldwell was still in Cedar Cove.

Trying to compose herself, Leah locked her hands together and forced a strained smile, determined to conceal her inner turmoil. "Now, how about that tea?"

"Thank you, dear," Cybil said, regarding Leah somberly. "Tea would be lovely."

As Leah went to the kitchen and filled the ancient kettle, conflicting emotions surged like a swollen lake after a winter storm. Every moment in Cedar Cove was filled with painful memories and she felt helpless against their mental assault. Leah had known that returning to her childhood home would mean facing those people who had caused her desperate flight so many years ago. But she'd sadly under-estimated the emotional blow of confronting her past.

And nothing could have prepared Leah for the trauma of seeing Boyd again. That had been an ordeal she'd never anticipated. There had been sorrow in Boyd's eyes, and veiled anger. But something else had been reflected in his riveting gaze—something filled with passion and with promise.

The golden liquid sloshed gently as Boyd absently rolled the brandy snifter. He stared into the glass and saw Leah's eyes staring back, sparkling with youth and laughter and love, as he'd remembered them all these years. Then, as he watched, mesmerized, the image transformed, becoming sad and wary and filled with loss.

"What in hell's the matter with you, Boyd? You got a bug in that brandy?"

Startled, Boyd looked across the study into his father's frowning face. "Were you speaking to me?"

Fletcher Cauldwell's pink jowls vibrated and he spoke with a fat cigar clamped between his teeth. "I sure as the devil have been trying, but it's like filibustering an empty room."

"Sorry," Boyd replied blandly, then set the glass on the gleaming coffee table. Leaning against the soft leather back of the armchair, Boyd focused his attention.

Indomitable, intimidating and irascible, the senator wasn't accustomed to being ignored. A mass of snowy hair frizzed across his scalp like an electrified cloud, and thick white eyebrows shot out at odd angles, as unruly as the man himself.

The elder Cauldwell squinted fiercely, his expression of displeasure deliberately calculated to frighten small children and subdue political foes. Such tactics had never worked with Boyd, who merely returned his father's annoyed glare with a calm, direct stare.

The senator broke the visual stalemate, converging on a more satisfying target. "Craig! Get your tail over here, boy. We've got work to do."

Craig, who had been pouring himself another brandy, nearly dropped the crystal decanter. Liquor sloshed from his nearly full glass as he spun around, startled by the senator's tone. Boyd saw a glimmer of anger and hoped that, for once, his brother would stand up to their father. Even when they were children Boyd had demanded respect from the senator, while Craig had merely begged for approval.

With a blink, the brief flare in Craig's eyes died, to be replaced by a familiar, vapid expression. Years of obedience training wouldn't be challenged tonight. Boyd was disappointed but hardly surprised. The brothers couldn't have been more different—in personality as well as appearance. Craig was taller than Boyd, loose-boned and wiry. His sand-colored hair was slicked straight back, whereas Boyd's dark hair always seemed windblown and untamed.

Neither man resembled the senator, each having inherited the predominant features of separate mothers. Boyd's warm eyes, dark hair and wry humor were the legacy of his affable mother. Craig was heir to the stubborn chin and tight, wide mouth of the woman who'd borne him, but he hadn't inherited her forceful personality. If life was a stalking beast, Craig Cauldwell was its prey.

"Dammit, boy, we don't have all night!" Fletcher Cauldwell was not a patient man.

Chugging half of the brandy in two quick swallows, Craig quickly crossed the room and took his seat.

"Now, then," the senator drawled, "let's just see who we're up against. There's that Wilcox fellow, but with the kickback business last year, he couldn't get elected chief cook at a fish fry. It's Koblowski I'm worried about." Cauldwell leaned back, tapping a blunt finger on the arm of his lounge chair and stared at Boyd for confirmation.

"He could be tough," Boyd agreed. "Incumbents usually have the edge in a close election, and Paul Koblowski has been on the Placer County Board of Supervisors for four years. He's got a fine record and he's clean."

Cauldwell grunted irritably. "He's been in politics too long to be clean, but he's damn sure smarter than most. We've got to dig a bit deeper, that's all."

Craig, perched stiffly on the edge of his chair, nodded somberly and took another swallow. "I've got Jason working on Koblowski."

Boyd frowned. "Mike Jason and Associates?"

"Sure," Craig said. "They're expensive, but they've already come through. Did you know Koblowski's sister had a nervous breakdown a few years back?"

The senator rubbed his hands together. "Sounds like a pretty unstable family to me."

Obviously pleased by his father's approval, Craig smiled. "And they've just started their investigation. By election time, we'll have him nailed to the wall." The youngest Cauldwell relaxed slightly, absently brushing the lapel of his suit as he did so.

Boyd recognized the gesture as one the senator used when he felt in control of a situation. Boyd also knew that Craig frequently aped the senator's behavior, even in his choice of apparel. Both men favored expensive three-piece suits, a contrast to Boyd's preference for washable slacks and loose sweaters.

Craig was like a love-starved puppy seeking scraps of kindness from a stern master, and he dogged the senator's every move. Even when Craig married, he'd brought his bride into his father's home. Five years and two children later, Craig's family still resided under the senator's roof.

Boyd loved both his brother and his father, but he wasn't blind to their faults. He did, however, choose to ignore those faults because he understood the root causes. After Boyd's mother had died, Fletcher Cauldwell's second wife gave him another son, then deserted them both. Craig's resemblance to his strong-willed mother was unfortunate. The senator's younger son was a bitter reminder of the woman who'd defied and humiliated the Cauldwell name. Craig had always been either criticized by his father as a weakling and a disappointment, or else totally ignored.

Until recently, that is, when Craig, desperate to win his father's attention and approval, decided to follow in the senator's footsteps by embarking on a political career. Boyd had agreed to help, hoping that mutual goals would solidify a relationship between them.

But this Koblowski business left a sour taste in Boyd's mouth, and family relationships aside, he had no intention of becoming involved in a muckraking, mudslinging free-for-all.

"No," Boyd said quietly.

The senator frowned. "What do you mean, 'No'?"

"No Jason and Associates, no negative campaigns, no rattling of closet skeletons." Boyd rubbed his neck and wished he'd volunteered to mail leaflets instead of managing his brother's campaign. "I realize this is a quaint notion, but I believe Craig should run on the issues."

Craig blinked. "Issues?" He gulped more brandy.

The senior Cauldwell's eyes narrowed. "Well, excuse me, Mr. Political Expert. As past president of your high-school class, you'd naturally know a hell of a lot more about campaigning than someone who's only been a state senator for sixteen years."

Amused, Boyd made no attempt to pacify his father's ruffled feathers and allowed him to vent his indignity.

Flushed with annoyance, the senator huffed and grumbled, his belly straining the buttons of his suit vest. "Placer County stretches from North Tahoe to Roseville and that's a powerful hunk of land. You think those folks'll vote for some fuzz-cheeked kid five years out of college unless they don't have a choice?"

The senator chewed his cigar, eyeing Boyd with grudging respect. Then a tiny smile twitched the corner of his mouth. "So what did you have in mind, son?"

Stalling for time, Boyd picked up his brandy, swirling it while he gathered his thoughts. He couldn't shake a sense of uneasiness with the entire situation. The loyal speech he'd just given notwithstanding, Boyd knew his brother was ill-suited for the pressures of politics. Still, the election meant so much to Craig and a victory would boost his brother's sagging self-esteem. Besides, in a weak moment, Boyd had promised to help and he took his promises seriously.

Setting down his glass, Boyd reached into a briefcase beside the chair and pulled out a manila folder. "Three candidate forums are scheduled in September and October. We have six weeks to prepare for the first. The Cauldwell name has widespread recognition throughout the northern part of California, and that's the ace we'll use to offset Koblowski's incumbent status."

The senator nodded politely, but seemed unconvinced.

Boyd continued. "Since Koblowski's divorced, stressing Craig's family-man image could be beneficial. We might want to consider some flyers with photos of Bitsy and the kids."

Craig brightened. "Bitsy would like that. She'd even go to luncheons and rallies—"

The senator interrupted, ignoring Craig's suggestion. "Family man, huh? Traditional values—God, the flag and apple pie." Fletcher pulled a lighter from his pocket and absently fingered it, then turned toward Boyd. "I like it. What's the setup?"

Boyd had seen the familiar frustration etched in Craig's face. Even now, in what should be the beginning of his brother's biggest triumph, Craig seemed invisible. It was Boyd to whom the senator turned for answers. It had always been that way.

Watching his brother, Boyd said, "What would you like to do on this, Craig?"

Gratefully, Craig looked up and realized that he had Boyd's undivided attention. And the senator's. "I'd like to stress the family image, too. My wife has a lot of contacts and I know she'd like to help. She belongs to some powerful women's organizations and I think she could gather some valuable endorsements."

Interrupting with an impatient gesture, Fletcher said, "Never send a woman to do a man's work. If an endorsement is worth having, go out there and get it yourself."

Craig's smile died and he downed his remaining brandy. As the senator rattled on about time schedules and campaign slogans, Boyd watched Craig wander unsteadily over to the liquor cabinet.

"So we'll need a firm plan before then," Cauldwell went on.

Boyd dragged his gaze from Craig. "Before when?"

With obvious annoyance, Cauldwell repeated himself. "Before the legislature's summer recess ends on August 1.

Then I have to go back to Sacramento and be a good little senator."

Boyd shrugged. "Only for a month." Congressional recesses, state or federal, always seemed such a waste to Boyd. There were Christmas recesses, spring recesses, summer recesses and a three-month lull between sessions, which, coincidentally, was also election time.

Sacramento was a two-hour commute from Cedar Cove, too much of a daily grind when the legislature was in session, so Fletcher kept an apartment a few blocks from the senate chambers. This house had been built for the senator's second wife shortly before Craig had been born. It was referred to by Cedar Cove residents as The Cauldwell Mansion and reflected a gracious elegance that starkly contrasted with the squalor of the senator's childhood. With single-minded determination, Fletcher Cauldwell had clawed his way to wealth and power, until his colorful vocabulary and coarse manner were the only relics of his itinerant past.

The past. Again Boyd's thoughts shifted to Leah—to the fragile strength and quiet dignity of the woman he'd once loved. Seeing her again had inflamed old wounds and Boyd realized that the emotional trauma of losing her, though long suppressed, had never really healed.

"What is it, son?"

Boyd was startled by the concern in his father's voice.

Cauldwell watched Boyd shrewdly. "Your mind's been meandering like a drunken mule on a crooked road. You sick?"

"No, just tired. I think I'll go home and get some sleep." Rubbing his forehead, Boyd tried to exorcise the blue-eyed image from his brain. "By the way, I brought a wreath to Louis Wainwright's funeral this morning."

The senator's lips pursed. "Louis Wainwright is dead? How did that happen?"

Craig seized the opportunity to show his expertise in local affairs. "Some workmen were replacing the sign in front of his store when it slipped and hit Louis in the head. The story was in last weeks' paper."

"I wasn't *here* last week," Fletcher said with exaggerated patience, then turned back to Boyd, regarding him somberly. "Wish I'd known. I'd have made a point to pay my respects and see if Cybil needed anything."

"I've already offered to help settle Louis's affairs."

Boyd saw surprise in his father's eyes. Cauldwell reached for his glass, choosing his words carefully. "I'm glad you were there to represent the family, son. I'll call Cybil tomorrow with my sympathies."

"I'm sure she and Leah would appreciate that."

The senator's hand froze in midair and Craig choked on his brandy.

"Leah?"

Boyd frowned. "Yes, Louis's daughter."

Craig pulled a handkerchief from his breast pocket, and blotted the sticky liquid from his wool slacks. His voice was strained. "I, uh, thought the Wainwright kid left Cedar Cove for good. Why did she come back?"

Boyd stared at his brother in disbelief. "Craig, her father just died. Why do you *think* she came back?"

"Oh, sure," he said with a nervous laugh. "The funeral."

The senator reached over and put his hand on Craig's knee. Craig stopped mopping and looked up, flinching at Cauldwell's commanding stare. There was a communication between the two men, a palpable sense that something significant was being shared.

Boyd's shoulders knotted. "You both seem to have a problem with the fact that Leah's back in town."

The senator recovered smoothly. "Not at all, son. It's just that, well, we remember how hard you took it when she left." Standing, he slapped Boyd's shoulder, blinked rapidly, then emitted a jovial laugh. "We should've realized that you'd long since gotten over that little gal. Right, Craig?"

Craig looked sick. "Right," he mumbled.

"After all, now that Louis is gone, Cybil will be needing her family. Yessir, I'm real glad that Leah's back."

Cauldwell was grinning broadly and his eyelids twitched as if he were sending Morse code. Boyd tensed, alerted by his father's reflexive spasm.

The senator always blinked when he lied.

Chapter Two

As Leah guided the car toward the outskirts of town, Stacey pressed her nose against the window. "Look, Mommy! There's a park under those trees with a playground and everything."

"That's not a park. It's the elementary school. I went there when I was your age."

"Really?"

Leah laughed at the disbelief in her daughter's voice. "I was in the fourth grade once, just like you."

Stacey considered this. "It must have been an awfully long time ago."

"Thank you very much. Twenty-seven isn't exactly ancient, you know."

Giggling, Stacey returned her attention to the passing view.

Cedar Cove hadn't changed much over the years, Leah noted as they drove past the line of small stores that made up the business district. There were subtle differences. The old feed store was now a boutique and the bait shack had been replaced by a modern gas station. But Ray's Pharmacy looked exactly the same, and beside it was the stucco-and-wood building that housed Wainwright Hardware.

Stopped at a red light, Leah stared at the faded sign that bore her family's name.

"What's wrong, Mommy?"

"Umm? Oh, nothing, honey. Nothing at all." The light turned green and Leah gratefully drove away, determined that nothing would spoil the day she'd planned for Stacey.

Suddenly, Stacey asked, "Did my daddy live here?"

Leah felt icy perspiration bead her upper lip. She'd always tried to be honest with her daughter, but Stacey's father was an uncomfortable subject and Leah was frequently evasive. After all, her daughter was just a child, much too young to understand the sordid details. Still, it was an understandable question and Leah decided to give a direct answer. "Yes, he did."

Stacey was immediately intrigued. "Is he still here? Can I meet him?"

Leah's fingers tightened on the steering wheel. She'd had similar conversations with her daughter, but here, in Cedar Cove, the subject took on new urgency. She expressed herself cautiously. "I don't know where he is now, darling." That was technically true, Leah thought miserably.

"Oh." Stacey was obviously disappointed. "That's okay. You and my daddy just wanted different things from life, right?"

Leah had told Stacey that many times and smiled, knowing that the conversation would now take a predictable and comfortable course. "That's right. And what else?"

"And you wanted me more than anything in the whole world."

"Yes, I did. And when you wrapped your tiny hand around my finger, I said..." Leah paused, as usual, so Stacey could complete the sentence.

She did, but her delivery lacked the normal enthusiasm. "You said that I was your very own and you'd love me forever and ever."

Something in the small, sad voice caught Leah's attention. Glancing over, she saw her daughter pensively staring out the window and Leah's heart filled with love. It still amazed her that such a terrible mistake could have produced such a miracle of joy. There had been difficult moments—moments like this when Stacey had asked about the man who had fathered her.

Over the years, Leah had answered as truthfully as possible, yet had always managed to elude the issue of exactly who that man had been. Some day, Leah knew, the child would have to be told. Some day, but not now.

"I wish . . ." Stacey's voice trailed off.

"What do you wish, darling?"

She shrugged softly. "Nothing. I was just thinking about Annie." Annie lived in Sacramento and was Stacey's best friend. "Annie's dad doesn't live with her, either. But he comes over sometimes and takes her places."

A hot mass formed in Leah's throat and she felt a deep, aching guilt. The one thing Stacey wanted—a father who loved her—was the one thing Leah couldn't provide. Women had dominated her daughter's world. Stacey had no father, no grandfather, and since Leah rarely dated, no male role-models of any kind.

"Are we almost there?"

"Umm?" Leah realized they were winding into the forest and she tried to get her bearings, searching for the dirt road that would lead to a secluded area of the lake.

Slowing the car, Leah scanned the thick forest, looking for a telltale break in the trees. "I think so, but it's been so long. Maybe the road isn't even here anymore—oh, there it is." Turning right, she eased the car down a steep incline.

"It's so pretty. The trees are so big, just like at Girl Scout camp." Stacey rolled down the window for a better view. "There's the lake!"

Leah parked the car in a small clearing and pulled the picnic basket from the back. After clambering out, Stacey caught the blanket Leah tossed to her, then ran down to the water's edge. By the time Leah reached her, she was already pulling off her tennis shoes.

"Can I go swimming now?" Stacey yanked her T-shirt off and Leah saw that she wore a bathing suit under her clothes. It was tight and the child tugged at it in a futile attempt to improve the fit. "I'm fat," she wailed.

"No, you're just growing fast, exactly as you're supposed to."

Stacey wriggled out of her jeans, tossing them in a heap and Leah saw the suit's elastic was cutting into her thighs. "I guess it *is* time for a new swimsuit, though."

"A bikini? Please? All the girls in junior high wear them."

"We'll see."

Stacey apparently took that to mean "Yes," and happily clapped her hands. The child's exuberance was contagious and Leah laughed. "Help me with the blanket, then you can give your suit a farewell swim."

"Okay," Stacey said, then spread her half over the soft grass. "Now?"

Smiling indulgently, Leah nodded but instead of rushing toward the water, Stacey hesitated. "I wish Grandma could have come. She'd like it here."

"I know, but your grandmother was feeling tired this morning." Too tired, Leah thought. Cybil had lost weight in the months since their last visit, and Leah was concerned by her pinched, pale appearance. Although Leah had tried to attribute the change to the stress of Louis's death, she had nagging doubts. Before she returned to Sacramento, Leah vowed to get Cybil in for a checkup.

A high-pitched squeal captured Leah's attention.

"It's cold." Knee-deep in the clear water, Stacey splashed happily. "Watch me swim!"

Leah knew that the small inlet was shallow, but the lake deepened quickly in open water. "Don't go beyond that big rock," she called, then stretched out on the blanket to watch her daughter play. There was a sense of déjà vu, being in this very special place. It had been *their* place, hers and Boyd's. Memories flooded her, warm and comforting, and she gave herself over to the sweet images.

There had been days filled with fun and laughter. There had been soft, warm nights filled with sweet kisses, the tender promise of young love. In the winter there had been snowmen and snow fights, followed by a crackling fire in the Cauldwell cabin.

The cabin. It was a quarter mile farther down the dirt road and Leah remembered it fondly. Before the senator had made his fortune, the cabin had been the Cauldwell home. It was the house where Boyd had been born and his mother had died.

When the senator had remarried, he'd built the huge house now known as The Cauldwell Mansion, but it was the cabin that Boyd had always considered to be his real home. He'd asked Leah to live there with him after they married.

They'd both been so young, so untouched by life's realities. It had been a sweet time, a safe time. Leah closed her eyes and gave in to her memories.

Lazily leaning against the lacquered stern of the sleek motorboat, Boyd watched Craig struggle with his tangled fishing line. Frustrated, Craig muttered an explicit opinion of the situation.

Boyd smiled. "Here, hold my rod and I'll see if I can get you back in business."

Craig wiped his forearm across his sweaty brow and squinted glumly at his brother. "I can do it."

Shrugging, Boyd pushed his ratty fishing hat low on his head and closed his eyes, enjoying the late-morning sunshine. Craig would battle the twisted nylon for another five minutes and then, as he'd already done four times this morning, he would swear loudly and thrust the knotted equipment at Boyd. Patience had never been one of Craig's virtues.

Except around their father. In the senator's presence, Craig had always been as docile and tame as a kitten.

"Boyd?"

"Hmm?"

"I was just wondering...." Craig hesitated.

With supreme effort, Boyd lifted one eyelid. "Wondering about what?"

"Well, uh, you said that Louis's kid was back in town."

Every sun-warmed muscle in Boyd's body cooled instantly, bunching with tension. His reply was a clipped affirmative.

Craig was nervously plucking at the mass of loops wrapped around his reel stem. "Do you know... I mean, did Leah say how long . . . she'll be staying?"

"I didn't ask." Pushing his canvas hat back with the tip of his finger, Boyd regarded his brother's unsettled demeanor.

"Not long, I imagine." Was that relief Boyd saw in Craig's face? "Why do you ask?"

"No reason," Craig answered cheerfully, tugging at the useless line.

Shifting his own rod, Boyd straightened, rubbing sudden tension from his neck. "Since you're so interested, I'll make a point of asking when I see Leah."

Craig's reel clattered to the boat floor. "You're . . . seeing her again?"

"Yes."

"W-why?"

Good question, Boyd told himself. He'd spent half the night thinking about Leah, dreaming about her; and by dawn, he'd decided that he simply had to see her again. The past still haunted him, and would continue to do so until he understood exactly what had gone wrong so many years ago. Perhaps if he had some answers, he could get that blue-eyed apparition out of his mind and go on with his life.

Aware that Craig had repeated his question, Boyd rotated his shoulders in the most casual shrug he could muster. "Cybil has asked me to help with a few legal details."

"Oh." Craig licked his lips and gave the tangled line a savage jerk. "Damn it!" His face turned red. Grabbing the whip end of the pole, Craig hoisted the entire rod over his head and violently beat the side of the boat.

Boyd's head snapped up. "Hey! That's the senator's best spinner."

Cursing viciously, Craig bashed the equipment until Boyd pried the slaughtered remains from his convulsive grip. Panting, Craig clenched his fists and stared at the bent metal scraps scattered on the boat floor. A vein at his temple bulged, pulsing rapidly.

Irritated, Boyd slid back onto the stern bench. He didn't bother to ask what had caused the tantrum. Stress was something Craig simply couldn't handle. Boyd knew that Craig could go months—years, even—without a break in his amicable docility. Eventually, however, every day pressures would mount and cause the inevitable explosion. This one hadn't resulted from the frustration of a tangled line, Boyd realized. The entire election process had taken its toll on everyone, but particularly on Craig.

With a gasp, Craig's eyes widened in comprehension. Apparently the potential consequence of his action had seeped in. "I-it wasn't my fault," Craig mumbled. "The stuff shouldn't break like that. It must be cheap junk."

Boyd knew that the fiberglass equipment had cost a small fortune, but it wouldn't help Craig to hear that.

"But it wasn't my fault," Craig insisted, his voice rising to an annoying whine.

Boyd soothed and placated, never disagreeing that Craig couldn't be held responsible for the smashed rod and reel.

Propping his elbows on his knees, Craig moaned and dropped his face into his hands. "The senator will kill me," he whispered, then looked up at Boyd with wide, pleading eyes. "What am I going to do?"

Boyd glanced at the shattered fishing rod. It was quite obviously beyond repair. "I'll take care of it," he said, making a mental note to order replacements that afternoon.

Craig smiled gratefully. "Just like the time I wracked up the senator's car? Do you remember that?"

Sadly, Boyd nodded. Unfortunately, he did indeed remember that incident and too many other, similar ones. The automobile accident had occurred when Craig was fifteen and Boyd was nineteen. The senator had been out of town, as usual, and Craig had sneaked a joyride in their father's prized luxury car. The results had been disastrous, but Boyd had accepted the responsibility.

Boyd had always accepted responsibility. If Craig had been in danger of failing a high-school class, Boyd had dutifully agreed that the teacher's expectations were probably too high and had completed his brother's assignments. It had simply been the easiest way to maintain family peace and protect Craig from the senator's harsh discipline.

Clearing his throat, Craig said, "You're the best brother I ever had."

The standard joke calmed Boyd, bringing a smile to his lips. "I'm the *only* brother you ever had."

Craig grinned. "I'll make it up to you."

Nodding, Boyd bent to clean up the broken parts, dumping the evidence into the lake. Then he cautiously approached a sensitive subject. "Craig, are you certain that this supervisorial post is what you want?"

"What?"

"Perhaps it would be better for you to get a few more years under your belt before you tackle a county-wide election."

"I have to win this election." Craig seemed on the verge of panic. "Once I get that job, I'll *be* somebody, and the senator won't treat me like a brain-damaged toddler. He'll be proud of me." Craig reached out and grabbed Boyd's wrist. "I can't do this without you—you know that. Please. You've never let me down before."

Sighing, Boyd stared down at the hand convulsively gripping him. "I'm not going to let you down, Craig. If you're certain this is what you want, I'll stand by you, just like I always have."

Craig's breath slid out with a soft whoosh. Releasing Boyd, he sat back, visibly relaxed.

Boyd was far from relaxed. In the past, Boyd had suppressed niggling doubts about Craig's emotional stability, and today's episode had brought those doubts bubbling to the surface. Unpleasant memories pushed into Boyd's mind as he recalled yanking a baseball bat from his brother's hands before Craig could attack the neighbor's barking dog. Then there had been the time Craig had been cut from the high-school basketball team and Boyd had caught him trying to burn down the gymnasium.

Of course, the senator knew none of this. Boyd had protected Craig then, and would protect him now. Craig was his brother, after all; and to a Cauldwell, blood was very thick indeed.

* * *

Leah sighed, stretching on the soft, familiar grass and enjoying her mental sojourn. Her reminiscences were broken as Stacey flopped onto the blanket and shook her soggy brown hair. "I'm hungry," she announced and immediately began rooting through the lunch basket. She pulled out a sandwich bagged in plastic. "Is this cheese?"

"No, that one's ham."

She wrinkled her snub nose. "I like cheese sandwiches better."

Leah pulled the basket onto her lap and began to search. "Well, we'll just have to find a cheese sandwich, then, won't we?" She received no answer and when she looked up, her daughter was staring back toward the road.

"Hi," Stacey said.

"Hello," replied a male voice. "It's a beautiful day for a picnic."

Leah froze.

"Yeah," Stacey agreed cheerfully. "Mommy said this is her very favorite place."

Swiveling around, Leah followed her daughter's gaze and saw Boyd walk out from the trees.

He hesitated, as though unsure of his welcome. Leah's mouth went dry at the sight of him. Yesterday at the funeral, his behavior had been as formal as his dark suit. Now, dressed in a loose sweater and worn jeans, he seemed taller, more powerfully built than she remembered. He exuded an aura of pure masculinity that literally took her breath away.

"Hello, Leah," he said softly. Their eyes locked and the air was charged with current.

Boyd was nervous, and the feeling irritated him. This was just a woman, he told himself—not an apparition. His palms were suddenly damp and he jammed them into the pockets of his jeans. "I didn't mean to intrude," he apologized. "I saw the car." He gestured helplessly toward the road.

It was Stacey who broke the tension. "Are you hungry? We've got lots of sandwiches."

Leah seemed to come out of her trance. "Yes, of course. Please join us."

She didn't have to ask twice. During the morning's fishing fiasco, Boyd had created and discarded a dozen excuses for seeing Leah again. The problem had conveniently been solved when Boyd had spotted the car, recognizing it as the one Leah had driven from the funeral.

Stacey offered Boyd a cup of lemonade, shyly returning his smile as he accepted the drink, then sat on the blanket.

"Is this your favorite place, too?" Stacey asked.

"Yes. I live just over the rise."

Leah looked up, surprised. "At the cabin?"

He nodded and saw her eyelids flutter downward. He felt a surge of pleasure that she'd remembered.

Boyd sipped the cool liquid and Leah nervously emptied the basket, then busied herself by dusting leaves from the blanket. Only Stacey, happily chewing her sandwich, seemed oblivious to the strained silence.

Boyd cleared his throat and turned toward the young girl. "It looks like you've been swimming." It was a mundane comment, but it started the ball rolling.

"Uh-uh. I can float and do the back stroke. Mommy taught me. She's a real good swimmer."

"Yes, she is." Boyd slid an amused glance at Leah and saw the flush creep up her face. "But then, she had a good teacher."

"Who?"

"Me. In fact, your mommy learned to swim in this very cove."

Stacey's eyes widened. "Really?"

"Absolutely. Of course, I didn't have much choice. I was afraid she'd drown herself." Leah warned him with her eyes, but Boyd saw the corner of her mouth twitch and knew she wasn't particularly annoyed. "Your mother was fifteen years old and had spent her entire life next to a lake but was scared spitless of the water."

Finally, Leah defended herself. "That's an exaggeration! I could swim."

"Like a rock swims."

Leah smiled and shrugged. "I will admit that your instruction helped improve my technique a little bit."

Arching an eyebrow, Boyd reached for a potato chip. "'A little bit'?"

"All right. A lot." Turning to Stacey, Leah said, "You see all my friends water-skied and I wanted to learn how—"

Boyd interrupted. "But she couldn't swim a stroke, so no one would take her out." Seeing Leah's indignant look, he added, "She *did* learn quickly, though."

Stacey was fascinated by the entire conversation. "Did you get to water-ski, Mommy?"

"Uh...well, yes. Once."

Boyd choked on his lemonade. Leah glared at him.

Not willing to let the subject go, Stacey persisted. "What happened?"

"I just didn't care for it. That's all." Leah threw the empty sandwich wrappers into the basket, then concentrated on straightening the blanket. Stacey was watching skeptically and Leah finally tossed up her hands. "Okay, okay. If you must know, I fell."

Leah saw Boyd turn away, then his shoulders began to shake and she heard his muffled laughter. It *had* been funny, Leah acknowledged, although she hadn't thought so at the time. Boyd had dragged her from the water, gasping and nearly blue.

Lips twitching, Leah said, "Go ahead. Tell her the rest of it, since you're enjoying this so much."

"Tell me what? What's so funny?"

Straightening, Boyd composed himself. "It's just that when your mother fell, she forgot to let go of the towrope and shot through the water like a torpedo. I think she swallowed half the lake that day."

Leah folded her hands primly. "You told me not to let go of the rope, and I didn't."

Chuckling, Boyd turned to Stacey. "You see the thanks I get for saving her life?"

Covering her mouth with both hands, Stacey rocked with delight. Charmed by the girl's openness and cheerful enthusiasm, Boyd reached out to tweak her nose.

Stacey immediately hugged him warmly. "I like you. You're nice."

If Boyd was stunned by her unexpected affection, Leah seemed horrified. "Stacey!"

Eyes rounding at her mother's tone, Stacey stiffened and looked at Leah, obviously confused as to what she'd done wrong.

Leah spoke softly, but Boyd noted the strain in her voice. "You mustn't be so familiar with strangers, darling. It isn't polite."

Wide eyes regarded Leah, then looked up at Boyd. He saw the girl's small lips quiver. "I didn't think he was a stranger. I thought he was our friend."

A peculiar ache squeezed Boyd's chest and as Stacey, with her eyes downcast in embarrassment, started to move away, Boyd stopped her with a hug. "I *am* your friend," he said, stroking the child's gold-brown hair. "And I'm your mommy's friend, too."

Stacey pressed her face against Boyd's chest, winding her small arms around his chest and seeming to melt against him. The child's unquestioning trust and innocent vulnerability touched Boyd. He felt a sudden surge of protectiveness and affection that was totally new to him, totally unexpected.

Looking up, he saw Leah watching with a strange, sweet-sad expression. She seemed mesmerized, almost rapturous—as though seeing something that was incredibly beautiful yet painfully beyond reach. Suddenly he saw a shimmer of tears as she looked directly into Boyd's eyes. He held the moment, savoring the sweetness of their silent communion. It was a spiritual intimacy, like a fleeting kiss between souls.

With a blink and a breath, the moment passed.

Leah turned away, staring into the picnic basket as though trying to memorize its contents. Boyd felt suddenly empty, as if something had been surgically removed from his chest. Leah's shoulders trembled and Boyd realized that she, too, had been affected by the experience.

Reality returned with a wiggle and a bounce as Stacey abruptly refocused her attention. "Can I have some cookies?"

Leah stared blankly. "I didn't bring any cookies."

"I did." Digging into the basket, the child proudly produced a brown bag, obviously quite full of something lumpy. "I brought them for the squirrels," she told Boyd.

He nodded wisely.

Leah's eyes gleamed. "Perhaps you should offer a cookie to Mr. Cauldwell."

"Would you like one, Mr. Cauldwell?" A gooey string of chocolate wrapped around Stacey's finger as she offered a crumbling cookie.

Boyd winced. "No thanks, but my friends call me Boyd and we *are* friends now, aren't we?"

Stacey grinned coyly, then poked the ground with her toe and licked chocolate from her finger. "Uh-huh."

As Stacey skipped across the meadow with her precious cookie bag, Leah watched Boyd follow the child with his eyes. She saw a sad, faraway look followed by a brief flash of anger. Then his face composed into a neutral expression.

"Mommy?"

"Umm?" Reluctantly dragging her gaze from Boyd, Leah saw her daughter standing by a two-foot-high tree stump. A prickling sensation skittered down her spine. There was something about that stump, something vaguely familiar yet disturbingly out of place.

Then memories flooded through her—the remembrance of a soft spring night and of moonlight dancing across the inky surface of the lake. There had been adolescent laughter mingled with wind songs; and as lovers had done for centuries past, Boyd had carved their names into the bark of the stately tree.

That moment had been magical, intensely sweet. Leah had traced the grooved letters with her fingertips and Boyd had kissed her, saying that as long as the tree stood, their love would flourish.

Now, amid the thickets of pine and cedar, one barren stump marred the beauty of the forest. Their tree, like their love, had been deliberately severed.

With a small gasp, Leah turned toward Boyd. His expression was grim, his gaze fixed on the weathered stub. There was anger in his eyes, a deep smoldering fury that chilled Leah to the bone. Intuitively, she knew who had mutilated the tree.

"How could you?" she whispered.

Boyd's jaw twitched. "Firewood." His eyes challenged her. "Do you have a problem with that?"

Leah looked away. "No."

Of course she had a problem with that. Ignoring the illegality of felling trees in a national forest, Boyd's action had been a very clear message. By savaging their tree, he had cut Leah out of his heart—figuratively and literally. But Boyd had also betrayed the depth of his pain.

Suddenly Leah's throat closed up and she felt as though she'd swallowed a brick. All these years she'd been so overwhelmed by the extent of her own torture, it had never occurred to her that Boyd, too, had been suffering. Guilt gnawed at her. She'd made one mistake after another, and so many people had been hurt. Like a rolling snowball gaining size and speed, there had seemed no way to stop the impending avalanche.

Stacey's impatient voice demanded Leah's attention: "Mommy!"

Forcing herself to look at the naked stump, Leah managed to choke out a reply.

Oblivious to the adults' tension, the girl furrowed her forehead in concentration. "If I put the cookies here, can the squirrels climb up and get them?"

Leah mumbled that they probably could.

Satisfied, Stacey crumbled the broken cookies on the stump, then ran into the lake and began thrashing through the water. "Mr. Cau—I mean, Boyd!" she called. "I can swim as good as Mommy."

With a stiff smile, Boyd waved and Stacey promptly flopped onto her back and began to work her arms like a Rototiller.

Crushing a dry leaf in his palm, Boyd angled a glance at Leah, then cleared his throat. "She's a lovely child."

"Thank you." Leah took a deep breath. "My mother tells me that your law practice is doing quite well."

He stared across the lake. "I can't complain."

Leah realized that he wasn't going to make her attempt at polite conversation particularly easy. She tried again. "What is your speciality? I mean, are you like those wild-eyed prosecutors I see on television? Or would you be pleading that the defendant jaywalked in a moment of insanity?"

Leah had hoped that humor would lighten the mood. It didn't.

Boyd responded in a dull monotone. "Neither. My partner works out of our state-line office and handles labor contracts. I'm more a legal jack-of-all-trades—wills, domestic disputes, small-business matters—nothing spectacular, but I find it...satisfying." The statement wasn't particularly convincing.

Leah was surprised, to say the least. "But I thought you were torn between private practice and government work. By now, I expected you to be either a stoic defender of the underdog or California's attorney general."

Boyd looked out toward the lake. "People change, Leah."

His soft words carried a powerful punch. Leah swallowed hard, then turned away, as though she, too, were absorbed in her daughter's swimming exhibition.

They watched Stacey for several minutes, not speaking, carefully avoiding the intimacy of eye contact. Then Leah heard Boyd clear his throat again and felt her muscles tighten.

"Why did you leave, Leah?"

She winced. Boyd had always been honest and direct, sometimes painfully so. It had been a quality that Leah had once admired. The years had taught some bitter lessons, and she now realized that, at times, untempered truth could cause great heartache. This was one of those times.

"I guess I was too young and too immature for a serious relationship." That wasn't really a lie, Leah told herself. "I wanted to see new places, meet new people."

Boyd considered her response. "I don't believe that."

Shrugging, Leah replied, "That's your choice."

"Give me some credit, Leah. You were halfway through your senior year, then suddenly dropped out of high school and disappeared into the night. I remember that 'new places, new people' line, too. It appeared in my mailbox. But I didn't buy it then, and I don't buy it now."

As Boyd talked, Leah maintained a blank expression but kept her hands busy, forcing stiff fingers to fold plastic bags, brushing invisible dust from the spotless blanket. "I'm sorry I hurt you," she said softly. "It was thoughtless and I apologize."

"Apologize? Do you know what I went through, searching for you, begging your parents for some clue, some small scrap of information about why my world had exploded under my feet?" Boyd's voice was raw, and Leah felt hot moisture flood her lashes. "I *loved* you, Leah. I wanted to marry you."

Wiping her eyes, Leah snapped the lid on the basket. "We have to go now. I don't want to leave my mother alone too long." She started to stand, needing desperately to escape the pain—Boyd's and her own—wanting only to run, as she'd done so long ago. Then Boyd's hand closed over her arm with a gentle, caressing warmth that immobilized her.

"How old is Stacey, Leah?" His voice was deceptively soft.

She didn't answer. She didn't have to.

When Boyd slowly removed his hand, a cold chill brushed her skin. He didn't speak for a moment and Leah saw him watching the child playing in the lake. Finally, he asked, "Who is Stacey's father?"

A cold pit opened in her stomach. "It doesn't matter."

Boyd's eyes speared her. *"It doesn't matter?"*

She didn't blink. "No, it doesn't. I gave birth to her, I've raised her and I've loved her. She's *my* child."

Boyd's jaw clamped angrily. "Did you love him?"

Leah's shoulders slumped. "No."

"Then why?" Boyd's eyes reflected agony and anger, bitterness and betrayal.

Seeing his anguish, feeling his torment, was like reliving the nightmares that had haunted her for so many years. She'd lived with guilt, lived with tearing loss, but Leah knew she could never live with the memory of how Boyd was looking at her right now.

She could only shake her head. How could she explain what she didn't even understand herself? How could she tell Boyd that, in her heart, she'd always been faithful to him? How could she ask Boyd's forgiveness when she could never forgive herself?

It had happened. It had been ugly and repulsive, a terrible mistake, but it *had* happened. And as much as Leah bitterly regretted having lost Boyd, the only man she'd ever loved, how could she regret her beautiful child?

No matter how difficult it was to dredge up the past, Leah realized that knowing the true story might in some way help Boyd overcome his feelings of rejection and anger. Cybil had said that Boyd should know what had happened on that dreadful night. Perhaps her mother was right—up to a point.

Stiffening her spine and her resolve, Leah forced herself to meet Boyd's eyes. He *did* have a right to the truth—to at least some of it.

"I—I hadn't meant for it to happen," she whispered, then pressed her palms against her cheek, as though their coldness could revive her courage. Boyd sat motionless, expressionless . . . waiting. In a halting voice, Leah continued. "After you left in September, I was lonely and depressed. We'd had such a wonderful summer and I was feeling pretty sorry for myself. Mother talked me into going to the town Oktoberfest at the lake with . . . a friend." God, this was difficult. Leah would have rather faced a firing squad, but she managed to continue. "The, ah, friend was having some problems and was trying to drown them with whiskey. I wanted to help him, get him to talk about his troubles. He said he would, if I'd have a drink with him. I did. I was a fool."

Leah saw Boyd's eyes narrow, then he looked away, staring into thin air. She tried to rush the remaining words before they choked her. "After two drinks, I got dizzy and felt ill. I lay down on the grass, trying to get my bearings, and he pretended to comfort me. H-He took advantage."

Boyd continued to stare silently into space for several minutes and Leah saw the tense twitch of his jaw muscles.

Finally he spoke, in a low and deadly voice. "Did it ever occur to you to say 'No'?"

Leah's jaw sagged. "Did it—? My God, *of course* I said no. When I realized what was happening, I cried and I pleaded, and I pushed. He simply wouldn't take no for an answer."

Boyd turned and stared straight at her. His fists clenched and he spoke through clamped teeth. "Are you saying that he forced you?"

"Yes," she whispered. "But I don't know if he realized that at the time. Afterward, he was sorry. He said there had been a misunderstanding. Because I'd gone willingly with him into the woods and because I'd taken the drink he offered, he thought...he thought I understood."

"If you said no, then it was rape." Boyd's expression flickered, changing from shock to horror to fury. His mouth opened, then snapped shut as he rubbed his face. Boyd looked up with tormented eyes. "Why didn't you call the police? Why did you protect him then, and why are you *still* protecting him?"

"What could the police have done? I was confused, I felt guilty and I felt...dirty. You went to law school Boyd. You should know what the system does to girls in my position. I just didn't want anyone to find out, to know what had happened to me." Leah's voice quivered and her hands began to shake.

Suddenly Boyd's arms were around Leah and he pressed her to his chest, rocking her, whispering encouragement. For the first time in so many years, Leah felt safe. Melting against him, she allowed the tears to flow as he caressed her hair, giving the comfort she so desperately needed. Finally Leah straightened and wiped at her wet face.

"Didn't you even tell your parents?" he asked softly.

"No, not until I had to."

"Why didn't you tell me the truth, Leah? Why did you run away and let me believe the worst?"

"I was seventeen years old, pregnant and scared to death, so I ran. It wasn't very courageous, but it's what I did and I can't change it." Leah didn't mention that she'd had little choice about leaving Cedar Cove. Louis Wainwright had seen to that. "And what would you have done if I'd stayed? Would you have told me it didn't matter, that you'd marry me anyway and raise another man's child?"

"I don't know." Standing, Boyd took a couple of steps, then turned back and jammed his hands into his pockets. "I wish I could say that I would have been understanding, that I would have stood by you, but I was young and egotistical and ... I just don't know."

"I understand," she whispered, cutting off the words that were tearing her heart. "Let's put the past to rest. It's over."

"*Is* it over, Leah?" His eyes impaled her. "In all those years did you ever think about me, ever wonder what might have been if we'd made different choices?"

Not trusting her voice, she could only nod.

Reaching out, Boyd softly stroked her cheek with the back of his hand. "Can you walk away now and never look back?"

Slowly, she shook her head.

He gently caressed her chin with his fingertip, then tested the fullness of her lower lip. With a deep breath, he pulled his hand away and raked his fingers through his hair. A lock fell across his forehead and Leah suppressed an urge to smooth it. She knotted her hands together.

"We can't change the past," Boyd said finally. "But maybe we can come to terms with it."

Leah felt a small flutter deep inside. The feeling could have been fear or excitement, a warning or a promise. Whatever it was, Leah pushed it away. Perhaps by resolving what had been unfinished between them, she could finally end the dreams that had haunted her—and the nightmares.

Maybe she could even learn to live with the rest of her secret.

The light from Boyd's reading lamp cast a golden glow on the cabin's knotty-pine walls. Rubbing his burning eyes, Boyd stared down at the briefcase gaping at his feet. The polished plank floor was strewn with letters to be signed and contracts to be proofed. He sighed. It was past midnight and he still held the page he'd started to read three hours earlier. The paragraphs had finally blurred into undulating, nonsensical blocks of print. Boyd's stiff fingers clutched a dictation unit, its tape still wound and ready to receive his first momentous words.

Those words would not be forthcoming tonight.

Disgusted, Boyd tossed the small recorder into the open briefcase and pushed himself from the leather armchair. The unread page slid soundlessly from his lap to the floor.

Stepping over the clutter, Boyd walked to the window. Beyond the glass was the forest, sculpted in night shades of gray and black, as chilling and somber as his mood.

Suddenly he felt captured, claustrophobic, as though the cabin walls were slowly closing in and squeezing the life from him.

Throwing the window open, he filled his lungs with cool, fragrant air. In the distance a lonely cricket called to its mate and the mournful song of a night bird floated through the darkness.

The melancholy sound pierced his heart.

Leah. Thoughts of her crowded his mind. He'd sought her out this afternoon, determined that after all the years and all the pain and all the haunting questions, he would finally have answers. Now that he had at least some of them, he wished for the return of blissful ignorance.

For nearly ten years Boyd had sullenly licked his wounds, self-righteous and secure that he'd been the victim of despicable deceit and duplicity. Although he'd gone forward with his life and achieved some measure of success, Boyd had always fantasized about seeing Leah again. It was childish, he knew, but in his daydreams she would come to him with declarations of love and pleas for forgiveness. He, of course, would be kind. It was, after all, *his* daydream and he was entitled to create his own heroic behavior.

The reality had been a mortal blow.

He could still see Leah's face, twisted in pain and humiliation as she offered Boyd his coveted answers. His ears still rang with the shame in Leah's trembling voice as she described her violation.

How could an act so vile have been secreted for over a decade? Boyd wondered. Why hadn't Leah come to him for comfort?

Turning from the window, Boyd leaned against the cabin wall and folded his arms tightly across his chest. He closed his eyes, locking unshed tears safely inside.

Boyd and Leah had been as close as two people could be, and yet she hadn't trusted him enough to share her grief. Instead, she'd run away. God, how that hurt.

Still, something didn't quite fit. Boyd couldn't shake the feeling that what Leah had left out was far more important than what she'd told him.

Boyd focused on that. He had to. If he allowed himself to think about what had happened to Leah—what Boyd had *allowed* to happen—the guilt and the anguish would surely drive him mad.

If only he hadn't gone back to school. If only he'd stayed in Cedar Cove, perhaps he could have protected Leah. Now it was too late—too late for regret, too late for recrimination. Too late for Leah.

With a cry of agony, Boyd slammed both fists back into the wall. *If only* and *too late*—phrases created to excuse the unforgivable. Boyd *had* left Leah alone and something horrible had happened.

When Boyd opened his eyes, his gaze fell on the corner plant-stand. As though drawn by some invisible force, he crossed the room and crouched in front of the huge green philodendron. The length of log supporting the clay pot was obscured by the plant's leafy tendrils spilling to the floor. Tenderly, Boyd reached out, parting the thick vines to expose a length of carved bark. Boyd traced the uneven gashes forming each letter, each word—*Leah & Boyd, Always*.

"Leah," he whispered. "What have we done to each other?"

Chapter Three

On Monday morning, Leah pulled into a narrow parking place and walked the short distance to her father's hardware store. She clutched the key Cybil had given her, but was startled to find the door unlocked. Pushing it open, Leah heard the familiar jingle that announced a potential customer.

She saw no one, although the fluorescent ceiling glowed with light and a sign in the window proclaimed Open—Please Come In. Narrow aisles wound through cluttered displays of tools and hoses, lengths of pipes and bins of assorted loose hardware. Leah remembered the chaos of organized clutter, but now there appeared to be so much more of it. The store seemed larger.

Bewildered, she looked around, then suddenly realized that the store was indeed larger. A wall had been knocked out, expanding the floor space by perhaps thirty percent. To say the least, Leah was surprised, because Cybil had never mentioned that the store had undergone such massive renovation.

Yes, there'd been many changes, but there was also a comforting familiarity. The ancient cash register still sat on the counter and Leah idly wondered if the decimal key still stuck. Suddenly Leah was a child again, with the counter looming above as she craned her neck for a glimpse of the tall, angular man who stood behind it. She could almost hear the tiny voice from the past. "Can I help, Papa? Please, can I?"

The voice turned deep and masculine. "Can I be helping you, miss?"

Taken aback, Leah whirled to see a portly man at the rear of the store. Although his mouth wasn't visible beneath the wiry red brush on his upper lip, Leah saw his eyes twinkle and knew he was smiling.

"Simon Sprague?"

"Indeed, indeed." Hurrying toward her, Sprague grasped Leah's hand and pumped it heartily. "And you'd be Miss Wainwright. Met you at the funeral, of course, but you look different now, with your hair all loose and all." Suddenly he dropped her hand and his eyes filled with sympathy. "Sad thing...about your daddy...and I sure am sorry. Weird, it was, him being in the wrong place when that sign came crashing down...." Sprague's voice trailed off and his expression was one of pure misery. "Louis was my friend. He was good to me...and I surely miss him."

Leah didn't know what to say. Sprague's grief was genuine. Perhaps she shouldn't have been shocked, but she was. Louis Wainwright had been a distant man, cordial enough with customers but too much a loner to have established the intimacy of real friendship. Obviously Simon Sprague had been privy to another facet of her father's personality, and Leah felt a small, indefinable twinge.

Seemingly embarrassed by his emotional display, Sprague coughed loudly, then shuffled his feet. "The store was closed all last week, so I figured it'd be best to get back to business. I didn't mean no disrespect."

"Of course you didn't."

"I know Louis would be right put out if I let the place go to hell in a hand basket—begging your pardon for the language."

Leah smiled. "Mother said that she could count on you to take care of things, and I see that she was right."

Sprague's small eyes softened. "How's your mama? Is she needing anything?"

"Mother's been tired lately, a bit washed-out." Sprague nodded somberly and Leah continued. "Actually, she'll be bringing my daughter by in a little while."

The thought of Cybil's presence in the store seemed to perk Sprague up considerably. "Well, glory, folks'll be pleased as punch to have her waiting on 'em. I'd best be sprucing the place up a bit—"

"Oh, she won't be staying."

Sprague's face fell. "No?"

"My daughter and I are going up to Virginia City this afternoon. Since Mother has some errands in town, she offered to drop Stacey off and save me a trip back to the house." Sprague looked so forlorn, Leah added, "You can be of help, though."

"Anything at all. You just say the word."

"Apparently Mother hasn't been, ah, involved in the business. There are some decisions to be made and she—that is, *we*, don't have enough information to make those decisions."

Although Leah had selected her words judiciously, Sprague was way ahead of her. "You might get a good price if you sell out now. Hate to see it, though. The business is sound, inventory turnover is good and old Louis, he didn't cotton to owing money, so there isn't much debt to speak of. Why, we got us a profit every month—not real big, but enough to keep your mama safe and warm." Simon suddenly looked abashed. "Of course, you'll be wanting to see the records and find out for yourself. I talk too much. Louis always said so."

"No, not at all. That's exactly the kind of information we'll need." Leah laid a reassuring hand on Sprague's arm. "I know Mother doesn't want to sell Wainwright Hardware, but I don't know if she can handle the additional stress right now."

"Well, now, no need for her to fret about that. I'll be here to help just as long as she needs me, and you seem to have a fine head on your shoulders. The two of you will do fine, just fine."

"I appreciate your confidence, Mr. Sprague, but—"

"Sy." He grinned. "My friends call me Sy."

Leah smiled. "Sy. But I'll be returning to Sacramento in a couple of weeks and it's possible that Mother will be going with me."

Sprague's round face crumpled. "Is that a fact? Cybil's leaving Cedar Cove? Mercy!"

Since Leah hadn't yet discussed that option with her mother, she hurriedly backtracked. "It's not certain, of course, but Mother has been under such strain lately that she might be more comfortable with Stacey and me." Leah offered her brightest smile. "It . . . ah . . . would be best if you didn't mention this discussion to anyone."

Sprague cocked his head, regarding Leah with pursed lips and shrewd eyes. Finally, as though he'd come to some decision about her motives, he flashed that infectious grin. "What discussion?"

Leah couldn't help laughing with him. She decided that she liked Simon Sprague very much. He was sincere and warm, and she loved the ways his eyes gleamed with good humor. Although she was normally cautious around people she'd just met, Leah instinctively trusted him.

Following him to the small office at the back of the store, Leah accepted a cup of coffee, then listened carefully as Sy explained the bookkeeping method Louis had used and showed her where the bank records were kept.

For the next two hours, Leah familiarized herself with the ledgers while Sprague greeted customers and inventoried the stock. Finally stretching her kinked muscles, Leah stood and rubbed the small of her back. She had validated the bank balances, cross-checked the cash receipts and deciphered her father's rather strange accounts-payable system. Many more hours would be required to complete the analysis, of course; but she'd made a good start and was encouraged by what she'd found. The records were clean and neat and her initial perusal indicated that the little store did indeed make a respectable profit.

Sy had been mistaken about one thing, though: Leah had noted that her father *did* have a rather large debt. The entry was a ten-thousand dollar liability, an unspecified Note Payable in the long-term debt section of his ledger. Leah wasn't particularly concerned, though, assuming that a copy of the promissory note was probably tucked away in the files. During the course of her audit, she would most certainly come across the paperwork and fill in the appropriate details.

The sound of muffled voices filtered through the closed office door, followed by a familiar childish laugh. Leah twisted the doorknob and peeked into the store. Cybil was nowhere in sight. Sprague was barely visible over the line of five-foot display units, his shiny head tilted backward as he spoke to a taller man.

"Mommy!" Stacey ran toward the office. "Is this where you worked when you were a little girl?"

"I'm not sure you could actually call what I did 'work,' but I did spend a lot of time here," Leah said.

She kissed her daughter's cheek, before Stacey wriggled away and peered curiously into the office. With a deep breath, Leah turned toward the man with whom Sy had been speaking. "Hello, Boyd."

He looked up and Leah's heart stuck in her throat. The distance between them seemed to melt away; their surroundings became a blur as she focused only on Boyd's mesmerizing gaze.

His expression was wary, as though he, too, wanted to break the spell but was powerless to do so. Leah's insides turned to warm mush. Just looking at him was torture, and she was bewildered by her inner turmoil. After all those years, Boyd still had an almost mystical control over her heart and her mind.

Finally, Leah was vaguely aware of a raspy coughing. She blinked. Sy was ambling toward the front of the store, apparently uneasy with the strained silence. The distraction seemed to pull Boyd from his trance, as well. He took a couple of stilted steps toward Leah, then hesitated. "Good morning."

She licked her dry lips, glancing back into the office. Stacey had discovered that the swivel chair could be manipulated like a Disneyland teacup ride. "You'll make yourself dizzy," Leah warned absently, then took a deep breath and returned her attention to Boyd.

Under her questioning gaze, Boyd suddenly felt uncomfortably hot. He knew Leah was wondering what in the world he was doing at the store and quite frankly, so was he. Attempting a matter-of-fact demeanor, Boyd said blandly, "Cybil and I spent the morning going over Louis's papers. Afterward, she was a bit fatigued so I volunteered to do some errands for her."

Leah lowered her eyes, but not before Boyd noticed a flicker of disappointment. Was she wishing for a more personal motive? Boyd certainly hoped so.

"That was very kind of you," she murmured. "I know how busy you must be."

"It was my pleasure."

Silence followed. Leah awkwardly poked a strand of hair behind her ear, then stared at her tennis shoes as Boyd pretended to study a bin of loose wing nuts.

Leah wrapped her arms protectively over her chest and offered a too-bright smile. "Well, has all the legal paperwork been settled?"

"Not completely, but we've made good progress." Business was a topic with which Boyd was most comfortable and he gratefully took refuge. "We couldn't find a will, but the assets will have to be inventoried anyway. Since you and Cybil apparently are Louis's only living heirs, I don't foresee any legal problems, but as you're probably aware, probate can be a time-consuming process."

"I know Mother appreciates your help. She seems so overwhelmed by everything."

"She has a right to feel a bit lost at the moment. This is a very stressful time for her."

Stacey appeared in the doorway, flushed with excitement. "Mommy and I are going to a real-live ghost town."

Smiling, Boyd lifted an eyebrow. "A *live* ghost town?"

Oblivious to the grammatical gaffe, Stacey nodded vigorously.

"I see." Boyd forced a serious expression. "And just where is this 'real-live ghost town'?"

Leah chuckled softly. "I thought Stacey might enjoy a trip to Virginia City."

"Virginia City is hardly a ghost town," Boyd pointed out. "It's very much alive and bustling."

"True, but it's kept its Old West flavor. Where else can a city girl see wooden sidewalks and real cowboys?"

Stacey was pink with anticipation. "And horses? Can I ride a real horse?"

"We'll see, sweetheart."

"Can Boyd come, too?" Stacey piped in.

Leah's smile died. "I'm sure Mr. Cauldwell has other plans for the day."

Round eyes somberly regarded Boyd. "Do you?"

"Not really."

Stacey whooped. "See? Can he come with us? Please, Mommy?"

Leah's discomfort annoyed Boyd. Obviously she found the idea of spending an afternoon with him distasteful. The thought sparked a sudden flare of devilry and he offered a saccharine smile. "Yes, Mommy," he said silkily. "Can I please?" He slid Stacey a conspiratorial look, and the child beamed with pleasure.

Eyes narrowed, Leah glared at him. "Two against one, is it?"

Stacey nodded enthusiastically and Boyd said, "It looks that way."

Not wanting a hasty capitulation, Leah pretended to struggle with her decision. Stacey held her breath, her round eyes silently begging. Try as she might, Leah couldn't maintain the stern expression and she laughed. "Oh, all right. Never let it be said that mothers aren't democratic."

Clapping her hands gleefully, Stacey darted toward the front door. Victorious, Boyd smiled, and wrapping his hand around Leah's elbow, he motioned toward the front of the store. "Shall we?"

Since Boyd's plush sedan was more comfortable than Leah's compact, he was elected temporary chauffeur and they settled into his car for the trip. After they'd traveled around the lake, Boyd turned up Highway 50 and crossed into Nevada. Throughout the entire journey, Stacey chattered nonstop, sharing relevant information about the highlights of her young life.

Leah gratefully noted that Boyd didn't seem irritated by her daughter's constant babble. In fact he appeared to be enjoying himself, laughing easily and often. He appeared genuinely proud that Stacey was always the first to be chosen for the playground kickball team and was appropriately indignant that she'd been rejected for the choice role of tooth fairy in the school's dental-hygiene play.

Relaxing against the comfortable velour seat, Leah realized that she felt a deepening sense of contentment and well-being. When she and Boyd had been together years ago, there had always been joy and laughter. Whereas Leah had been a shy child and a quiet adolescent, Boyd had always been outgoing. He also had a wicked sense of humor, and as he had done at the lake yesterday, he had a way of diffusing tense moments. If he had on occasion displayed a moodier facet of his personality, well, under the circumstances, Leah found it difficult to fault him for it.

In fact, at this moment she couldn't find fault with anything. It had been years since she'd been so deliciously— happy. At the thought, she felt a familiar twinge of warning. Leah's experience was that happiness, at best, is a fleeting experience, and that its loss was more painful than having never experienced it at all.

How jaded, she thought sadly; how cynical she'd become. She pushed away her melancholy thoughts and focused on the unfolding scenery.

"Leah?" Boyd angled a concerned glance toward her.

"Pardon me?" Blinking, Leah realized that Boyd had been speaking to her. "I'm sorry. I guess I was a bit preoccupied. What were you saying?"

Relaxing slightly, Boyd returned his gaze to the road. "Stacey was telling me about your condominium in Sacramento. How long have you lived there?"

"About three years. Actually, it belongs to my boss." Seeing Boyd's head snap around, Leah hastened to explain. "We're renting it from her."

"Oh." His grip on the steering wheel loosened. "Cybil says you've done quite well for yourself as an accountant."

"Mother exaggerates. I'm a bookkeeper for a medium-size electronics manufacturer."

Boyd shrugged. "Same thing."

"Not really. I have a bachelor's degree but I'm not a CPA."

"Berkeley?"

"University of California. The campus was relatively close to Aunt Jo's."

"You lived with your aunt after you left Cedar Cove?"

"Yes, for about three years."

"So, you and Stacey have been on your own since then?"

Although the question was casual enough, Leah realized that Boyd was discreetly guiding the conversation into an area that she didn't want to discuss, particularly since her daughter was in the back seat, alert and extremely interested. Obviously Boyd was fishing for clues to Leah's past relationships—including, God forbid, previous marriages. There was absolutely nothing to report, yet oddly enough, Leah didn't really want Boyd to know that. If he realized that she'd never looked twice at a man in ten years, Boyd would understand how much power he still held over her heart.

A green highway sign ahead offered the opportunity for a quick change of subject. "There's the turnoff."

Sighing, Boyd mumbled, "I see it." He slowed the car, preparing for a left turn.

Virginia City was perched in a mound of barren foothills and had, a century ago, been a prosperous mining town. As the car strained up the final dusty incline, Stacey let out a whoop.

"It's just like in the movies," she said, turning in her seat to get a better view of the weathered antique buggies standing in front of colorful saloons.

Boyd parked the car and Stacey leaped out, then stopped to stare as four huge horses clopped down the street pulling a creaking stagecoach. Watching the child's awestruck expression, Boyd felt a surge of joy. Seeing the world through Stacey's eyes was almost like a rebirth, as the ordinary became wondrous and special.

Turning, Stacey looked up at Boyd, her blue eyes filled with gratitude. "Thank you," she said, then smiled with such pleasure that Boyd felt his heart wrench.

The interior of the Sundance Saloon glittered with light prismed into a rainbow of color by walls of mirror and beveled glass. In the corner, a player piano filled the air with tinny ragtime, and a costumed hostess added to the dance-hall ambience. Stacey tasted her first sarsaparilla and immediately pronounced it "yucky."

They rode the stagecoach past the old Miners' Union Hall, saw a gold nugget as large as a dinner plate at the museum and took Stacey to the small petting zoo. When a pygmy goat decided to lunch on the hem of Stacey's T-shirt, the child shook her finger in the startled animal's face, scolding it with such a serious expression that Boyd laughed until his sides ached.

Stacey inspected the damage with obvious disgust.

Leah struggled to suppress her amusement. "I think what we need here is to drown our sorrows with some lunch." Glancing at her watch, she amended the statement. "Make that dinner."

The shirt was immediately forgotten. "Hot dogs?" Stacey asked hopefully, then pointed down the street toward a vendor with a colorful cart.

Sensing an opportunity to display his gallantry, Boyd volunteered to obtain the delicacies. He took orders with a flourish, then bowed at the waist and headed toward the hot-dog wagon. Stacey's giggles followed him and he smiled.

After making his purchase, Boyd balanced a carrying box of soft drinks in one hand and a carton of hot dogs "with the works" in the other. Leah and Stacey, however, were nowhere to be seen. Mumbling to himself, he scanned the dusty roadway, wondering why they'd chosen such an inopportune moment to wander off.

Then Boyd spotted two familiar heads and sighed in relief. The two had settled onto a bench by the souvenir shop. As Boyd approached, he heard Stacey's breathless voice.

Leah was leaning over, brushing tangled strands of gold-brown hair from her daughter's face and Boyd realized that neither had noticed him.

"This is the most fun I've ever had in my whole, entire life," Stacey said, wiggling impatiently. "Isn't Boyd wonderful, Mommy?"

"Yes, sweetheart. Hold still, now."

"Do you like him?"

Boyd saw Leah's hand pause and her eyelids flutter, but she spoke so softly he couldn't hear her reply. He had no difficulty, however, in hearing Stacey's response. The child's voice was wistful, but clear and strong.

"I wish he was my daddy," she said.

The drinks sloshed. Boyd stopped in his tracks as if he'd hit a brick wall. His lungs began to ache and he realized that he'd forgotten to breathe.

For a few short hours, Boyd had actually overlooked the fact that someone else was Stacey's daddy—someone who had ripped Leah away and destroyed their love. Suddenly Boyd was assaulted by an uncontrollable fury that shook him to the soles of his feet. He couldn't move.

"Boyd?" Leah stood quickly. "My goodness, you're swimming in soda pop."

Boyd's expression was as tight as a death mask and he stood as though rooted to the ground.

Bewildered by Boyd's odd transformation, Leah watched him carefully as she set the dripping cups on the bench. Stacey, however, seemed oblivious and scrambled toward the coveted hot dogs.

"Is something wrong?" Leah touched Boyd's arm and he flinched. She pulled her hand away in confusion.

"Nothing's wrong," Boyd replied, although he knew his harsh tone said otherwise. He tried to soften it with a stiff smile. "The hot dogs will get cold."

Nodding, Leah was unconvinced but unwilling to pursue the matter.

The meal was strained and silent. Boyd studied Stacey and wondered why her hair was so much lighter than Leah's. "He" must have had light hair, Boyd concluded. Then he directed his attention to Stacey's mouth. It was very wide, like a thin slash across her round face. Turning, Boyd stared at Leah. He saw full lips, a short, almost pointed chin and a fragile bone structure.

Self-conscious, Leah touched her face. "Do I have catsup on my nose?"

Boyd ignored her question. Swiveling, he looked back at Stacey. The child's chin was squarish, with a deep cleft, and her facial bones were heavier, more substantial than Leah's. "His" characteristics, Boyd decided. Everything was suddenly so obvious. All Boyd had to do was piece together the physical attributes which were "his" and search the entire town of Cedar Cove until he found a match. Boyd would find the man who had defiled Leah and when he did—

Cutting off the thought, Boyd snapped his head toward Leah and stared at her. What exactly *would* he do to this unknown, unnamed seducer? The answer scared the hell out of him.

At that particular moment, Boyd wanted to kill the guy.

Despite the heat of the day, Boyd was instantly cold. What was happening to him? These thoughts were insane. A civilized person simply didn't go around comparing chins and hair color with murder in mind!

Leah gazed out the car window. The moon had yet to rise and it was too dark to see more than a few blurred shadows—shades of black and gray as somber as Leah's mood.

The day had begun so beautifully, filled with easy laughter and a comfortable sense of fun. But then, without warning, everything had changed.

After dinner, Boyd had been quiet and withdrawn. Something had obviously upset him, and Leah had a deep sense of foreboding as to what that something might have been.

Angling a glance at Boyd, Leah saw his tense grip on the steering wheel, and as oncoming headlights illuminated his face, she noted the harsh set of his jaw.

Wanting to break the strained silence, Leah said, "Stacey had a lovely day. She was thrilled by the nugget bracelet you bought for her."

Boyd's response was a curt nod and a single, garbled word.

Swallowing a surge of annoyance, Leah managed to keep her tone relatively civil. "The weather couldn't have been nicer. I was afraid it would be too hot, but it was just perfect."

This time, Boyd managed a noncommittal grunt.

So much for polite conversation, Leah thought grimly and turned to look into the back seat. Stacey's head lolled sideways and only the comforting restraint of the shoulder harness kept the sleeping child upright.

Now that Stacey was lost in blissful slumber, Leah decided on the direct approach. "At one time, I considered your temperament to be part of your charm. Maybe I succumbed to the mystique of the strong, silent type."

Leah was staring straight ahead, but from the corner of her eye she noted that Boyd slanted a quick glance in her direction. Good. At least she'd gotten his attention. Maintaining an even tone, she continued. "I guess I've changed a bit, because now I don't find moodiness at all charming."

Boyd's cheek twitched. "I'm sorry. I've been a bit... distracted."

After a long moment, Leah took a deep breath. "Has your curiosity been satisfied? You've been staring at both Stacey and me like we have antennae sprouting from our ears." She saw Boyd's shocked expression as he quickly glanced into the rearview mirror. "She's asleep. Nothing short of driving over a cliff would wake her now."

This information did little to ease the tension.

Leah curled her fingers into her palms until she felt nails bite flesh. She was angry, at herself more than at Boyd. For a while, Leah had allowed herself to pretend that the past didn't matter. A foolish notion, to be sure, but for a few glorious hours, she and Boyd had recaptured the special spark that they'd once shared. Each tremulous touch, every meaningful look, had warmed Leah to her very core, and during those sweet moments, it had been as though the "incident" had never happened.

But of course, it had.

Obviously, Boyd was well aware of that fact. After all, a tangible and constant reminder was asleep in the back seat.

"Mommy! He fell out of the tree!"

The soapy glass slipped from Leah's hands into the dishwater. Stacey's voice rose a full octave. "Mommy!"

Leah ran to the kitchen door, pushing it open with her shoulder as she dried her hands on a dish towel. "Stacey?"

Clutching the porch rail, Leah scanned the yard until she saw Stacey hunched beneath a huge fir about seventy feet from the house. The child's back was to Leah and her head was bent forward as she cradled something in her hands.

With growing concern, Leah flipped the towel over her shoulder and ran. Stacey whirled around and extended her arms. A small partially feathered bird was huddled in her palms.

"He fell a long way," Stacey said tearfully. "Is he going to die?"

Leah looked at the pitiful creature and shook her head. "I don't know, sweetheart."

"I don't want him to die," the girl wailed.

The bird wobbled and tried to lift its head. It was a baby jay, obviously not old enough to be on its own. The fledgling's scrawny body was covered with a grayish down through which a few brave feathers were trying to emerge.

Shading her eyes, Leah peered up into the branches. "It must have a nest up there," she said. Several adult jays screeched, hopping from bough to bough in agitation.

Stacey tilted her head and followed her mother's gaze. "Can we put him back?"

"I'm afraid not. It's too far up and besides, I've heard that the parents will abandon a baby if it has a human scent on it."

A new flood of tears splashed down Stacey's face and Leah wrung her hands in frustration. Her daughter had always been a sensitive child with a deep reverence for all forms of life. She would be absolutely traumatized if the bird were to expire in her little hands. Something had to be done.

Leah chewed on her lip, then said, "Perhaps I could call the vet."

Stacey sniffed and hiccuped. "Does he know about baby birds?"

"Well, he should certainly know more than I do." Leah pulled the towel off her shoulder and folded it into a soft pad. "Here, honey. Set him on this and we'll put him in a shoe box so he doesn't get cold."

They managed to get the bewildered chick nestled into the soft terry cloth, and were so engrossed in the chore that the slam of a car door startled them both.

Stacey's eyes lit like neon. "Boyd! Come see my bird."

Leah's breath caught. She hadn't heard from Boyd for three days. After their trip to Virginia City, she'd wondered if she would ever see him again. Her emotions had run the gamut from confusion to sadness and anger. Apparently Boyd was unable to accept the past.

Leah had finally decided that that was his problem. But then, she hadn't asked him to barge back into her life.

Overcoming her own feelings of guilt and shame had been a long and painful process. Leah wouldn't be made to feel those awful emotions again to satisfy a bruised male ego; and she certainly would never allow her daughter to be hurt.

Her resolve and her spine stiffened simultaneously.

"Hello, Boyd," she said coolly.

His smile fell flat and he raked his fingers through his hair. Stepping around the front of his car, Boyd hesitated, cleared his throat, then directed his attention to Stacey, who was running toward him, clutching her towel-wrapped bird.

"He fell out of the tree."

Boyd nodded somberly. "It looks like a stellar jay. Where did you find it?"

"Over there." She pointed to a pile of pine needles pillowing the base of the tall fir. "Mommy says we can't put him back."

"Oh?" Boyd slanted a glance at Leah, then lowered his voice. "Well, sometimes mommies can be wrong, you know."

"Really?" Stacey's eyes widened, as though the thought had never occurred to her.

Leah, who had already worked herself into a healthy state of irritation, was less than pleased by Boyd's comment. Gesturing toward the top of the fifty-foot tree, she challenged, "Be my guest."

Boyd grinned. "Do you have a ladder?"

Leah's jaw dropped like lead. "You're joking."

But Boyd had sauntered under the tree in question and was staring up into the thick foliage.

Hurrying to his side, Leah said, "You can't possibly climb up there. You'll break your neck."

Amber sparks warmed his eyes. "Would that upset you?"

She stiffened. "Not particularly. But it would upset Stacey."

"I guess I deserved that." Boyd's expression sobered. "Leah, I'm sorry about the way I behaved the other day. I honestly don't know what's come over me lately."

Leah concentrated on unrolling the sleeves of her plaid shirt and fiddling with a cuff button. Boyd touched her shoulder, then slid his hand silkily down her arm and over her trembling hand.

He bent toward her, lowering his head until his lips were inches from her ear. "Things are going on in my heart and in my head, Leah—things that I don't understand."

Leah felt as though she'd swallowed a sand dune. Her tongue thickened and her mouth was suddenly as dry as a desert. She tried to speak but the words simply clogged in her throat. Boyd was stroking the back of her hand and her fingers tingled under his warm touch.

"You've been through so much already, you don't need me adding to your problems. I tried to stay away but—" He took a ragged breath. "I care about you."

Turning, Leah discreetly brushed the moisture from her eyes and wondered if her quaking knees would give way. She needn't have worried. Boyd was suddenly behind her, his strong hands holding her shoulders, his cheek pressing the side of her head.

"Give me another chance," he whispered. "I won't let you down again."

Again? Leah's mind buzzed in confusion. Then she felt Boyd's lips brush the top of her brow, and sparks shot down her spine. She sagged back against him. Boyd moaned. He reversed his grip on her shoulders, sliding both hands across her collarbone until she was wrapped in his comforting embrace.

Unconsciously, Leah rubbed her face against his muscular forearm, finding pleasure in the friction of crisp hairs against her soft skin. She uttered a sigh of contentment, purring low in her throat. His strength made her feel cherished, his warmth permeated her very core and the years seemed to melt away. It was yesterday again.

Then something tugged at Leah's shirt.

Startled, Leah looked down and saw Stacey, still cuddling the homeless bird.

Boyd's arms sprang apart as if they'd been hugging a burning log. "Uh, the ladder," he mumbled helpfully.

Smoothing her shirt with as much dignity as she could muster, Leah stared at the ground. "It's in the garage."

Boyd muttered something under his breath, then there was a rush of cool air against Leah's back as he turned away. She felt suddenly bereft.

By the time her breathing had returned to normal and she had managed some semblance of composure, Boyd was rounding the house, balancing the ladder under his arm. He propped it against the trunk of the fir tree, expanding the rickety-looking thing to its full height. It hardly reached the first flimsy twigs of the huge tree.

"It isn't tall enough," Leah remarked.

"It'll do. Once I get past the bare trunk, I'll climb the branches."

Leah went white. "You can't."

"Why not?"

"Well . . . you'll drop the bird."

"Oh, ye of little faith." Grinning, Boyd turned to Stacey and carefully took the terry-cloth bird bed. The tiny jay blinked huge trusting eyes. "May I borrow your sweater, Stacey?"

Without a word, she began tugging the pullover off while Leah sputtered helplessly.

Meanwhile, Boyd was eyeing Stacey's ponytail. "And I sure could use that rubber band."

"Okay," Stacey replied cheerfully. Reaching back, she tugged briefly, then her hair fell like a shiny cloud around her shoulders.

Following Boyd's instructions, she bunched the neck of the sweater, using the elastic to close the opening much as it had previously held her ponytail. When she'd finished, the sweater had been transformed into a pink knit sack with the fuzzy fledgling pouched safely inside. With the sweater arms tied around his neck, Boyd had a dandy sling and both hands were free to grab branches.

Boyd gloated. Stacey beamed.

Leah frowned. "I still don't like this." Punctuating the statement, Leah folded her arms tightly. Tilting her head, she looked up toward the crest of the tree. She couldn't even see that high.

"It's not as bad as it looks," Boyd said, noting Leah's discomfort. "The nest is just a few feet above the top of the ladder."

Leah squinted at the designated area. "How do you know that?"

Pointing, Boyd said, "See that limb with the broken twigs at the end?"

"No— Oh, there it is."

"Right. Well, can you see that heap of dead pine needles?"

"Umm, I think so." Leah blinked at him. "Is that the nest?"

Shrugging, Boyd mounted the ladder. "I sure hope so. I don't like heights any more than the next guy."

As Boyd scaled the ladder, Leah bit her lip and mentally repeated every prayer she'd ever learned. By the time he'd hoisted himself onto the third branch, Leah was eating her knuckles and when his foot slipped, she nearly dropped to her knees.

Finally he was straddling the target limb as though it were a horse, balancing himself by clinging to the branch directly above his head.

"Aha!" Boyd peered into the patch of pine needles, waved, then reached into the pouch with his free hand.

Above him, all manner of feathered creatures screeched and squawked in alarm.

From her vantage point, Leah watched Boyd lean close to the nest, deposit the truant bird, then scoot backward toward the main trunk. Stacey bounced and yelled encouragement as Boyd descended, oblivious to the fact that Leah had paled to a ghostly hue and now had a death grip on the ladder.

When Boyd's foot crunched into the earth, Leah's breath escaped in a loud whoosh.

He grinned. "Miss me?"

Before Leah could answer, Stacey launched herself into Boyd's arms and assaulted him with breathless questions. "Were there other babies in the nest? Did you see the mommy bird? Did you tuck him in real good so he won't fall out again?"

Laughing, Boyd lifted Stacey, setting her firmly on the ground. "Give me a chance, sprout." He pulled the pink sling over his head, then made a production of taking a deep breath. "Yes, no, yes," he said, then tweaked her nose.

Clapping her hands, Stacey hopped in place. "How many babies were there?"

"Three, including the one you rescued."

Suddenly, Stacey's expression froze. "What if the mommy and daddy bird don't come back? What if they 'bandon it 'cause it smells like you?"

"I beg your pardon?"

Managing to twist a bark of laughter into a coughing spasm, Leah clutched at herself and tried to gain control.

Boyd looked offended. "I showered this morning."

Obviously annoyed, Stacey spoke with the exaggerated patience children use only on unenlightened adults. "Mommy told me that birds don't like the way people smell and they might go away and never come back and the baby would be all alone."

"I see—I think." Boyd's forehead creased. "Well, we certainly can't let that happen, can we?"

Stacey shook her head somberly.

Leah's eyes twinkled. "What do you have in mind?"

"Well, I have some binoculars Stacey could borrow. That way she could kind of keep an eye on things."

Looking up, Leah shook her head. "All she'll see from here is a pile of dead pine needles."

Considering the problem, Boyd rubbed his chin in concentration as he scanned the surrounding area. His gaze lit on a stately cedar growing beside the house and he smiled. "Then I guess we'll just have to change her perspective, won't we?"

Leah's eyes narrowed. "I don't think I like the sound of that."

Grinning, Boyd rubbed his hands together. "Trust me," he said, then strode toward the house.

Stacey laced her fingers under her chin and sighed. "Isn't Boyd a nice man?"

With a sinking heart, Leah whispered, "Yes, sweetheart, he is a very nice man." Even as she spoke, the pain in her chest was nearly unbearable because Leah knew that she and Stacey would have to leave soon. Every day in Cedar Cove increased the odds that Leah's secret would be exposed.

And that secret could destroy Boyd.

Chapter Four

Leah dropped the last peeled potato into the colander and listened to its rhythmic pounding. Boyd and Stacey were still hard at work. For the past two hours, the Wainwright house had vibrated with the constant din of grinding buzz saws, thudding hammers, childish giggles and masculine laughter. They were comfortable sounds, family sounds.

A lid clinked. Turning, Leah saw that Cybil had come into the kitchen and was peering into the Dutch oven, poking at the bubbling pot roast with a fork.

"It looks wonderful, dear," Cybil said, inhaling the pungent aroma of garlic and onion. She replaced the lid. "Have you asked Boyd to join us for dinner?"

"Yes." Leah concentrated on slicing potatoes. "I mean, considering the time he's spent building a bird-watching platform for Stacey, it seemed the hospitable thing to do."

Smiling broadly, Cybil agreed, "Of course it was."

Feeling her face heat, Leah wielded the paring knife with more force than necessary, mercilessly slashing at the unfortunate spud.

Oblivious to her daughter's discomfort, Cybil crossed the kitchen. The back door stood open and Cybil peered through the screen, leaning to get a view of the activity at the rear of the house. "Why did they choose that particular tree?" she asked.

"For several reasons, according to Boyd. It has a strong, supportive branch system only ten feet off the ground, and will give Stacey the best view of Rumpelstiltskin's home."

Cybil's head turned quickly. "Rumpelstiltskin?"

"Stacey's baby bird." Leah smiled. Actually, the name was well suited to the homely, pinfeathered ball of gray fuzz.

With a soft tsking sound, Cybil returned her attention to the yard. "They certainly have accomplished a lot this afternoon."

"Well, once Boyd sets his sights on something, it's full speed ahead." At least that part of Boyd's personality hadn't changed, Leah thought wryly. "When Boyd found the ladder in the garage, he saw Papa's workshop and a stack of old plywood. The next thing I know, he's up to his armpits in sawdust and Stacey is practically bouncing off the walls with excitement."

Cybil was silent for several moments, then suddenly said, "Stacey has become quite attached to Boyd."

The knife went through the potato with enough force to score the wooden cutting board. Leah clamped her lips together and remained silent.

Cybil's voice took on a wistful tone. "You need a man in your life, Leah."

"Mother!"

Startled, Cybil met Leah's stern gaze with one of absolute innocence. "Yes, dear?"

Leah sighed. For the past week, Cybil had been less than subtle in making known her opinion that Boyd Cauldwell should play a significant part in Leah's future. Although she meant well, the repeated comments had taken a toll on Leah's nerves—probably because Leah herself had been on an emotional roller coaster. There had been times when she had allowed herself to indulge in nostalgic fantasies and wishful daydreams. At the lake, Boyd had held and comforted her, and for a few delicious moments, the years had melted away.

But it had all been an illusion. He'd soon grown somber, withdrawing into himself as he had done at Virginia City— become unforgiving, unforgetting and angry. Boyd was a man in turmoil; and although Leah had to give him credit for trying to come to terms with the past, she knew that same past would haunt them always.

Yesterday was gone.

Leah was determined not to fall prey to Cybil's false romanticism. "We're just old friends."

"It could be more than that, if you'd let it."

"No, it couldn't." Leah pivoted, facing Cybil with an unwavering stare. "You know that."

Cybil's smile faded. Turning away, she whispered sadly, "I just want you to be happy, Leah."

"I know you do, and I love you for it. But how happy would any of us be if Boyd found out the whole truth?"

Chewing her lip, Cybil's gaze slipped nervously away. "He wouldn't have to find out."

The knife slipped from Leah's fingers and clattered to the counter. She couldn't believe what she'd just heard. "You think I should *lie* to him?"

"Not exactly." Cybil wadded her fingers together and looked extremely uncomfortable.

"Just what kind of relationship could be built on a foundation of half-truths and evasions? I couldn't do that to Boyd." Leah decided not to mention the fact that Boyd was obviously having difficulty accepting the small part of the truth that he already knew.

"Then tell him everything, Leah. Let Boyd make his own decision."

Leah's jaw tightened as she picked up the knife. "No." The whole story would tear Boyd's heart out. God, it all seemed so hopeless.

A cool touch on her arm broke into Leah's thoughts and she looked into Cybil's compassionate eyes. "I'm sure you know best, Leah. I won't mention it again."

Nodding, Leah tried to swallow the lump in her throat and continued to chop furiously.

Cybil slid the paring knife from Leah's hand. "Perhaps you should let me finish this."

Blinking, Leah looked down and saw that the cutting board was smeared with potato mush. She moaned.

"Never mind," Cybil said soothingly. "Why don't you go out and check on the construction crew? I'll finish up here."

Deciding that she'd done enough kitchen damage for one day, Leah took a deep breath and went out into the yard.

The old blue cedar stood so close to the house that its silvery foliage brushed the weathered clapboard. Stacey stood at the base of the tree, staring up into the vibrating branches. Her foot rested on the first rung of a wooden ladder, which jutted from the soft earth into the bristling heart of the tree.

Dried twigs and leaves crunched beneath Leah's feet and Stacey turned toward the sound. "Come look, Mommy. We're almost done."

Tilting her head back, Leah shaded her eyes and followed the child's gaze. Only when she'd positioned herself directly underneath the tree could Leah see the plywood platform wedged among the thick branches. A large semicircular opening beside the main trunk swallowed the top of the ladder, and the structure was enclosed by a sturdy-looking railing.

Stacey was flushed and excited. "Isn't it absolutely the superest thing you've ever seen in your whole life?"

"It's pretty super, all right."

At the sound of Leah's voice, Boyd leaned over the rail. "You're just in time for the housewarming."

"Yeah!" Stacey leaped onto the ladder and had scrambled up three rungs before Leah snagged her belt. Clinging to the ladder rail like a fly on a wall, Stacey looked down quizzically. "What's the matter, Mommy?"

Tightening her grip, Leah licked her lips nervously. The platform seemed so much higher from this angle. She saw Boyd's amused expression as he leaned his elbow on the railing and rested his chin in his hand. He arched a brow in question.

Feeling foolish, Leah stammered, "The, uh, ladder might fall."

With childish impatience, Stacey sighed. "No, it won't. Boyd nailed it to the tree."

"Oh." Skimming a glance upward, Leah saw Boyd nod tolerantly.

"Three-inch screws, top and bottom," he said, helpfully pointing to a tiny metal disk gleaming against the wooden rail. "If it makes you feel any better, I reinforced the plywood floor with pine strapping and the guardrail has been secured with steel brackets." His eyes crinkled mischievously. "This platform would even hold you, Leah."

Tossing Boyd a sour stare, Leah released her daughter's belt. The child scurried like a squirrel, then disappeared up through the platform opening. In a second, two happy faces peered over the railing.

"Wow!" Stacey turned around in wonder. "Awesome!"

The mellow timbre of Boyd's rich laughter sent an army of goose bumps down Leah's spine.

"Try these," Boyd said, and Stacey ducked within the branches.

Leah couldn't see what "these" were. Backing up, she shaded her eyes, then saw Stacey reappear. A pair of huge black binoculars dwarfed her face and her small fingers barely reached around the circumference of the large lenses. Rotating her upper body from left to right, the girl suddenly stopped, apparently focusing on something of interest.

She emitted a squeal of pure delight. "It's him! It's Rumpelstiltskin, and his mommy is feeding him." Lowering the binoculars, Stacey whirled toward Boyd. "I guess she didn't care what he smelled like."

Boyd smiled sickly.

As Leah buried a snort of laughter in her hand, she saw Boyd's strong calves dangling from the platform opening. She heard mumbled voices, one deep and one high-pitched, but couldn't discern the conversation. Then Stacey reappeared at the railing and Leah's attention was captured by the sight of Boyd's muscular thighs descending into view. Tightly rounded buttocks, moving provocatively, were followed by wide shoulder muscles that rippled beneath the thin knit sweater.

Leah's breath slid out silently and her hand involuntarily clasped at the sudden ache in her abdomen. He was magnificent.

Stepping onto the ground, Boyd turned and stood like a deity surveying his kingdom. Backlit by the day's last spray of golden sunlight, he appeared potent, alluring and intensely sexual. A small gasp caught in Leah's throat and she had an overwhelming desire to touch him.

Her inner battle was brief. She saw her own hand outstretched, fingers quivering, reaching. Like two halves of a mirror image, Boyd extended his hand until their fingertips kissed softly, then joined and held.

For that brief moment, they stood united in a soundless communication of mind and of spirit. The experience was dreamlike, beautiful and sweetly intense. If only it could last forever.

But "forever" was a fantasy, and reality broke in with unpleasant gruffness. "Boyd!"

Blinking, they looked up to see Senator Fletcher Cauldwell huffing across the yard and scowling with obvious displeasure. When Leah saw him, she felt as if her facial expression had suddenly been glued in place. She'd hoped never to lay eyes on this man again.

Boyd was surprised by his father's unexpected appearance and more than a little apprehensive. Beside him, Leah had suddenly stiffened like a broomstick and the senator's expression was even more dour than usual. As Cauldwell puffed across the uneven terrain, Boyd felt an indefinable sense of uneasiness.

He greeted his father, then added, "I didn't expect to see you here."

The senator's face was red with exertion. "I could say the same to you," he said brusquely, mopping his shiny forehead. Cauldwell took a deep breath and his belly strained threateningly against the buttons of his starched shirt. Tucking his handkerchief into his pocket, the senator scanned Leah with narrowed eyes. His lips stretched and his jovial voice contrasted with his cool, calculating gaze. "Well, well. Little Leah Wainwright, all grown-up and filled out right nice. Good to see you again." As he spoke, his eyelids flicked rapidly.

Leah had paled three shades and Boyd saw that her eyes had darkened to the color of cold steel. She was clearly upset by his father's crass comment. "Thank you."

Frowning, Boyd studied Leah's tight expression. His father's attitude confused him. Leah and the senator had always gotten along well in the past. In fact, Leah had had a way with the crusty old man. She'd catered to his ego and the senator had often stated that Leah reminded him of Boyd's mother—the one woman Fletcher Cauldwell had truly loved.

Now it occurred to Boyd that after Leah had left Cedar Cove, his father had never mentioned her name again. At the time, Boyd had assumed that the senator was simply avoiding a painful subject. Seeing the thinly veiled hostility between the senator and Leah made Boyd wonder about that assumption.

Cauldwell cleared his throat and spoke to Leah with politic politeness. "I'm sorry about your daddy. I'd like to pay my respects to Cybil, if she's up to it."

For several seconds, Leah simply stared. When she finally spoke, the words were tight with forced courtesy. "That's very kind of you, Senator. I'll tell her you're here." With that, Leah excused herself and went into the house.

Both men were silent until the vibrating screen door had stilled completely. Rubbing his neck, Boyd met his father's eyes and sighed. "All right. What are you *really* doing here?"

Cauldwell appeared offended. "Why, just what I said, son. I came to pay my respects."

"You could have done that over the telephone."

The senator changed the subject. "You missed the strategy session last night."

"Something came up." Actually, Boyd had spent most of the evening sitting on a tree stump staring out at the lake, but he had no intention of sharing that fact with his father.

"You've been hard to get a hold of lately." Cauldwell extracted a cigar from his pocket. "Haven't been in the office much."

Boyd shrugged. "I've taken some time off this week."

Fingering a polished gold lighter, the senator lifted one ruffled brow and glanced pointedly toward the house. "Trying to rekindle an old flame?"

"Maybe."

Absently, Cauldwell slipped the lighter into his pocket, leaving the unlit cigar firmly clamped between his teeth as he spoke. "You can't build a good bonfire with used wood."

Boyd's eyes narrowed and his fists clenched angrily. "What the hell is that supposed to mean?"

Startled by Boyd's harsh tone, Cauldwell started to reply but was stopped by the rustle of branches overhead. His jowls sagged as two pudgy legs appeared, then Stacey scrambled down the ladder.

She jumped from the second rung and grinned up at the senator. "Hi," she said cheerfully. "Who are you?"

Cauldwell's mouth was still open.

"Stacey, this is my father, Senator Cauldwell." Boyd completed the formality: "Senator, this is Leah's daughter, Stacey."

Boyd noticed the senator take several shallow breaths and wondered if the older man was about to hyperventilate. His face was reddening again, and he stared down at the girl as though he'd seen a small ghost.

Stacey squinted up. "Are you a real senator?"

Cauldwell had a coughing spasm. Finally he cleared his throat, wiped his brow and nodded.

"Do you make laws and everything?"

Without answering, the senator bent forward and stared into Stacey's startled face. With a fat fingertip, he touched her chin, turning her head to the right, then to the left. Then, apparently noticing Boyd's stunned expression, Cauldwell straightened and mumbled something about Stacey's being as pretty as her mama.

Stacey's gaze dropped demurely, then she coyly peeked up and smiled.

Leah opened the back door. Her shoulders were as straight as a T square and Boyd saw her eyes sweep from the senator to her daughter, and back again. Holding the screen door open, she spoke briskly. "This way, please."

With a final glance at Stacey, the senator heaved himself up the steps to the porch. Leah stepped from the doorway to allow him access, then slanted a questioning look at Boyd.

He understood. "I'd better get these tools cleaned up first. It'll be dark soon."

"I'll help," Stacey offered, emphasizing the point by scooping a hammer out of the dirt.

"No, I want you to clean up and change clothes before dinner." Leah flinched, knowing that her tone had been sterner than the situation required.

"Aww—"

"That's okay, sprout," Boyd said, ruffling Stacey's hair. "I can struggle through on my own."

Sensing defeat, she dropped the hammer, and with shoulders slumped, dragged herself into the house. Leah followed. When they reached the living room, Leah saw Cybil standing stiffly by the sofa, her thin hands fully engulfed by the senator's meaty palms. Her mother looked nervous, Leah decided, and extremely ill at ease. But then, so was Leah.

As Stacey went upstairs, Cauldwell settled on the sofa. Perching two cushions away, Cybil folded her hands tightly and laid them in her lap.

Suddenly Leah felt cold. The two figures on the sofa blurred together and her knees began to buckle. She steadied herself on a nearby table and was backing toward the kitchen door when she realized her mother was speaking to her.

"Leah? Are you all right?"

Sweat beaded across Leah's lip. "The, uh, rolls in the oven..." Helplessly, she gestured toward the kitchen, then whirled, pushing through the doorway. Stumbling to the table, she collapsed into a chair and lowered her head into her hands.

From the living room she heard muffled voices, one soft and tentative, the other strong and authoritative. Although the words were unclear, Leah was vaguely aware that the senator was offering sympathy and help, but she'd long ago lost any illusions about Fletcher Cauldwell's humanity.

Once, Leah had actually liked him. She'd even trusted him. That had been a bitter mistake.

Oh, he could be charming enough. After all, in the political arena, charm was an asset, and the senator wasn't one to waste assets. But Leah had learned that the elder Cauldwell had a darker side. He was a powerful man and wasn't averse to using that power in order to further his own interests.

Ten years ago, Leah had become a threat to those interests, and she'd felt the full impact of that power.

She remembered the last time the senator had been at the Wainwright home. She remembered muffled voices from the past, only instead of cowering in the kitchen as she was now, she'd been huddled at the top of the stairs, listening—and crying.

Cauldwell had bellowed in rage, calling Leah unspeakable names, peppering his tirade with threats and obscenities. Louis Wainwright's anger had been, as usual, cold and contained. Leah had believed that her father was defending her, but his clipped responses had been drowned out by the senator's verbal barrage. The only thing Leah understood clearly were her mother's choking sobs.

Suddenly the voices had become softer, more intense.

Then Cybil had been sent upstairs. With red eyes and wet cheeks, she'd gathered Leah to her breast, soothing and rocking her, saying that Louis would take care of everything. Everything would be all right, she'd told Leah.

And Leah had believed her.

But everything *hadn't* been all right. The next morning, Louis had sent Leah away and she'd never seen her father again.

As Leah pushed away the unpleasant memories, she realized that the house was completely quiet. No voices, muffled or otherwise, were filtering from the living room. Wiping her cheeks, she walked to the door, opening it a crack to peek into the living room.

Cybil was alone, clutching her abdomen as though in terrible pain. Her expression was one of stark horror.

* * *

Darkness brought a chill to the air and Leah shivered, wrapping her denim jacket tightly around her chest. Stars sprayed across the clear night sky in such brilliant abundance that it was impossible to define where one point of light ended and another began.

During her years in the city, Leah had forgotten the beauty of her mountain home. So much was different, yet so much had remained the same. Since Leah had returned, she was aware of subtle changes inside herself—a tightening, a tension, a feeling of being powerless. Those emotions frightened her. It was like being a child again, being swept away by circumstances over which she had no control. The woman deep within, who had grown strong and self-sufficient, was withering, to be replaced by the frightened girl of yesterday.

The senator's visit had brought those suppressed emotions to the surface, but Leah realized that they had been quietly simmering deep in her soul since the moment she'd arrived in Cedar Cove.

The snap of a twig startled her. Turning, she heard the crunch of dried leaves and saw a familiar shadow moving toward her.

When Boyd was standing beside her, Leah shifted her gaze toward the lake. Surface waves rolled through reflected moonlight until the glow undulated sensuously.

Boyd stood silently, so close she could feel the warmth radiate from his body. As he shifted his weight, the air swirled gently and a spicy male scent teased her. The heaviness in her chest dropped lower. Much lower. She felt restless, strangely agitated.

Hugging herself even more tightly, she stepped away to allow the comfort of some space between them. Boyd respected her unspoken request and didn't follow.

"I expected you and Mother would be discussing business for most of the evening," Leah said.

"Cybil seemed a bit preoccupied. I don't think she was feeling well."

"She's been eating antacids like candy lately." Concerned, Leah gazed toward the house. "I'm going to get her in to see the doctor next week."

"She *did* look a bit more peaked than usual at dinner." Boyd slid a sideways glance at Leah. "So did you. Is anything wrong?"

Leah turned away. "It's just been a tiring week, I guess."

Skeptical, Boyd said, "I'm sure it has been, but you both seemed in good spirits earlier today."

"Maybe the strain just caught up with us at the same time."

"Maybe." Boyd kicked at a pinecone. "Or maybe my father's unexpected visit had something to do with this universal mood swing."

Closing her eyes, Leah rubbed at her forehead and wished he would drop this unpleasant subject. Boyd was too intelligent to be fooled by shrugging off the senator's sobering effect on the Wainwright household. Still, Leah wasn't ready to delve too deeply into the cause of Cybil's distress—or of her own.

Sighing, Leah replied. "Yes, Mother was upset by the senator's visit."

"Why?" Boyd demanded. "What did he say to her?"

"I really don't know." That was certainly the truth. Cybil had been completely closemouthed about the details of Cauldwell's visit, refusing to discuss it with Leah. "When I asked her, she just mumbled something about reliving old memories, and went up to her room."

"What 'old memories'?" Boyd frowned. Leah was being deliberately evasive—again—and his tolerance was thinning considerably. His voice reflected his frustration. "And what about you, Leah? Why did you act as though you'd just been confronted by Jack the Ripper holding a bloody knife?"

"Did I?" She attempted an expression of surprise and innocence, but Boyd's twitching jaw announced that she hadn't pulled it off. Leah mentally kicked herself, wishing she'd been able to control her emotional transparency when Cauldwell had shown up. Denying what Boyd had clearly seen in her stunned expression was foolhardy, but Leah was grasping at straws. The conversation was veering out of control and into forbidden territory. With a tight laugh, she said, "I don't know what you mean."

Boyd was in no mood for social niceties. His voice was low, his tone clipped, and he went for the jugular. "The hell you don't. What the devil has happened between you and my father?"

"That's none of your business," she snapped, then spun on her heel and started toward the house.

Boyd reached out quickly, snagging her arm and halting her movement. "I think it *is* my business."

"I don't." She stared at the offending hand. When he released her, she marched across the yard. Anger mingled with fear welled from the pit of her stomach. Focusing on the back porch, Leah prayed that she would reach the safety of the house before Boyd recovered and stopped her.

It wasn't to be. She'd gotten as far as the tire swing when Boyd stepped in front of her. He didn't have to say a word. His expression spoke volumes.

Leah recognized the determined slash of brow, the steel-hard jawline. He would have an answer, if not tonight, then tomorrow or the next day or the next—but he wouldn't be denied. If she didn't satisfy his growing suspicion, he would just keep on digging, and sooner or later, he would find out a great deal more than Leah wanted him to know.

Leah's shoulders slumped in defeat. "All right."

Boyd folded his arms across his chest and he waited.

Swallowing hard, Leah expressed herself cautiously. "When I realized that I was pregnant, I was afraid to tell my father, so I went to the senator." Leah saw Boyd straighten in surprise. His jaw slackened as his arms dropped to his sides. Hurriedly she continued: "It was probably foolish, but he'd always been so kind to me and I—I trusted him. I thought he could tell me what to do, but—" A hot mass suddenly rushed into her throat, choking off the words. *God help me!* she cried silently. She was telling Boyd the truth, but Leah knew she could go only so far in relating what had happened that night.

With compassionate eyes Boyd reached out, but Leah dodged the comfort of his embrace. This was like tiptoeing barefoot through shards of glass. One careless step could result in horrible injury.

Only it was Boyd who would be the one to suffer the most.

That realization dried her unshed tears and strengthened her resolve. In a dull monotone, Leah continued. "He made some rather unpleasant references to my moral standards, then told my father. Needless to say, the incident soured our relationship."

For several silent moments, Boyd stared numbly at Leah, unable to believe what he'd just heard, yet knowing instinctively that it was true. Closing his eyes, he rubbed at his forehead and remembered when he'd come home to find Leah gone. He remembered his father's strange behavior and the subtle, cutting remarks about Leah. At the time, Boyd had been too engrossed in his own pain to analyze the situation, but now things were beginning to fall into place.

His heart ached for Leah, for the betrayal and humiliation she must have felt. And Boyd's own family had added to her grief. How could he possibly atone for that?

"Leah," he whispered. "I'm so sorry." He saw her shoulders rotate in a gesture of acceptance.

"It was a long time ago," she said. "It's over."

"But not forgotten."

"No." She stared up at the sky.

Boyd fought an almost overwhelming urge to gather her into his arms and kiss away the hurt. "He had no right to treat you that way. But I understand why he did."

Leah's head snapped toward him, her eyes wide with disbelief. "Excuse me?"

Well, that was certainly tactless, Boyd told himself. Spearing his fingers through his hair, he tried to explain. "Do you remember my stepmother?"

Leah's eyes narrowed. "Vaguely, but she left town when I was about six."

"She didn't exactly 'leave town.' The senator kicked her out after he found her in bed with one of his campaign aides."

"Is that supposed to shock me?"

Boyd sighed. This wasn't going well at all. "I'm simply trying to explain why he views women as less than trust-

worthy. He had no way of knowing that you had been...
victimized.''

Leah's eyes widened and her lips parted, as though she
wanted desperately to say something. Then her mouth
tightened and she nodded in a jerky movement designed to
indicate that she'd understood Boyd's explanation.

Somehow, he doubted that. Her expression had become
veiled and guarded. The years had hardened her, he thought
sadly. And why not? When she'd needed support and understanding, she had been consistently let down by those
she'd loved and trusted. She'd been abused, harshly judged,
and abandoned. And Boyd had been powerless to stop it.

Now he wanted desperately to help her, but he didn't
know how. Nor did he fully understand why it was so important to him. Perhaps he needed to soothe his own guilty
conscience; perhaps it was something deeper. All he knew
for certain was that he had a passionate need to see Leah
laugh again, to see her happy.

Finally she spoke. ''It's late.''

''I should be going,'' he replied, but made no move to
leave.

Leah nodded. Of course he should leave, she told herself. In fact, he should never have come at all. It was just
making everything so much more...difficult. With a deep
breath she turned and managed what she hoped was a convincing smile. ''You've made this a wonderful day for
Stacey. Thank you for that.''

''I enjoyed it.'' Fingering the rope from which the tire
swing hung, a picture flashed in Boyd's mind, a Techni-
color image from years past. Leah had loved this swing. She
used to beg Boyd to wind the rope as tightly as he could get
it, then scream in delight as it uncoiled, spinning her like a
centrifuge. It had made Boyd dizzy just to watch, but Leah
had absolutely loved it. She'd been adventurous then—
trusting, innocent and vulnerable, very much like Stacey's
injured bird.

The years had changed her. The spark of adventure had
been replaced by a thick veil of caution, and the freshness
of her youthful enthusiasm had dissipated. But she still had

an aura of innocence about her. And she was still vulnerable.

Looking up, Boyd saw that Leah was watching him. He nodded toward the swing. "Do you still like to be spun until you turn green?"

She watched him soberly for a moment, then rewarded him with a soft laugh. "No. Now I get ill making a U-turn."

"That's quite a change."

"We all have to grow up," she said sadly. "And we all have to change."

Boyd regarded her thoughtfully. "Have I changed, Leah?"

She looked away. "Of course."

"How?"

"Well, you have some gray hair, for one thing."

"Ouch." Boyd raked at the offending lock. "Really a sweet-talker, aren't you?"

"You asked." She chewed her lip, then added, "And you're moodier than I remember."

He winced. "Virginia City."

"Yes, but I noticed it at the lake, too." She watched him carefully, noting his sad expression as he stared off into the blackness. "It's Stacey, isn't it?"

For a moment, Leah thought he hadn't heard her, then she saw an almost imperceptible nod.

"She's wonderful, Leah, but I look at her and I see—" His voice broke and their eyes locked. "She should have been our child, Leah—yours and mine."

With a soft gasp, Leah felt her expression crumble under Boyd's probing gaze. "I know," she whispered.

She wanted to look away, but couldn't. She wanted to run, but was paralyzed. She wanted to cry out, but was suddenly mute.

Boyd reached out slowly, hesitantly, then closer and closer until his fingertip was nearly touching her cheek. He paused, his expression twisted as though he were about to extend his hand into a burning flame but couldn't control himself. Then Leah felt his touch, a whispering stroke of warmth against her skin.

Her breath caught. She stood motionless. Boyd's knuckles stroked downward, then reversed and he cupped her chin in his palm, tipping her face up. Leah saw desire in his darkening eyes and a wave of heat seared her to the very core.

Lowering his head, Boyd touched his cheek to hers and whispered her name. The friction of his rough skin was pleasing and she reveled in it, rubbing her face against his with catlike pleasure. There was a low, rumbling sound emanating from deep within his chest. It was arousing, exciting. Leah had never experienced this surge of inner heat, this tingling deep inside her.

Boyd's lips brushed her face, then traveled slowly down to her throat. She moaned at the delicious warmth of his mouth on her skin, at the sweet sensations washing over her as he slid his hands over her back. Then he brought his mouth upward, ever so slowly, until his lips were teasing hers, not quite touching but close enough to be felt.

Leah trembled, feeling the damp heat of his breath on her skin, waiting and wanting, suddenly hungry for his mouth. Finally she parted her lips in silent invitation.

He kissed her then, softly and sweetly, touching her as delicately as one might stroke the fragile petals of a rose—so tenderly, so comfortingly. Like a summer flower, she felt her own petals soften and bloom.

Without conscious thought, she slid her hands over his chest, marveling that such gentleness could emanate from such strength. She massaged his hard muscles and tested the springy mat pushing beneath his thin cotton sweater while her palms itched to touch his bare skin. A few hairs peeked over the opening at his neck, and Leah fingered them gingerly.

He shuddered and groaned, tightening his grip on her.

Suddenly, he became more demanding. As she gasped in surprise, he plunged his tongue into her mouth, tasting and savoring.

The gentle heat he'd created suddenly exploded into a raging hunger. A sound rolled from deep inside her, a muffled cry of need—and of terror. She pushed at Boyd, only to feel steely arms tighten, crushing her against his chest.

He wouldn't let go. Oh, God. *He wouldn't let go.*

Leah's arms were pinned. Panic swelled like a black tide. What was happening? She couldn't breathe, couldn't move.

Oh, please, her mind screamed wildly.

"Don't hurt me! Oh, God, please let me go! Please... please..." Leah was sobbing in terror as she impotently pummeled his chest. Then her knees gave way and she sagged limply, tears streaming down her face.

From what seemed like a great distance, she heard a voice. Strangely, it soothed her and she tried to concentrate on its lulling sound. Someone was saying her name, over and over again.

With a choked rasp, Leah opened her eyes and saw Boyd's stricken face. As though she'd just awakened from a savage dream, Leah blinked and looked around. She wasn't at the lake, and the man with her wasn't—

A cry of relief bubbled from her throat. She felt Boyd's fingers press into the flesh of her arm and realized that he was holding her up.

"Leah... My God, Leah. Who did this to you?" His voice quivered with fear and rage.

Shakily, she managed to pull her feet under her, testing their strength until she stood on her own. Turning away, she felt her skin flame with humiliation. This had never happened to her before. But then, she'd never given it a chance to happen.

"I—I'm all right," she replied, not at all certain it was true.

Boyd was distraught. "I just assumed that over the years there would have been . . . other men in your life."

"Of course, there have been," she said stiffly, unable to meet his eyes. "I haven't spent the past ten years in a convent."

Even as the words slid over her tongue, Leah inwardly flinched. It wasn't exactly a lie, after all. Over the years, she really *had* tried to find someone else. Perhaps she'd tried too hard at first, and for all the wrong reasons. Yes, there had been lonely times, but when Leah had attempted to ease that loneliness with the company of other men, her thoughts had than friendship with those who would happily have shared her life; and she had never allowed them more than a few chaste kisses.

But Leah had never lowered her defenses, never felt her body throb as though her blood had been boiled. The peculiar heat wasn't completely unfamiliar, however. Leah had experienced the same passion, the same longing for Boyd ten years earlier. Now he'd reawakened those yearnings and in doing so, had exposed the secret terror lurking deep inside.

The flashback had been horrifying and embarrassing, but it was the look on Boyd's face that had nearly destroyed Leah. She could accept anger, even contempt, but she could never accept his pity.

Chapter Five

Hubbard's Department Store had always enjoyed a thriving Saturday business, and this afternoon was no exception. Stacey rooted through racks of colorful swimsuits, oohing and ahing over skimpy scraps of fabric, while Leah leaned wearily against the lingerie counter, nodding patiently.

"Look at the pink-and-purple one, Mommy." Stacey exuberantly wiggled a clothes hanger from which a kaleidoscopic fragment dangled limply. "Isn't it unreal?"

"Umm." Leah eyed the suit. "It's so unreal it's almost nonexistent."

With a pained expression, Stacey rolled her eyes, then turned her attention back to the exciting world of summer fashion.

Leah realized that her baby girl was growing up, and was depressed by the thought. There had been so many "firsts" over the years: first tooth, first step, first day of school. Soon Stacey would experience the first bloom of young womanhood: first date, first high-school prom, first love.

First love. Leah smiled sadly. Adolescent romanticism had left Leah ill prepared for her own first love, for the tearing pain of desperate happiness followed by plunging despair. If only she could spare her daughter such exquisite torture. Intellectually, she knew that Stacey, like all independent human creatures, would insist on making her own way in the world, mistakes and all.

Leah's thoughts turned to Boyd, her own first love—and, she realized now, her last love. It was foolish to continue denying what her mind and her soul had always known: Leah had never stopped loving Boyd Cauldwell, and deep inside she realized that she probably never would.

Over the years, Leah had concentrated only on raising her daughter. When Stacey was grown, however, Leah would still be alone, still pining for the one man she could never have.

"Can I try them on now?"

Absently, Leah mumbled, "Umm?"

"The bathing suits. I need to see if they fit."

"Uh-huh." Leah gazed into space, thinking how strange life was. She'd spent years trying to convince herself that Boyd Cauldwell was nothing more than a fond childhood memory. Her reaction last night when he'd kissed her had been frightening and humiliating, but at least she'd *had* a reaction. Leah had assumed she was simply one of those frigid women for whom sex held no appeal. Not true. She had wanted Boyd, and only Boyd. Her body had wanted him and her spirit had wanted him.

Her mind, however, had only wanted escape. Post-trauma sex syndrome? The entire situation was ironic, almost tragic. But in a way, Leah was thankful. A love affair with Boyd would inevitably lead to disaster.

Stacey's voice was edged with exasperation. "Mother-r-r-r!"

Startled, Leah pushed herself away from the counter. Stacey, her arms loaded with a stack of multihued swimsuits, was impatiently tapping her foot. "Ah, did you want to see how those fit?"

"Yes, please," her daughter said, with a long-suffering sigh.

Leah's eyes darted around the store, focusing her mind on the business at hand. "The dressing rooms are over there."

Jostling through the crowd, they managed to snag a harried salesclerk, who pressed a numbered plastic card into Leah's hand and motioned toward a row of curtained cubicles.

Once they were inside, Leah hung the selected garments on a hook. "Which one do you want to try on first, sweetheart?"

Stacey's arms were folded tightly over her round tummy. She stared at the carpeted floor and mumbled something that Leah didn't quite catch.

"Pardon me?"

Shifting uncomfortably, Stacey spoke to her shoes. "I want to do it myself."

Stunned, Leah realized that her daughter had been suddenly struck by an attack of prepubescent modesty. Not knowing whether to laugh or cry, Leah settled on a coughing spasm. Wiping her eyes, she muttered, "I'll, uh, just wait out here."

She slipped through the drape, leaned against the wall of the long, narrow hallway, and shook her head in disbelief. Stacey was indeed growing up.

"Leah?"

A vaguely familiar voice called Leah from the far end of the corridor. Leah turned toward the sound.

"Leah Wainwright! I declare, I *thought* that was you but you've just changed so much, I really just couldn't be sure." A frothy blond woman with a beauty-shop fresh coiffure bounced toward Leah with two bored-looking youngsters in tow. "Well, you know, I heard you were in town but I just never expected to see you out and about. I mean, with your daddy and all."

The woman was as effervescent as a gin fizz—all sweetness and foam, but with a subtle hint of sharpness.

Leah pulled an obscure recollection from the past—a vision of blue-and-yellow pom-poms at the high-school football games and the leaping, screaming head cheerleader. "Bitsy Mayfield?"

Pleased, the woman nodded and flashed the sixty-karat grin Leah remembered.

Bitsy had been adorable, popular and rich, class president and homecoming queen, voted Most Likely to Break Hearts by the senior class. Since Bitsy had been a year ahead of Leah in school, they'd never been particularly close. Still, it was good to see her.

Relaxing, Leah chuckled softly, shaking her head and repeating, "Bitsy Mayfield. You haven't changed a bit."

With a high-pitched laugh, Bitsy patted her stiff hair, preening slightly. "Haven't I?" A small boy, perhaps three years old, tugged at Bitsy's arm and whined. Annoyed, she shook him off, then shrugged. "Obviously, there have been *some* changes," Bitsy said, gesturing toward the children. The boy was sulking dangerously and the girl, who appeared to be slightly older, had shyly hidden behind her mother's ample hips. All Leah could see was a thatch of stick-straight sandy hair.

"They're lovely children," Leah commented.

Bitsy arched an eyebrow. "Sometimes they are, and sometimes they're just like their father." She gave Leah a women-understand-these-things look and Leah nodded somberly.

The saleswoman stepped into the dressing room, rubbing her hands together and smiling solicitously. "Did you find anything you liked, Mrs. Cauldwell?"

With a careless wave of her hand, Bitsy said, "Nothing at all. You really should get a more stylish selection. The stores in Sacramento carry all the new European designers." As though the entire subject was tiresome, Bitsy turned toward Leah, effectively dismissing the deflated clerk.

Leah felt as though her face had been frozen in place. Bitsy was continuing to ramble on about something, but Leah's mind simply echoed the words, "Mrs. Cauldwell."

When Bitsy answered, Leah realized that she'd spoken aloud. "Craig and I were married six years ago. I thought you knew."

"Ah, no—no, I didn't," she said stiffly. "Congratulations."

With a toss of her head, Bitsy grinned smugly, then lifted her left hand to display an enormous diamond-studded wedding band. "Thank you. Marriage does have its small rewards." Wiggling her ring finger, Bitsy left little room for doubt as to her meaning. "Craig's running for the Board of Supervisors, you know. And what does *your* husband do, Leah?" Bitsy added shrewdly.

"I—I'm not married."

Bitsy's eyes gleamed. "Oh, that's right. Silly me."

Leah licked her dry lips. Craig's wife. Craig's children. Leah's gaze darted to the boy. He favored Bitsy, with almond-shaped green eyes and a very straight, almost pointed nose. The child had oatmeal-colored hair, but that seemed the only resemblance to the Cauldwell side of the family.

Then a movement caught Leah's attention. From behind Bitsy, a small face peered curiously, with deep-set blue eyes.

"This is Jenny," Bitsy said, then tapped the boy's head. "And the miniature monster here is Jamie."

The girl appeared to be about five and Leah felt her chest tighten at the sight—a freckle-splattered nose and a too-large mouth slashing above a broad, cleft chin. There was no doubt that this child was a Cauldwell.

But then, so was Stacey.

"No... Oh, no."

"Pardon me?" Bitsy inquired.

Before Leah could respond, the curtain was jerked aside and Stacey pranced into the hallway, then piroutted once. "This one is my favorite. Do you like it?" Suddenly the child noticed Bitsy's undisguised curiosity. "Hi. Are you a friend of my mommy?"

"Yes, dear. We're old friends." Bitsy pursed her lips and stroked her chin, regarding Stacey thoughtfully.

Leah jumped between them, turned Stacey so that her back was to Bitsy, then crouched and tugged on the fabric of the suit. She knew she was being ridiculous. Just because she saw a family resemblance herself didn't mean that anyone else would notice. Perhaps there wasn't really any similarity at all. Perhaps it was all in her guilty, troubled mind.

Finally Leah mumbled, "It's too tight, darling. Try on another one."

"No, it's not. See! It's supposed to go down like this."

"It fits beautifully," Bitsy said smoothly. "Why, that style is all the rage."

Stacey beamed.

Bitsy's daughter suddenly tugged at her mother's arm. "Look, Mommy. That little girl has an angel kiss, just like Jamie."

Stacey blinked at the younger girl. "What's an 'angel kiss'?"

A reddish stain splashed over the side of Stacey's hip, exposed by the French cut of the suit. The girl's pudgy finger pointed at the birthmark. "That is," she said, "my brother, Jamie, has one, too. Mommy says it's because an angel kissed him when he was born."

"Really?" Craning her neck, Stacey examined the small blemish, then grinned, obviously pleased by the romantic image of how it might have gotten there.

Skimming a glance at Bitsy, Leah saw the woman's eyes had narrowed and she was staring at Stacey as though the child had three noses.

Leah felt sick. "Birthmarks run in our family," she lied, then stretched her lips into a plastic smile and hoped she looked cheerful. A strained silence followed. Leah noted that Bitsy had paled considerably.

Lifting her chin, Bitsy's gaze swept from Stacey to Leah, then back again. "Yes, *flammus* discolorations are quite common, aren't they?" Her voice was cool. Abruptly grabbing her son's hand, she pulled the child to his feet. "We have to go now, Leah. It...it was nice to see you again."

Then the dressing room was suddenly empty. Stacey went behind the curtain to change and Leah sagged against the wall feeling as though the air had been squashed from her lungs.

Don't overreact, Leah silently reprimanded herself. *Be calm.*

Leah told herself that she was exaggerating the significance of the situation, misreading Bitsy's expression. There was no reason to panic. After all, the world was simply crawling with children who had cleft chins and birthmarks. Besides, Stacey looked just like Leah—everyone said so.

Well, almost everyone.

It was after five when Boyd pulled up in front of the Cauldwell mansion. He turned off the ignition, leaned back in the seat and tried to compose his thoughts. Anger seethed deep inside as he mentally rehashed what Leah had told him the night before.

For years, Fletcher Cauldwell had professed to know nothing about what had happened to Leah. In fact, Boyd clearly remembered every detail of that horrible day ten years ago, the day he'd returned to discover that Leah had left Cedar Cove. The senator had blustered and stammered, offering sympathy for Boyd's pain but professing ignorance of the reasons for Leah's hasty departure. It was obvious, his father had piously intoned that Leah was ill prepared to be the wife of a Cauldwell.

The senator had lied, pure and simple.

And Boyd had bought into the entire charade.

A loud, blaring honk startled Boyd and he realized that he'd slammed his fist into the car horn. He swore, then pushed open the door and stepped out, utterly determined that the senator should acknowledge those lies and admit that he'd betrayed the trust of a frightened, seventeen-year-old girl who'd pleaded for help.

As Boyd mounted the steps of the massive porch, he was still bothered by niggling doubts. Nothing about this situation made total sense. Knowing his father's rigid expectations, Boyd understood why the senator might have been outraged by a perceived betrayal of his son, particularly if Leah hadn't fully explained the gruesome details. But why had he concealed Leah's visit?

Even as he asked himself the question, an answer was clear. In his own warped way, the senator had been trying to protect Boyd.

But that was something Boyd wanted to hear for himself.

The heavy door swung open and a fleshy, gray-haired woman smiled up at him as she wiped her hands on a towel.

"Good evening, Mrs. Blumstein." Boyd strode into the entry. "Is the senator in his study?"

Wrinkling her pink forehead, the woman replied, "Why, no. He left this afternoon for Sacramento."

Boyd had taken two steps toward the study, then stopped abruptly. "What? That wasn't on his schedule."

Mrs. Blumstein appeared flustered. "I don't know about that. Senator Cauldwell said he was going to drop by the cabin on his way to the airport."

Boyd massaged the back of his neck. "I've been at the office all day." Trying to catch up, he silently added, for all the good it had done. He'd accomplished nothing of significance and given himself a roaring headache in the bargain. Glancing over, he realized that the senator's housekeeper was wringing her hands and looking extremely distressed. Boyd smiled and the housekeeper visibly relaxed. "Did my father say when he'd return?"

"He didn't mention anything to me, but maybe Mr. Craig could tell you." She grinned broadly, flipping the towel over her pendulous forearm. "The chicken Dijon is nearly done and I baked a wonderful peach pie for dessert."

"Thank you, but I won't be staying." Boyd had other plans for dinner and was hoping to convince Leah to share them. "I'll see if Craig knows when the senator is due back and—"

Boyd's words were obscured by a heavy thud, followed by the sharp crash of shattering glass.

"Mercy!" Mrs. Blumstein gasped, then waddled toward the parlor.

A woman's voice, high-pitched and angry, filtered through the closed doors. Boyd moaned, then stopped the older woman before she could interrupt the heated argument. "You finish dinner," he said soothingly. "I'll take care of this."

"But—"

"Please. It'll be fine."

Unconvinced but obviously unwilling to disregard Boyd's request, the housekeeper nodded and tottered off.

There was another crash, then Boyd heard Bitsy scream, "Get rid of her!"

"How?" Craig whined. "It's not my fault—"

"She'll ruin everything... *everything*. If you think I'm going to stand by and let my life go down the toilet because you can't control your lousy libido, you've got another thing coming, buster."

"Aw, honey—"

"*Don't* you 'honey' me, you cowardly worm. If you lose this election, I swear I'll leave. Do you hear me? I'll leave and take every dime you have."

Craig's voice broke. "You don't mean that."

After a moment of silence, Boyd heard her soft, deadly response. "Try me. If you don't take care of her, I will."

Turning away, Boyd shook his head and walked back toward the front door. Unfortunately, fights between Craig and Bitsy weren't uncommon. Apparently Craig had been caught in another one of his extramarital trysts, and although Boyd found Bitsy to be a rather shallow and materialistic person, he did have some empathy for her. Craig was, by any definition, a philanderer and a rotten husband.

At the moment, Boyd didn't want to involve himself in what was obviously a private matter but he made a mental note to discreetly broach the subject with Craig as soon as possible. It could, after all, have an impact on the current political climate, and as his brother's campaign manager, Boyd couldn't afford the luxury of turning a blind eye.

But as Boyd steered his car onto the road, he felt a peculiar prickling sensation skitter down his spine. There had been something different about the argument he'd just overheard, an undercurrent of desperation in his brother's voice that made the hairs on Boyd's neck stand up. Suddenly he had a dreadful premonition that something terrible was about to happen.

With critical eyes, Leah turned in front of the full-length mirror, adjusting and readjusting the scoop neckline of her black dinner dress. If she had another inch of bustline, the plunging cut would have provided a delightful décolletage instead of a gaping, simply immodest view.

Reaching behind, she unzipped the unsuitable garment and glanced at her watch. It was nearly seven and Boyd would be here at any moment. When he'd called, Leah had almost declined his dinner invitation. Now, she wished that she had.

Still, it would provide a quiet setting for Leah to tell Boyd that she had decided to leave Cedar Cove early. In fact, Leah desperately wished that she'd never come at all.

But Cybil had needed her.

To Leah's surprise, however, Cybil had suddenly agreed to return to Sacramento with her and Stacey. Tonight would be the last time Leah would ever see Boyd Cauldwell. The realization was both a relief and an agony. But for Boyd's sake, and her own, she simply had to go. Leah loved Boyd too much to risk staying.

When the doorbell rang, Leah pawed through the closet, finally selecting a modestly styled, ice-blue chemise. She slipped it on, applied a coat of pale pink lipgloss and automatically reached for her favorite fragrance.

She heard running thumps on the stairway and knew that Stacey was heading down to greet Boyd. Throwing open the bedroom door, Leah took a deep breath and followed.

"For me?" Stacey squealed.

Leah heard the sound of ripping paper, then a whoop of delight. When she went into the living room, Stacey was clutching a book to her chest and Boyd was smiling.

"I thought you might like it," Boyd said. "You can compare the illustrations to identify the various species in the area."

Stacey spotted Leah and thrust the book out. "It's a bird book," she said, obviously thrilled. "It has all kinds of pictures."

Leah managed a smile. Why did he have to be so darn nice, anyway? Of course, Boyd had no way of knowing that Stacey would have little use for an Audubon Society Field Book in downtown Sacramento, and Leah hadn't had the heart to tell her daughter that she would only have one more day to enjoy her bird-watching activities.

Stacey had dropped cross-legged to the floor and was thumbing through the colorful pages. "Here he is! It's a picture of Rumpelstiltskin."

Curious, Boyd looked over her shoulder, then nodded. "You're right, Stacey. That's a stellar jay and that one is a blue jay. Can you see the subtle differences?"

Brows furrowed, the girl studied the pages.

Looking up, Boyd saw Leah. His eyes crinkled with pleasure. "You look lovely." Stepping around the child, he walked over to Leah and handed her a single white rose.

Nervously she took the perfect bloom, inhaling its sweet scent. From any other man, Leah would have thought the gesture too slick—seductive and romantic but basically insincere. Boyd, however, was watching Leah with genuine pleasure. A long time ago, a much younger Boyd had gathered a cluster of wild poppies, offering them to Leah with the same guileless joy.

Suddenly Leah's heart felt as though it had been squeezed.

"We should be going," she said crisply, then handed the flower to Cybil. "I won't be long, Mother. If you need me, we'll be at . . . ?" She silently questioned Boyd.

"Here's the number," he said and handed Cybil a neatly folded square. But Leah saw that some of the light had gone out of Boyd's eyes.

Swallowing hard, she turned away, silently cursing her deliberate brusqueness. Leah didn't want to hurt Boyd by seeming callous or indifferent, but she had to make a clean break. It wasn't fair for Boyd to believe that they could ever recapture what they'd once had.

Leah reached toward Stacey. "Kiss me goodbye, sweetheart." Jumping to her feet, Stacey gave Leah a quick hug and a peck on the cheek. "Behave. And mind your grandmother."

"I will." Then Stacey lurched toward Boyd, winding her arms tightly around his waist. "Thank you for the bird book," she said fervently. "I love it. It's the best thing I ever got in my whole life."

Initially Boyd looked shocked and perturbed by Stacey's affectionate display, but Leah noted that his eyes warmed quickly as he stroked the child's hair. "You're welcome, sprout."

As Leah watched the man she loved and the child she adored, she felt her heart wrench. It seemed so right to see them together. But Leah knew it was wrong. Very wrong.

With her emotions spinning, Leah marched stiffly outside, pausing as Boyd opened her car door.

The summer sun hung low in the western sky as Boyd drove south through town. He pursed his lips, slanting a glance at his silent passenger. Leah seemed preoccupied, uneasy. Given the brutish manner in which he'd lost control of himself last night, Boyd really couldn't blame her.

He still didn't understand what had come over him. He only knew that he had wanted... No, he had *needed* to touch her, to taste her and hold her against him. Her lips had felt so warm, her body so pliable as she'd melted against him, and he'd been flooded by a rush of sensations.

Somewhere deep in his consciousness, Boyd had felt her go rigid and had been overwhelmed by icy fear. She was pulling away again and he'd felt a sense of panic at the loss. Without realizing what he was doing, Boyd had held her tighter and tighter still, as though by doing so, he could keep her with him forever.

Leah's expression of sheer terror when she finally tore away would haunt Boyd for the rest of his life.

Angrily, Boyd gripped the steering wheel. How could he have been so selfish, so insensitive? Boyd had known what Leah had been through and yet he'd blithely ignored her emotional trauma. In fact, he'd probably done her irreparable harm, all because he had so desperately wanted— wanted what?

He honestly didn't know. Boyd was torn by inner conflict, bewildered by his own feelings. Some emotions were identifiable—guilt and anger. Others were ambiguous, deep disturbances that were obscure and confusing.

When Boyd turned down the familiar dirt road toward the cabin, he felt Leah's growing tension permeate the vehicle. Clearing his throat, he managed what he hoped was a reassuring smile. "I thought we needed some time alone." He slanted a quick glance in her direction and saw that her eyes had widened in distress. Boyd slowed the car, then pulled to a stop. "I don't want to upset you. We can go somewhere else, if you'd like."

She managed a wan smile. "I was just a bit surprised, that's all. There's no reason to change your plans. Spending an evening at the cabin will be...like old times."

Boyd smiled. That's exactly what he'd hoped..."like old times." He and Leah had used the cabin as a hideaway from the world. They'd spent hours there, making plans for the future, or just gazing into each other's eyes.

Those moments had been magical, filled with soft kisses and tender exploration. They had fantasized about consummating their love, yet had agreed to wait until they were husband and wife. If they'd only known— "Boyd?"

"Umm?" Tearing his thoughts from the past, Boyd focused on Leah and realized that she was fidgeting nervously. No wonder. He'd been staring at her like some kind of dazed madman. Rubbing his eyes, Boyd sighed. "I want to apologize for last night, Leah. I had no right to behave so, uh, rudely."

Her eyes rounded, then she quickly averted them, as though she were trying to conceal her thoughts. "It was my fault, actually. I'm normally not so high-strung."

Absently tapping his finger on the steering wheel, Boyd scanned her face for clues. It hadn't been her fault at all, and he wondered why she would say so. Still, he felt a need to reassure her and tried for a light, teasing tone. "I promise to control my carnal urges tonight."

She rewarded him with a soft laugh. "Controlling urges has always been one of your strong points. I trust you."

Boyd winced at the reminder that in the past, he had been the one to pull back when passions had flared too hot. "Touché," he muttered, then shifted the car into gear and headed down the road.

When Boyd pulled up in front of the cabin, he glanced at Leah and felt as though he'd taken a body blow. As she stared at the familiar old structure, her eyes had a wistful, luminous glow. Leah's lips curved into a serene smile and for a moment, Boyd wondered if she even remembered that he was sitting beside her. She seemed lost in sweet reminiscence.

Leah was still smiling when Boyd went around the car to open her door. She stepped out and took a deep breath, inhaling the scented air with obvious pleasure.

As they walked to the small porch, Leah's eyes darted, absorbing the familiar surroundings. It was as she'd remembered, Leah thought, noting the knothole in the second step. After the prom, they'd sneaked here for a few private moments and Leah had gotten her high heel snagged in that silly hole. Cybil never had fully accepted Leah's story that the heel had simply snapped at the dance. Of course, Leah never had been able to lie her way out of a soggy tissue sack and she hadn't been able to look her mother in the eye for a week.

Glancing up, Leah saw Boyd swing open the cabin door. A welcoming glow sprayed from the softly lit interior and as she stepped inside, Leah felt as though she'd entered a time tunnel. The fire crackled invitingly, the old ginger-jar lamp cast soft warmth over the cozy room and wonderful memories washed over Leah like warm summer rain.

"Oh," she murmured, more in a breath than a word. "It's just like I remember it."

Greedily Leah's gaze swept the room, absorbing the ambience and reveling in the loving feelings swelling up inside her. The Wainwright house was merely a wood-frame structure. Now, Leah felt as if she'd finally come home.

The cabin was small, with living dining kitchen areas all contained in a single room. Leah knew that the small hallway led to a bathroom and two bedrooms. Her skin warmed to recall how she'd discovered those bedrooms—and just what else she'd *almost* discovered that night.

Boyd, as usual, had finally exercised his famous mind-over-matter restraint and the evening had once again ended chastely.

Barely aware that Boyd had closed the door and was standing close behind her, Leah walked slowly around the small living room, delicately touching familiar objects and discovering new ones.

"The desk wasn't here before," she mused, more to herself than to Boyd. She trailed a fingertip across the gleaming wood rolltop, then noticed that several pots of greenery had been added. "And the plants are all new."

"The desk is a garage-sale special." Boyd hesitated, following her gaze toward the trailing philodendron. The log on which it sat was safely covered by foliage. "I...like plants. They add a bit of life to the place."

"Oh, yes," she agreed. Leah's voice had the breathless timbre, like an excited child at Disneyland. Suddenly, she whirled and laughed, clasping her hands together in a gesture that Stacey would have used. "It's all so wonderful!" Her gaze fell on the distressed-oak dining table, beautifully set for two. A bud vase in the center held another perfect white rose. "Oh, Boyd, you've gone to so much trouble. It's all so very...lovely." She flashed a smile of genuine delight.

Boyd steadied himself on the kitchen counter with his outstretched hand.

Leah was instantly alarmed. "Are you ill?"

"No." The word broke and Boyd cleared his throat, then chuckled self-consciously. "It's just that when you smile like that, you can drive a man to his knees."

Lowering her gaze, Leah turned away so Boyd wouldn't see how much his words had pleased her. Although she knew that renewing a relationship with Boyd would, under the circumstances, be impossible, she was still torn. Part of her desperately wanted Boyd to see her not as a child, but as a desirable woman. The more intelligent part of her knew just how unwise that would be.

Boyd broke the brief silence, encompassing the kitchen with a careless sweep of his hand. "I'd better start dinner."

"Can I help?"

"Do you still toss a mean salad?"

"The best."

"Umm, I can't wait."

Reaching into a cupboard, Boyd pulled out a huge wooden bowl. Leah was already scrounging through the refrigerator, tossing all manner of things green and leafy onto the counter. Without a second thought, she automatically opened a drawer and extracted a knife. Leah and Boyd had prepared many meals here and the utensils were still nested in their usual spots.

Leah glanced up and saw Boyd's twinkling expression. "Are you amused by something?"

"Not amused," he corrected. "Pleased. Vegetables taste so much better when you slice them."

Leah emitted a sound of disbelief. "I'm sure you've had your share of female vegetable slicers over the years."

"Nope. Not a one."

Arching one eyebrow, Leah said, "Next you'll be trying to sell me Florida swampland."

Boyd smiled. "Spoken like a jealous woman."

Leah sliced into a hapless green pepper with a ferocious whack. "I have absolutely no reason to be jealous."

"That's true."

"After all, your romantic past is none of my business."

Boyd winced as Leah's knife whistled, then axed into a fat carrot. "I'll tell you mine if you tell me yours," he said smoothly.

The knife froze in midcut and Leah looked up. "Excuse me?"

"I'll tell you about my romantic past. Then you tell me about yours." Boyd poured a marinade over a thick steak and took Leah's silence as an affirmative. "Contrary to popular belief, I'm not the Don Juan of South Tahoe. I've had a few relationships, but only one that could be called serious."

In spite of herself, Leah held her breath. She wanted to know; she didn't want to know. More important, she didn't want to *tell*.

"Julia and I dated for about two years. We were both in our mid-twenties and she was ready for commitment. I wasn't."

"I find that difficult to believe," Leah said. "You were ready for commitment when you were twelve."

"That's a bit of an exaggeration."

"Not really." Leah chuckled. "I can't remember when you weren't Mr. Straight Arrow, everybody's gallant knight and the original dependability kid."

Boyd considered this. "You make me sound like a real nerd. Was I so boring?"

"Not at all." Leah flushed. *Boring* was definitely not a word that described Boyd Cauldwell. "It's just that I know how much you love children, and I expected you'd have your own family by now."

Piercing the meat with fork prongs, Boyd was silent for a few minutes, then said, "So did I. As a matter of fact, wanting a family was about the only thing Julia and I had in common."

Leah concentrated on peeling a cucumber, foolishly feeling pleased that Boyd's relationship hadn't worked out. She didn't like the image of Boyd with another woman, but felt a niggling twinge of sorrow that he hadn't found the happiness he so richly deserved. "I'm sorry...that things didn't work out for you."

"I'm not. I didn't love her, and I seriously doubt that she was in love with me." He smiled brightly. "So that's the story of my love life. Your turn."

"Ah." Leah licked her lips and answered truthfully. "I've had a lot of...friends, but never met anyone I wanted to spend the rest of my life with."

"'Friends'?"

"Umm." Leah feigned fascination with the cucumber.

"Men friends?"

"Of...course."

"Serious?"

She shrugged, becoming more uncomfortable by the moment. "The usual male-female relationship, I imagine."

"I see."

Boyd's skeptical look said that he hadn't bought Leah's story for one minute. Given her panicked reaction when he'd embraced her with such frightening passion, Leah knew that skepticism was well-founded.

Forcing a cheerful facade, Leah added, "I know what you're thinking."

"Really?"

"Yes, but I can assure you that I've never had the, uh, problem before. It's probably just being back in Cedar Cove. That's all."

Boyd angled a narrowed glance at her, then emitted a neutral sound and flipped the steak.

Pushing away the guilt of having stretched the truth, Leah pretended that the topic no longer interested her. In fact, Leah simply didn't want to admit that she'd spent the past ten years unfavorably comparing every man she met to Boyd. That knowledge would simply encourage Boyd to believe that they could rekindle their relationship. And as much as Leah wanted to do just that, she knew it was impossible. In two days, Leah would return to Sacramento and her secret would go with her. But tonight Leah wouldn't think about that. Tonight, she would allow herself to dream, just a bit.

To change the subject, Leah said, "Tell me about your law practice, Boyd. When did you decide against being a defense attorney?"

Frowning, Boyd spooned marinade over the meat. "I don't know that I actually decided against it. Things just worked out differently, that's all."

"But contract law? It's...so unlike you." Leah saw Boyd's eyes veil with a strange sadness. It hurt her. "I'm sorry. It's really none of my business, and I'm sure you love what you do."

"Not really," he said blandly. "I had every intention of going into private practice and saving the underdogs of the world from a justice system that caters to the rich. But—" He shrugged, as though confused himself. "My partner's father is one of the senator's political buddies, and one thing led to another...."

"But if it wasn't what you wanted to do—"

"I didn't say that," Boyd countered, a bit too strongly. "Besides, the practice isn't all I've got going. I'm a member of the Tahoe Valley planning commission, have a seat on several political-action committee boards and do a lot of campaign work for some of the state's most powerful officials."

Leah sucked in a breath, then threw up her hands in mock horror. "Imagine, poor little me in the presence of such greatness. My grandchildren will be so impressed."

Stunned, Boyd gaped at Leah as she shamelessly batted her eyes. Then he threw back his head and laughed. "Good Lord, listen to me. Do you know who I sound like?"

Eyes sparkling, Leah nodded. "The senator."

"God help me," Boyd moaned, then turned his attention to the steak, stabbing it with the sharp tines. "Let's talk about something more pleasant, Leah."

"Like what?"

"Like you. Now, don't go furrowing your brow at me. I bared my soul for you."

Bothered by the thought of such personal revelations, Leah shrugged, hoping to indicate that she found herself a rather boring subject. "There's not much to tell. As I told you before, I stayed with Aunt Jo for a while. Then, when Stacey was about three, I got a job and moved out. We've been on our own ever since. End of story."

Leah slanted a glance at Boyd and saw him watching her carefully. She swallowed hard, looked away and busied herself by shredding lettuce.

Boyd persisted. "I still don't understand why you left Cedar Cove. Wouldn't it have been easier to stay with your parents during such a...difficult time?"

Leah tensed. "Do you have any tomatoes?"

"In the fridge."

"Thanks." Gratefully, Leah stuck her head in the cool refrigerator, then closed her eyes and wondered how much, if anything, she should say. Finally she grabbed the first round red thing she saw, pasted a bright smile on her face and closed the door.

Boyd regarded her thoughtfully. "Why does that question bother you?"

"I'm not the least bit bothered," Leah said cheerfully.

"Umm. Then why are you chopping the hell out of that apple?"

"Apple?" Leah's eyes widened, then she groaned. "All right, I *am* bothered."

"Why?"

"I didn't exactly choose to leave Cedar Cove, Boyd. My father sent me away." Boyd's face darkened like a thundercloud. Leah continued in a soft, tremulous voice. "At the time, I was crushed, feeling rejected and abandoned. I still don't completely understand why he shipped me off like so much baggage, but I guess it was because he was...ashamed of me."

Not knowing what to say, Boyd simply went to Leah and gathered her into his arms. She sighed, closing her eyes and giving herself over to his comfort. He was stroking her hair and murmuring soft, encouraging words and Leah wanted to stay there forever.

But she couldn't and was frightened by the very fact that she wanted to so badly. Suddenly she pushed away, then winced at Boyd's bewildered expression. To lighten the mood, Leah attempted a tight laugh. "If you don't put that steak in the broiler, we'll both die of starvation and a search party will discover nothing but a pile of bleached bones."

Taking the hint, Boyd managed a stiff smile and completed his task. As he did, Leah set the filled salad bowl on the table and wandered toward the fireplace. She argued with herself, knowing she had to tell Boyd that she was leaving, yet unwilling to put a damper on what little time they had left together.

A silky voice whispered, "Five minutes."

Startled, Leah spun around and realized that Boyd was standing right behind her, so close that her bodice brushed the lapels of his sport jacket. She held her breath, mesmerized by the warm glow in his eyes. Her fingertips brushed his chest and she felt the involuntary twitch of his chest muscles.

A spark of pure devilry lit her eyes. "You're still ticklish," she said, then laughed at Boyd's apprehension.

"No, no. I'm not," he assured her, but his worried expression said otherwise and he took a step backward.

"Really? Let's just check this out." Leah advanced, fingers flexing for action, mouth curved with mischief.

"I'm still bigger than you," Boyd warned, but his eyes gleamed. "I'll defend myself."

Circling, Leah wiggled her fingers threateningly, chuckling as Boyd flinched and sidestepped. Finally, she attacked, thrusting her squirming hands beneath his coat. "Aha! Gotcha!"

Boyd emitted a hoarse croak and tried to fight her off, but he was laughing too hard to put up an effective defense. He grabbed at her wrists, but she quickly ran her fingers up his rib cage seeking escape. Half choking, half pleading, Boyd stumbled backward and tripped over a small magazine rack. As he fell, he bellowed, "If I go, you go," and snatched Leah's arm.

With a wail of dismay, Leah toppled forward, landing on Boyd's chest. He promptly wrapped his arms around her and they rolled on the floor, laughing and struggling.

"Release me, you cad!" Leah said, giggling madly.

"Only if you retract your deadly claws, my lovely."

Leah's arms were pinned at her side and she tried in vain to free herself. Breathing heavily, she stared up into Boyd's amused face.

"Give up?" he inquired politely.

"Never." Rotating her hips, she tried to throw him off, but he'd filled out considerably since the old days, and Leah couldn't budge him.

Boyd smiled smugly, fully aware that the tide of battle had turned and that he was in command of the situation. "Actually, this is rather pleasant, don't you think?"

At that point, Leah realized just how vulnerable her position was. After all, lying flat on one's back with a grown man stretched full length on top was a rather suggestive position. Besides, Boyd was right. It *was* rather pleasant. In fact, it was more than pleasant; it was downright sensual, and Leah was well aware that if she didn't do something immediately, she would soon be incapable of doing anything at all. Leah's body was already responding to the quickening of Boyd's heart against her breast and the smoldering heat that darkened his eyes.

With her free leg, Leah kicked out forcefully, trying to plant her foot on the wall and lever herself over. Instead, she missed and nearly knocked over the trailing philodendron.

As the plant rocked precariously, Boyd released Leah and grabbed it. He looked massively relieved as the pot was safely returned to the stand and he busily rearranged the trailing vines.

"I'm sorry," Leah said, curiously watching the process. "I didn't mean to— What's that?" Her eyes narrowed as she saw that the plant was set on a length of cut log. It wasn't the log itself, however, that had captured her attention. She'd caught a glimpse of jagged grooves carved in the bark. Familiar grooves. Too familiar.

Questioning, Leah's gaze swept from the now obscured log to Boyd's pale face. As she reached to brush back the foliage, Boyd stopped her by grasping her wrist.

"The steak is probably done."

Leah looked into his eyes and she suddenly knew what she would find beneath the leaves. Wresting her hand away, she parted the vines and sucked in a quick breath. *Leah & Boyd—Always.*

Tears stung her eyes. "You kept it," she whispered. "Oh God, all these years."

Caught, Boyd sheepishly averted his gaze. Leah found his sudden shyness endearing and laid her hand on his cheek. Although Boyd tried to smile bravely, his eyes betrayed anxiety. "I guess I couldn't let go," he said.

"Why...did you let me think that you'd burned it?"

"I was afraid you'd laugh at me for being foolish or sentimental." With a minute movement, Boyd turned to kiss Leah's palm.

She shuddered, closing her eyes. How could he believe that she would laugh at something so touching and beautiful? Liquid warmth spread through her entire body and she suddenly felt light enough to float without wings. Boyd still cared for her. The realization made her giddy with delight.

As Boyd touched Leah's cheek, she inhaled deeply, breathing in the masculine scent of him. He smelled of musk and marinade, pine and wood smoke. It was softly erotic, delicately arousing. The smoky fragrance became more predominant, filling her senses.

"Oh, no!" Boyd croaked suddenly. "The steak!"

He leaped to his feet, covering the distance to the kitchen with three giant strides.

Bewildered, Leah watched, then sniffed the air and realized that the smoke had been quite real. Their dinner was charcoaled.

Moaning, Boyd pulled the broiler out, setting it on the range. Gray wisps rose from the sizzling meat and Boyd looked so miserable, Leah pressed her knuckles into her mouth to keep from laughing.

Finally she managed to say, "Salad is healthier than red meat, anyway."

Morosely, Boyd skimmed a glance at the beautifully set table. Two silver candlesticks awaited the touch of flame, and crisp linen napkins had been neatly bound with matching silver rings. Leah felt a pang of sympathy. He'd worked so hard to make everything perfect, and now he looked so glum....

Quickly she stood and lightly dusted her silk dress. Assuring him that everything would be just fine, Leah found a can of gravy and quickly turned the burned steak into faux stroganoff. In a few minutes, Boyd's good humor had returned and they bustled around the kitchen as though they'd been doing so all their lives.

The meal turned out well, and they congratulated themselves as they enjoyed it. Soon the mood softened as Leah realized that the time had come to tell Boyd that she was leaving. It would be more difficult than she had imagined. She decided to work up to it gradually.

"It was very kind of you to bring Stacey the book. I know she was absolutely thrilled."

"It was my pleasure. She's really quite an unusual little girl." And a constant reminder of the past, Boyd thought dismally. He forced a casual tone. "While we were working on the bird-watching platform, she mentioned that she wanted to go water-skiing. I thought maybe tomorrow—"

"No."

Surprised at the bite in Leah's voice, Boyd could only stare. She was obviously disturbed, and he wondered why. Leah picked up her water glass, sipping delicately, and Boyd could almost see the little gears of her brain turning. Finally she set the glass decisively on the table. "I'm sure Stacey would enjoy a day on the lake, but I'm afraid that won't be possible."

"Why not? Tomorrow's Sunday, and I could bring the boat around to your dock early... We'd have all day."

"We'll be busy tomorrow . . . packing." Leah avoided his eyes as she added, "We're leaving on Monday."

Boyd felt as though the air had been kicked from his lungs with a steel-toed boot. "I thought you had another week's vacation."

"Yes, but I have a million things back home to take care of."

His eyes narrowed. "What about Cybil? Are you just going to walk off and leave her alone at a time like this?"

"Of course not," Leah said sharply, then took a deep breath. "Mother has decided to return to Sacramento with us."

"For how long?"

Leah shrugged and fiddled with her fork. "As long as she wants. I have a few loose ends to tie up at the store, then Simon can take over until Mother decides whether or not to sell."

Leaning across the table, Boyd took Leah's hand. It trembled. "I don't want you to leave."

"I-It's necessary."

She was pale, Boyd noted, and her eyes held the desperate, trapped expression of a snared rabbit. Releasing her hand, he sat back. "All right," he said softly. "But Sacramento is only two hours away and I don't mind the drive."

Leah looked up. "You'd do that?"

"Of course. I have no intention of letting you go again."

Leah could hardly believe it. Sacramento was a long way from Cedar Cove and from the secrets harbored here. Perhaps, away from this place, she and Boyd really *could* rekindle their past. Happiness and hope surged through her.

As Leah contemplated the wonderful possibilities, the telephone rang. Looking up, Leah saw that Boyd had started to clear the table and was in the kitchen.

"Shall I answer that?" she called.

"Yes, please," Boyd said, then watched as Leah crossed the room. As she lifted the receiver, Boyd's mind wandered to the bombshell she'd just laid on him. It wasn't as though Leah had decided to live in Nigeria, he told himself. She was simply cutting her vacation a bit short. People did things like that all the time.

Except that Boyd knew instinctively that Leah was running from something or someone. From him? Had his behavior last night frightened her so badly? No, Boyd didn't believe that. Over the past week, he'd come to realize that something much deeper was bothering Leah. And Boyd was determined to find out just what it was.

The telephone receiver thunked into its cradle. Glancing across the room, Boyd felt his throat go dry. "Good Lord, Leah, you're as white as a snowbank. What's happened?"

She appeared to be in shock, eyes wide and filled with despair. Her lips parted, quivering and she emitted a soft moan. "I-It's Mother."

Boyd reached Leah in two steps and grasped both of her hands. They were limp and icy cold. "What about Cybil?" he asked, coaxing gently. "Tell me what's wrong."

Suddenly, she looked up and stared right at Boyd. "She's had a heart attack. Oh, God, Boyd. My mother is dying."

Chapter Six

By the time Leah and Boyd returned to the Wainwright house, it was well after midnight. Leah felt like a zombie—as though her mind had melted inside her skull.

But Boyd had been wonderful and so supportive. During the traumatic ordeal at the hospital, he'd never left her side. Propping her up, he'd calmed her with soft words and even softer caresses, shielding her with his body as she tried to deal with her newest emotional blow. Now, as they mounted the porch steps, Boyd's strong hands warmed Leah's chilled skin, guiding and soothing and protecting.

The house seemed cold and empty, Leah thought numbly. But of course, it was neither. Lottie Varner, the woman who'd called Leah at the cabin, had volunteered to stay with Stacey so that Leah could rush directly to the hospital.

As Boyd and Leah walked through the front doors, Lottie dropped a magazine and stood slowly, fear and worry etched on her leathery face. She was a sturdy woman with a no-nonsense style that Leah had always found comforting. As usual, her thick brown hair was braided and coiled like plaited earmuffs.

Nervously, the older woman wiped her palms across the skirt of her faded dress. "Is Cybil...?" Unable to complete her question, Lottie gestured helplessly.

"She's awake and her condition is stable," Leah said quickly and saw relief in the woman's eyes. "They have her hooked up to some kind of monitoring equipment and the doctor said they won't know how extensive the damage to her heart muscle was until they perform some tests. But—" Her voice broke and she clutched at her throat as though trying to squeeze out the words. "But she's going to be all right."

Lottie closed her eyes and swayed slightly. "Praise the Lord."

Beside Leah, Boyd wrapped his arm around her waist and she leaned against him, absorbing his strength. He brushed his lips across her forehead and she felt his breath on her skin as he whispered something. It didn't matter what he'd said. Leah knew it was loving and gentle and filled with encouragement. She fused herself to him.

"Mommy...?" Stacey stood at the top of the stairs, clutching a worn rag doll. It was the doll Cybil had made for her fifth birthday. "Where's Grandma?" she asked with a choking sob.

"Oh, sweetheart." Leah held out her arms and her daughter flew into them, clinging and crying. Stroking the child's mussed hair, Leah murmured softly. "Grandma's going to be just fine, darling. Everything is all right."

With a hiccup, Stacey raised swollen red eyes. "Honest?"

Leah smiled. "Cross my heart."

As though requiring confirmation, Stacey sniffed and stared at Boyd. He nodded. Satisfied, the child returned her attention to Leah. "I was so scared, Mommy. Grandma got sick and I didn't know what to do."

Sitting on the stairs, Leah pulled her daughter into her arms and rocked her as though she were a frightened toddler. "You did everything just right. Grandma told me all about it."

"She did?"

"Yes, indeed. She said that you dialed 911 for the paramedics, then you called Mrs. Varner. I'm so proud of you, honey. You probably saved your grandmother's life."

That thought struck Stacey mute and her red eyes widened in awe, then filled with fresh tears.

Boyd hunkered down, brushing away a strand of hair that was stuck to the child's wet cheek. "Hey there, sprout. What's all this?"

"I-it's just that—" Her words were interrupted by a hiccup. "Grandma almost d-died and . . . I was scared."

"I know, Stacey." Boyd's voice was husky. "I'm scared, too, and so is your mommy."

Stacey was clearly skeptical. "Really?"

"Everyone gets scared sometimes, and that's okay. You can't be brave if you aren't a little frightened to begin with and you were very, very brave tonight." Boyd gently stroked the girl's face with the tip of his finger; then, as though it was the most natural thing in the world, he embraced the trembling child, kissing her cheek and massaging her back.

Throwing her arms around Boyd's neck, she burrowed against him. Leah watched them, her eyes stinging with a flood of hot tears. It was such a beautiful, moving sight. She absorbed it, cherished it and knew she would remember this moment always.

Finally, with a sniff and a shy smile, Stacey backed away. As the child stood on the stairs with her fingers twisting the fabric of her flannel nightie, Leah saw total trust in Stacey's eyes. Her daughter was looking at Boyd with an expression usually reserved for a favored movie star or the newest teen idol. Stacey, Leah realized, was suffering from an acute case of hero worship.

Almost afraid to look, Leah forced a glance at Boyd. His eyes were shining, his lips gently curved. The admiration was apparently mutual. Under ordinary circumstances, Leah would have been deeply touched and overjoyed that the man she loved and her child were establishing such a beautiful relationship.

These, however, weren't ordinary circumstances.

Quickly she stood. "I think, young lady, that it's time for you to get your beauty sleep. You don't want to look like a pink-eyed bunny when we see Grandma tomorrow, do you?''

"Is Grandma coming home?"

"Not for a while, but we can see her at the hospital."

"Oh." Stacey was obviously disappointed, but before she could say anything else, she was overtaken by a gigantic yawn. Her eyelids seemed suddenly heavy and she blinked owlishly.

Smiling, Leah took her daughter's hand. "What do you say we hit the old sack before you begin to snore?"

Stacey yawned. "I don't snore," she mumbled, without much conviction, then slid a glance at Boyd. "Will you please tuck me in?"

Startled, he pointed to himself. "Me?"

Stacey nodded. Leah was stunned.

"Oh, well... I don't know," Boyd said, then looked toward Leah for guidance.

She simply placed her daughter's hand in his large palm and said, "First door on the left."

Gamely, Boyd allowed Stacey to tow him upstairs, and tossed a final pleading look over his shoulder before disappearing down the hallway.

Leah continued to gaze at the steps, startled when she realized that Lottie was now standing close behind her.

"If you don't need me anymore, Leah, I should be getting on home."

"Oh, of course. I can't tell you how much I appreciate what you've done for us tonight. You've been so very kind."

"It's nothing compared to what Cybil's done for me over the years. Why, when my Frank took sick, Cybil moved right in for almost three weeks, cooking and cleaning and taking care of my four kids. She's a good woman, your mama."

"Yes, she is," Leah said quietly.

Lottie's lips tightened. "Cybil's been through a lot of hurt. Maybe I shouldn't be saying so, but I don't think she shoulda' let Louis do... what he did to you."

Looking away, Leah clasped her hands together. "Mother didn't have much choice, Lottie. Papa could be very insistent."

"She coulda' stopped him and she knows it. It's been hell for her, living with that guilt." Lottie touched Leah's arm. "It's good you've come back, Leah. She needed to know that you forgive her."

Leah could only nod. She wished she could honestly say that she'd never felt any anger toward Cybil, but it would have been a lie and Lottie knew that. It was natural for Leah to have felt abandoned. Children seem to feel as though their mothers are images of loving perfection, all-powerful and above such mundane matters as poor judgment or fear. Now that she was herself a mother, Leah had realized just how unreasonable her expectations of Cybil had been.

Everyone was human, everyone made mistakes.

"I'll just call Frank to come pick me up," Lottie said. "Could I be using your phone?"

Boyd appeared at the top of the stairs. "Let Frank rest, Lottie. I'll drive you home."

"Why, that's awful nice of you. I wouldn't want to put you out none." Lottie's dark eyes skittered from Boyd to Leah, then back again. She smiled in approval and Leah felt her skin heat.

"No trouble at all," Boyd assured Lottie. When he reached the bottom step, he turned toward Leah. "Stacey was asleep before I got the blanket pulled around her. And by the way, she *does* snore."

Leah's chuckle died in her throat as Boyd's expression became serious.

Eyes darkening like smoky topaz, Boyd cupped her cheek in his palm. "Are you all right, Leah? After I drop Lottie off, I could come back."

Blushing furiously, Leah peeked over and saw Lottie grinning broadly. "I'm fine," Leah said, her voice squeaking slightly. "Ah, you go on home and get some rest."

The warmth from his hand radiated from her face to the soles of her feet. He was moving one fingertip in slow, sensuous circles around her temple while he delicately traced the curve of her jaw with his thumb. As her tongue darted out to moisten her lips, she saw his attention riveted to her mouth. He looked hungry. Leah tried to suppress a surge of excitement.

"Maybe I should just wait in the car," Lottie said cheerfully.

Leah couldn't tear her eyes from Boyd's face, but was aware that the front door had opened and closed.

"Will I see you tomorrow?" Boyd whispered.

At that moment, Leah couldn't have said no if her life depended on it. She nodded.

Boyd's eyes crinkled with pleasure. "And the next day and the next day and the next?"

This wasn't fair, Leah thought. He was taking advantage of her in a weak moment. Boyd knew that his fingers were sensitizing her skin until she tingled all over and that his eyes were burning erotic thoughts into her brain. Leah was trembling under the force of his sizzling gaze and she was certain that every exquisite sensation washing over her was plainly etched in her diaphanous expression.

She was vulnerable to him and he knew it.

Softly, Boyd whispered, "I want to kiss you, Leah."

Leah realized that he was holding back, unwilling to proceed without permission. All she had to do was say no, and Boyd would respect her wishes. After all, Leah knew how dangerous it would be to renew their romance. Boyd was giving her an out.

Leah's answer slid out with a sigh. "Yes."

But Boyd moved no closer. Instead, his eyes seemed to be memorizing her face, greedily absorbing her image as though he might at any moment blink and lose her again. His eyelids lowered slowly and he took a deep, racking breath. Then he opened his eyes and she felt cherished by the love she saw in them.

Lowering his head, he brushed his mouth against hers, a touch so delicate Leah wondered if it was real. Once more, his lips captured hers, clinging this time, sipping her sweetness until Leah felt him tremble against her. His desire was evident, still he touched only her face with his fingers and his lips.

Shakily, he straightened, an expression of wonder in his eyes. For several minutes, they simply stared, savoring the sweet, almost spiritual experience.

Then Boyd spoke. "Lottie's waiting."

Leah wanted to touch his cheek, to trace its creases with her fingertip. "I know."

"I . . . don't want to leave."

A stabbing ache pulsed through her chest. "I know."

Boyd took two steps toward the door, hesitated, then spun on his heel, reached out and gathered Leah into his arms. He held her tightly for a brief moment, then, as though he doubted his own resolve, turned and walked quickly out the front door.

Leah felt bereft, cold and suddenly very alone.

Merely going through the motions, she turned off the living-room lamps and automatically secured the door locks. She checked on Stacey, then went to her room and undressed for bed.

No matter what Leah had done to discourage him, Boyd still wanted to be with her. It was as though a higher power had determined that they were destined to be together. Suddenly, Leah had a desperate need to believe in miracles. It wasn't logical. The facts were very clear. Relationships couldn't be based on a foundation of lies and evasion, but the truth would be too devastating.

Though it had caused great pain to do so, Leah had tried to discourage all Boyd's reconciliation attempts because of that pernicious truth and because deceptiveness was contrary to Leah's very nature. Fate, however, was constantly thwarting her noble motives.

Leah was beginning to believe in destiny—and in miracles.

She'd just pulled back the bedcovers when the doorbell rang. She glanced at the clock, wondering who would be calling at one-thirty in the morning.

Whoever it was began to knock loudly.

Boyd. Her heart leaped like a happy trout. He'd come back, after all.

Grabbing her cotton robe, Leah slipped it on as she hurried down the stairs. She tied the sash around her waist, laughing as she flung open the door.

The smile froze on her face.

"Well, well. Li'l Leah Wainwright." Craig Cauldwell swayed drunkenly, then steadied himself by grabbing the doorframe. "Jus' like old times."

Leah tried to slam the door, but Craig lurched forward and pushed his way into the house.

"Wha's the matter, baby? Not happy to see me?"

Stiffening, Leah lifted her chin and hoped he wouldn't recognize her fear. "What do you want, Craig?"

"Want?" He laughed unpleasantly. "Funny, tha's what I was gonna ask you."

He walked into the living room, staggering slightly, and fell onto the sofa. "Got anything to drink?"

"No." With her arms folded tightly, Leah glanced at the telephone. She mulled the thought of making a call, then discarded it. The last thing she needed was the publicity of having the police drag a drunken Cauldwell out of her living room. And although he was too intoxicated to realize it, that was also the last thing in the world Craig needed. Hopefully, Leah could manage to manipulate him out the door without a major scene. "I'll make some coffee," she said.

Craig belched. "Don' want coffee."

Ignoring him, Leah went into the kitchen and quickly prepared two cups of instant coffee. Her hands were shaking and the hot liquid sloshed, burning her skin as she carried it into the living room. She offered the coffee to Craig. He was bent over, with his elbows propped on his knees, his palms covering his face. Finally, she set the cup on the table and positioned herself across the room.

Rubbing his eyes, Craig sat up, then picked up the coffee and sipped. As Craig's mouth slackened, and his chin drooped, Leah's gaze stayed riveted on his features. Her heart began a wild palpitation as she realized exactly what Bitsy had seen when she'd looked at Stacey. Bitsy had seen a miniature replica of her own husband's face.

At this moment, however, Craig looked so pathetic, so childlike, that Leah wondered how she could ever have been frightened of this pitiful man. The empathetic moment was not to last, however. When Craig's eyes narrowed and his lips clamped into a wide, hard line, Leah's fear returned.

She knew only too well that Craig Cauldwell had the capacity to be very, very cruel.

Leah tried to keep a steady voice. "I-it's very late. Please drink your coffee, then I think you should leave."

He stared at her. "Leave?"

"Yes, leave." Leah raised the cup to her lips, pretending to drink. She fervently hoped that Stacey wouldn't awaken and that Boyd really wouldn't return tonight.

Craig's eyes focused on thin air. "My wife is going to leave me. Did you know that?"

"No—no, I didn't." Leah cautiously set down her cup. "I'm sorry, Craig."

"She's real mad," Craig mumbled, staring vacuously into space. "It's all your fault." Suddenly he stood, bumping the table and spilling coffee over the polished wood surface. "Bitsy said your kid is the spittin' image of Jenny."

Leah froze, remembering the blue-eyed girl in the dressing room. But the thought was fleeting. Craig had a strange look on his face and Leah's brain was on red alert.

"You tol' her didn't you?" Craig fixed Leah with a wild stare.

"No, of course not." Leah licked her lips and pressed her trembling hands together. "Bitsy may have noticed a . . . family resemblance and the birthmark—"

"She knows. You must have told her." He took a menacing step and swayed slightly. "You're just tryin' to get me in trouble, to ruin my life."

"I didn't tell Bitsy any—"

"You're lyin'!" Craig lunged at Leah and before she could move, he'd wrapped his fingers around her wrist and dragged her from the chair. "I won' let you destroy everythin'."

"Craig, stop!"

"What're you after? Money? How much do you want?"

"Let me go." Leah tried desperately to peel Craig's fingers from her bruised skin. "I don't want anything from you."

Craig jerked her forward and Leah bounced off his chest. "Maybe you're after the big bucks. Yeah, tha's it. You want the Cauldwell name for your bast—"

Leah's palm cracked across Craig's cheek with enough force to snap his head sideways. Releasing his grip, he staggered backward.

Fists clenched and quivering with rage, Leah snarled like an animal protecting its young. "If you ever again speak about *my* daughter in such a vile manner, I swear you'll regret it. Get out of this house!"

Rubbing his knuckles over his stinging face, a quickly sobering Craig sized up the woman who'd gone from mouse to maniac in a single heartbeat. Then he smiled, a coldly menacing smirk that froze Leah's blood. "Is that a threat, Leah? I don't like threats."

"Get out," she whispered.

"I'll get out when I'm ready." His eyes slid to the open neckline of her robe. "I do what I want to do—or have you forgotten?"

Leah recognized the violence in his eyes. Stacey was upstairs and Leah was terrified for the safety of her daughter. Reaching behind her back, she felt blindly for something—anything for protection. No matter what she had to do, she silently vowed that this man would never hurt her again.

Then Craig's eyes suddenly went blank. His mouth fell open and an expression of total desolation dropped over him like a black curtain. He turned away, fingers spearing his straight, sand-colored hair. He mumbled to himself. "Koblowski will use this against me. I'll loose it all...the election, my career, my wife. The senator won't be able to cover it up anymore and everyone will know." Suddenly, Craig looked stricken. "Does Boyd know?"

"No."

Relieved, Craig massaged his forehead. He looked drained, lost and bewildered. Behind her back, Leah wrapped her fingers around the neck of a heavy vase. Even though Craig no longer seemed threatening, she knew his Jekyll-Hyde personality was unpredictable and dangerous.

Dropping his hands, Craig met Leah's eyes. "You have to leave Cedar Cove."

Leah tried for a calming, reasonable tone. "I will leave Craig. I'm going back to Sacramento as soon as possible."

"Tomorrow?"

She shook her head. "My mother is in the hospital. I can't leave until she's well enough to travel."

"You've got to go!"

Craig took a threatening step and Leah tightened her grip on the vase, silently begging him to stop.

He did, but his expression was deadly. "If you don't pack up your kid and get out of town, something real bad might happen."

With that, Craig spun around and strode out the front door, leaving Leah shaken to the core.

Tears splashed down her face as she realized the bitter truth. Boyd could eventually accept what had happened ten years ago but he would never be able to live with the fact that Stacey had been fathered by his own brother.

There would be no miracle now.

Frustrated, Leah shut the metal drawer with more force than necessary. She'd examined every document in Louis's files and still hadn't found any support for the mysterious debt in the ledger. Since Cybil had suddenly become adamant that the business would have to be sold, the details of the note had to be included on an audited financial disclosure for prospective buyers. Leah was stuck. She had no idea where else to look.

The front doorbell jingled.

"Sy?" Leah stepped from the office to the store and saw Simon hurriedly stashing a potted plant behind the cash register. It appeared to be a lushly foliaged African violet in full bloom. "What have you got there?"

Sprague jumped like a boy caught filching cookies. "Nothing important," he said quickly, shoving the pot out of sight. With an embarrassed grin, he changed the subject. "Find what you were looking for?"

Leah frowned. "No, as a matter of fact I didn't, and I'm at a loss as to where it could be."

Rubbing his ample stomach, Simon pursed his lips in concentration until the mustache circled his mouth like a bushy red wreath. After a moment, he said, "You know,

Louis kept an old metal box in the safe. Never knew what was in it though."

"I didn't see any safe."

"Under the throw rug." Simon moved through the narrow aisle toward the office. "Louis had the dang thing put in about five years ago, after some drunken yokel held up the pharmacy down the street."

Leah stepped aside to allow Sy into the room. The rug in question was simply a tattered square of carpeting. Grunting, Simon squatted, flipped the corner back to reveal a metal lid with a combination lock. Grinning up, Sy said, "Under the pencil holder."

Confused, Leah stared at the plastic cylinder packed with writing instruments. "*What* is under the pencil holder?"

"The combination."

Leah removed the pencils, turned over the holder and saw that a label had been stuck on the bottom. "Uh, 'Right 38, left 11, right 22,'" she read.

Simon twisted the knob. "Louis mostly used this on weekends, with the banks being closed and all." After lifting the lid, Simon reached inside and extracted a battered metal box that was about the size of a thick book. He handed it to Leah.

"Do you have a key?" she asked hopefully.

"Don't need one."

"Well, it *is* locked," Leah pointed out.

"True, but this here's a hardware store." Straightening, Sy grinned and disappeared through the doorway. Leah heard the sounds of tools clunking, then Simon reappeared holding a pointed awl and a small hammer. "Just set it on the desk and stand back."

She did. In less then ten seconds, Sy flipped the lid up and emitted a satisfied grunt.

Leah smiled and shook her head. "A surprising, but useful talent."

Sprague looked quite pleased with himself. "I've picked up a few skills here and there."

"Umm." Leah looked into the box. There was an old bankbook, a photograph of Cybil and Leah taken years ago at the lake, the title on Louis's pickup truck and several legal-size envelopes.

Simon peered over her shoulder. "I've seen that picture before. I caught Louis staring at it once, looking real sad."

Leah sucked in a sharp breath. "Did...he ever talk about me?"

"Louis wasn't a real talkative man," Simon mumbled. "But I do remember him saying something about wishing things was different between you and him." Simon scratched his shiny forehead, pondering the question. "Don't rightly remember exactly, but it seemed like he was protectin' you somehow."

"Protecting me?" Leah scoffed at the notion.

Shrugging, Simon switched to a safer subject and stared pointedly into the metal box. "Find anything you need in there?"

"Not yet." Leah opened one of the envelopes with shaky fingers and tried to refocus her mind. "Ah. This is the deed to the house and the original mortgage papers. I'm sure Mother will need this when she sells the property." Leah felt Simon's restless shuffle. Turning, she saw him cast a furtive glance at the clock. "Goodness, I hadn't realized it was so late. Why don't you go on to lunch now?"

"Well, I do have an errand." He looked extremely nervous as his gaze swept toward the cash register. "If you're not needing me for anything, that is."

Suddenly Leah realized exactly what "errand" Sprague was planning. Smiling, she assured him that she would be fine on her own, then covertly watched as he went through the store, pausing to remove the plant from its hiding place. As he opened the front door, Leah called out, "Mother will be very pleased, Sy. African violets are her favorite."

His cheeks looked like toasted tomatoes and he smiled sheepishly. "I know," he said, then disappeared into the street.

Chuckling to herself, Leah turned back to the remaining contents of the box. The second envelope contained lease papers on the hardware store, but it was the final envelope that held the secret of the ten-thousand-dollar note.

Leah read the document, fell into the swivel chair, then read it again. She felt sick. The note was payable to Senator Fletcher Cauldwell.

Trying to tell herself that investment in a local business was probably just a politically astute move, Leah stared at the notarized signatures. Her heart sank. Instinctively, she knew that wasn't the case.

The papers had been signed the day after Leah had been forced to leave Cedar Cove.

Carefully, Leah reread the key paragraph. The entire document was unlike any she'd ever seen. The "loan" was interest free and all payments had been deferred until the business was sold. There seemed to be one other condition which would cause the note to be due and payable in full; violation of the terms of an agreement that had apparently been executed separately.

Leah chewed her lip. What agreement? There was no copy of any agreement with the note, nor had she seen any such document in Louis's files.

The customer bell interrupted her thoughts and for the next hour, Leah was too busy handling the cash register to worry about the case of the disappearing loan agreement.

When Simon returned, she sighed in relief. "I'd forgotten how rushed things can get around here."

"That they can, Miss Leah," Simon agreed, then shyly handed her a white bag stamped with a Hamburger Hamlet logo. "I thought you might be getting a tad empty."

Gratefully, she accepted his offering. "That was very kind of you."

Staring at his scuffed work books, Simon fidgeted, then coughed and said, "You go relax, now. I'll take care of things out here."

"I think I'll do that." Leah started toward the office, then hesitated. Perhaps Sprague had some idea as to where the mysterious agreement might be. As soon as the thought popped into her mind, she discarded it. If Sy didn't know about the note, he certainly wouldn't know about a related agreement. Besides, Leah didn't really want anyone to know that her father had dealings with the senator.

Sprague was waiting politely. "Are you needing something else?"

"No. No, thank you." Turning, she went back to the office, then glanced over her shoulder. "By the way, how's Mother feeling this afternoon?"

"Good, she's feeling real good." Simon blushed furiously. "She, uh, liked the flowers."

Leah smiled and closed the door.

After another hour of frustration, Leah decided to call it a day. As it was, by the time she picked Stacey up at Lottie's they would have to rush to get to the hospital before visiting hours were over.

Leah placed the metal box back in the floor safe. As she straightened the rug, the office door flew open. Startled, Leah whirled and her jaw tightened angrily.

"What do you want?" Leah said through clamped teeth.

Fletcher Cauldwell stared briefly at Leah, then glanced contemptuously around the cluttered room. "Just wanted to say I was real sorry to hear Cybil was sick."

Leah's stomach felt as if it had been filled with concrete, but she remained silent.

Cauldwell slid into Leah's chair, leaning back as though he owned the office and everything in it. His smile never reached his eyes. "Things have been pretty rough for your family lately. Maybe I can help out."

"We don't need any help," Leah snapped.

Cauldwell's eyes narrowed dangerously. Leah knew the senator didn't take kindly to rudeness, but at the moment she could care less. As far as Leah was concerned, this man was personally responsible for her mother's heart attack. She could still see the look of pain and shock on Cybil's face after the senator's visit last week. Although Cybil had refused to tell Leah what Cauldwell had said, she was certain that it had been the final blow to her mother's deteriorating health.

Now Cauldwell was breathing heavily, glaring at Leah with a thunderous expression. Leaning back, he steepled his fingers and regarded her with calculating coolness. "It's understandable that you'd be a mite tense right now, so I'll

SILHOUETTE DELIVERS FIRST-CLASS ROMANCE— DIRECT TO YOUR DOOR

Mail the Heart sticker on the postpaid order card today and you'll receive:

—4 new Silhouette Special Edition® novels—FREE
—a lovely lucite digital clock/calendar—FREE
—and a surprise mystery bonus—FREE

But that's not all. You'll also get:

Free Home Delivery

When you subscribe to Silhouette Special Edition®, the excitement, romance and faraway adventures of these novels can be yours for previewing in the convenience of your own home. Every month we'll deliver 6 new books right to your door. If you decide to keep them, they'll be yours for only $2.74* each—that's 21 cents below the cover price, and there is *no* extra charge for postage and handling! There is no obligation to buy— you can cancel at any time simply by writing "cancel" on your statement or by returning a shipment of books to us at our cost.

Free Monthly Newsletter

It's the indispensable insider's look at our most popular writers and their upcoming novels. Now you can have a behind-the-scenes look at the fascinating world of Silhouette! It's an added bonus you'll look forward to every month!

Special Extras—FREE

Because our home subscribers are our most valued readers, we'll be sending you additional free gifts from time to time in your monthly book shipments as a token of our appreciation.

OPEN YOUR MAILBOX TO A WORLD OF LOVE AND ROMANCE EACH MONTH. JUST COMPLETE, DETACH AND MAIL YOUR FREE-OFFER CARD TODAY!

*Terms and prices subject to change without notice. Sales tax applicable in N.Y. and Iowa.
© 1989 HARLEQUIN ENTERPRISES LIMITED

Remember! To receive your free books, digital clock/calendar and mystery gift, return the postpaid card below. But don't delay!

DETACH AND MAIL CARD TODAY.

BUSINESS REPLY CARD

FIRST CLASS MAIL   PERMIT NO. 717   BUFFALO, NY

POSTAGE WILL BE PAID BY ADDRESSEE

SILHOUETTE BOOKS
901 FUHRMANN BLVD
PO BOX 1867
BUFFALO NY 14240-9952

NO POSTAGE
NECESSARY
IF MAILED
IN THE
UNITED STATES

ignore your lack of manners. Besides, I've got a business proposition for you."

"I'm not interested."

"You haven't heard it."

"I don't have to." Then Leah decided to play a hunch. She had a lot of questions and Cauldwell was probably the only person in Cedar Cove who had the answers. Maybe she could bluff those answers out of him. She met his gaze. "I still remember the last business proposition you made to my family."

She saw surprise in his expression and was pleased.

"So your mama told you." He tapped his fingers together. "Then you know that I've been tolerant about the contract violation."

Somehow, she managed an indifferent shrug. "The contract's not valid, and you know it."

As he bent forward, Cauldwell's bushy brows lowered ominously. "The hell it's not. I could have called that note the minute you set foot in Cedar Cove, wiped out your business like that—" He snapped his fingers to emphasize the point. As though he realized that his anger gave Leah the advantage, the senator relaxed. "Fact is, I feel kind of sorry for everything you've been through. Since you'll be taking Cybil back to Sacramento, I've decided to help out and take the store off your hands."

Leah took a deep breath, willing her knees to stop shaking. "Who told you I'm going back to Sacramento?"

Cauldwell seemed pleased with himself. "Let's just say some of my best friends are realtors."

"It's true that we considered selling the store." Forcing a casual movement, Leah encompassed the office with a loose hand gesture. "Actually, the hardware business is pretty good right now and I think we can make a go of it."

"We?"

"Yes. I've missed Cedar Cove and Stacey loves it here. We might decide to stay." It wasn't true, of course, but Leah took perverse pleasure in watching the senator's veins bulge.

"That'd be a mistake," Cauldwell growled. "I'm holding a paper that says your daddy got ten thousand dollars to

keep you and that brat of yours out of my town. As of now,
I'm calling that note."

Leah swallowed the bitter liquid rushing into her throat.
It was true. Louis had banished his own daughter for a few
miserable dollars. "Just because my father made a deal with
the devil doesn't mean I'm going to give up my soul."

The senator snapped from the chair as though he'd been
spring-loaded. "Now you listen to me, missy. I've been patient because of your daddy dying and all, but you're playing with fire now and you're sure as hell gonna get singed."
Cauldwell's voice burned like acid and he was panting with
the force of his fury. "You come struttin' back, pretending
you're decent when everyone in town knows what kind of
woman you are."

Leah felt the blood drain from her face. "Get out."

Anger turned to scorn as Cauldwell ignored Leah's de-
mand. "Boyd may be blinded by your pretty face, but he
won't turn on his own blood. Deep down, he knows you're
just another cheating tramp."

"That's not true," she whispered. "You know what
happened."

"Lies." Cauldwell snorted. "Lies then, lies now."

Leah turned away. It was no use. The senator had never
believed her version of what happened. Cauldwell simply
couldn't accept that Craig would have forced himself on his
brother's fiancée. It had just been easier to blame Leah than
to accept any weakness in the Cauldwell lineage.

Obviously agitated, the senator began to pace. "You tried
to turn Boyd against his own brother, just like you're trying
to turn him against me, but it won't work."

Leah picked up that statement with interest, remembering that she'd told Boyd about her visit to Cauldwell years
ago. Apparently Boyd had confronted his father with that
fact, but Leah already regretted even the snippets of information she'd shared with him.

Leah met the senator's icy gaze with unblinking intensity. "If you hadn't shown up at the house last week with
trouble written all over your face, I wouldn't have had to tell
Boyd anything at all."

Halting, Cauldwell stared at Leah. "And if you'd stayed in Sacramento where you belong, your mama wouldn't be lying in a hospital bed right now."

Squaring her shoulders, Leah lifted her chin. She wanted to scream, to deny it at the top of her lungs, but Cauldwell had struck a sensitive chord. By some bizarre stream of abstract logic, he was right.

Sensing her vulnerability, the senator went in for the kill, his voice lowering to saccharine sweetness. "But I'm a reasonable man. I'm still willing to buy you out and offer a fine profit to boot."

Winding her fingers together to still the quivering of her hands, Leah managed a thin smile, determined to wipe the smug expression from Cauldwell's face. "As I've said, I have no plans to leave Cedar Cove right now."

The senator's eyes hardened like ice chips. "That's just a real unfortunate choice, young woman, and one you'll soon be regretting.

With that, Cauldwell strode out the door.

Chapter Seven

Leah stared at the vacant doorway and felt her knees buckle. Grabbing the corner of a tall file cabinet for support, she dropped into the chair.

Why had she done such a stupid thing? Taunting one of the most powerful men in the state was at best foolhardy and at worst downright dangerous.

Boyd was right. Leah *had* changed, more than she realized. Some deeply hidden demon of resentment had suddenly risen up and conquered rationality. That frightened her. Over the years she'd been convinced that she was reconciled with her past. Obviously, a secret niche in her subconscious still harbored silent resentment, and fueled by recent events, buried rage now boiled to the surface.

But vengeance was not only futile, it was risky. Leah had a daughter to protect, and Stacey's physical and emotional safety was Leah's prime directive. Nothing else really mattered.

Still, Leah desperately wished that she'd never returned to Cedar Cove, never learned of her father's ultimate betrayal. It was almost too much to bear.

A sound alerted Leah to Simon Sprague's presence. Wiping at her face, she glanced peripherally toward the doorway and saw that Sy was watching with compassionate eyes.

He cleared his throat. "The door was open . . . I couldn't help hearing."

Leah rubbed her head. Great. She sighed. "Was anyone else in the store?"

"Not a soul," he assured her.

Thank heavens, Leah thought grimly. That, at least, was something to be grateful for. "I'd appreciate if you'd keep anything you happened to, uh, overhear to yourself."

Sy looked offended. "I wouldn't be telling such tales."

"Of course, you wouldn't. I'm sorry, it's just that—"

"I can help," he blurted. "I've got a few pennies set aside. It's not quite as much as you need, but it's a start."

"Oh, Sy." Leah felt tears threaten. "That's so kind of you."

Bewildered, Sprague shook his head, murmuring, "I can't believe Louis would do such a thing."

Before Leah could respond, the telephone rang shrilly. She stared for a moment before lifting the receiver.

"Leah?"

Her chest tightened. "Hello, Boyd."

From the corner of her eye, Leah saw Sprague back discreetly out of the office.

"I missed seeing you yesterday." Boyd's voice was low and sexy. "Did you catch up on your work?"

Leah felt a pang of guilt. When Boyd had called yesterday, she'd told him that she had too much to do and couldn't see him. In truth, Leah's confrontation with Craig had forced her to face facts. Encouraging Boyd to hope for a long-term relationship was cruel and unfair.

But leaving would be twice as difficult this time, like cutting out a chunk of her heart. Still, Leah gathered her courage and kept a cool voice. "Actually, Boyd, I didn't get nearly as much accomplished as I'd hoped."

"Oh." Disappointment tinged his tone. "Well, how about this evening?"

"I'm sorry, I've made other plans."

Boyd's voice hardened. "What kind of plans?"

"I don't believe that's really your concern, Boyd."

She heard his breath catch and she tightened her grip on the receiver. This was the most painful thing she'd ever done, and she wondered if she would be able to carry it off.

When Boyd spoke again, his voice was softer, filled with concern. It nearly undid her. "What's wrong, honey? Is it Cybil?"

Snatching a tissue from the desk drawer, Leah wiped her wet eyes. "Mother's fine. The tests showed no permanent damage. She'll have to take it easy for a while, but the doctors don't see any reason why she can't expect a full recovery."

"That's wonderful. I know you must be relieved to hear that." He paused, then said, "I have a meeting with the senator this afternoon but I can cancel it if you need me."

"Oh, don't even *think* about canceling." Sudden anger made Leah's voice tremble. "After all, we wouldn't want the senator annoyed."

The anger was contagious. "Don't you think you've held this grudge long enough?" Boyd snapped. "I realize you feel my father behaved insensitively, but he was trying to protect my feelings. That doesn't excuse what he did, but surely after all these years, you can at least understand it."

Taking her silence as acquiescence, Boyd continued in a calmer tone. "I've talked with him, Leah. He regrets what happened."

The words nearly choked her. "I'm so relieved." Of course, Boyd would defend his father. Cauldwell had been right—Boyd would never defy his own family. Even though it was unfair to blame him for what he couldn't know, that essential truth remained. "I don't want to discuss this any more."

"Damn it, Leah—"

"In fact, I don't really want to discuss anything else. I— I appreciate your help and everything you've done for us, but it would be best to leave it at that." Leah twisted the tissue into a soggy spear.

"Best for whom?" Boyd bit off each word.

"Best for everyone."

There was a long pause. She heard his breathy rasp, then he said, "Is this your quaint little way of giving me the gate?"

"Call it what you like."

"I'm calling it what it is. Why don't you just pack a bag and steal off in the dead of night? That *is* your specialty, isn't it?" A thud echoed through the line, as though Boyd had slammed his fist into a desk. "Tell you what, Leah. Why don't you try something really different, like telling the truth for a change? Who knows, with a little practice you might even get the hang of it."

Wincing at Boyd's angry tone, Leah pressed her fingernails into the soft flesh of her palm. She wanted to cry out that she needed him, that she loved him. Instead, she forced herself to be calm and tough. "The truth is that I've had it up to my eyebrows with the entire Cauldwell clan. I...don't want to see you again, Boyd."

Air rushed from Boyd's lungs as his ribs suddenly contracted. He couldn't believe what he'd just heard. Something was wrong, dreadfully wrong. It seemed as if Leah was reciting trite lines from a poorly written and unconvincing script. But why? Boyd knew that Leah still cared. He remembered joyful tears when she'd found the carved log at his cabin and the way her lips had trembled when he touched her.

What had happened to frighten her away? Boyd had no idea, but he was certainly going to find out.

A small sound, like a muffled sob, echoed in the receiver and at the same moment, Boyd heard his brother's voice filter from the reception area outside his office. Glancing at his watch, Boyd moaned. It was nearly time for the strategy session.

"I'll be over tonight, Leah." Boyd looked up as Craig walked into his office, then spoke firmly into the phone. "We'll discuss this then."

"There's nothing to—"

"About seven." Boyd gently cradled the receiver, staring at the silent telephone for several seconds before glancing up.

Craig was watching Boyd with a strange, almost distraught expression. As he met Boyd's eyes, Craig suddenly turned and dropped a stack of folders on the conference table at the far end of the office.

"Got any Scotch?" Not waiting for an answer, Craig opened the liquor cabinet and pulled out a glass. He grabbed a bottle and poured himself a healthy drink, then downed half of it in a single swallow. With a ragged sigh, Craig slumped forward, bracing himself on the cabinet, then straightened, refilled his glass and dropped heavily into a nearby chair.

Boyd regarded his brother thoughtfully. Craig looked like a lost child, confused and agitated. In fact, the youngest Cauldwell had been tenser than usual for the past couple of weeks and Boyd wondered if the strain of the impending political campaign was taking its toll.

"You look tired," Boyd said.

Craig shrugged and took another drink. "The debate in Auburn has been pushed up. It's going to be held next week."

Boyd rubbed his chin. That was bad news. Public speaking was definitely not Craig's forte. Boyd had arranged for coaching and preparation, but a week wouldn't be nearly enough time. "It might be best if we plead conflict of schedule."

"You mean drop out of the debate?"

"Canceling is preferable to being unprepared."

Shaking his head adamantly, Craig muttered, "The senator would kill me if I chickened out." With an angry gulp, he downed the rest of his drink. "I've got to do it—I've got to be ready." He looked at Boyd with pleading eyes. "Help me."

Again, nagging doubt clumped around Boyd like a cold, damp cloud. Craig simply wasn't ready for a seat on the county board.

Boyd leaned back in his chair. "Listen, Craig. I'm worried about you. You look as though you haven't had a decent night's sleep in a month and you've been so damned jumpy the past couple of weeks, I'm afraid you're going to give yourself an ulcer. Why don't you take a rest?"

"Don't worry." Craig emitted a harsh laugh. "I can look after myself." Standing, he whirled back to the liquor cabinet for another refill.

Yeah, Boyd thought dryly, like an unweaned puppy can take care of itself. Craig simply wasn't competent for the job to which he now aspired, and Boyd could no longer live with his own part in this mess.

Facing Craig directly, Boyd said, "I think the timing here is wrong."

"What timing?"

"The election. You're not ready yet. Let's give it some distance." Seeing Craig's crumpled expression, Boyd changed to a more placating tone. "A few more years of experience would—"

"No!" Craig's face reddened. "I'm going to win. I have to."

Tapping a finger on his desk, Boyd carefully considered his next statement. Finally he said, "That's your decision, Craig, but you'll have to do it without me."

"W-What are you saying?"

"I'm saying that if you insist on running for this particular seat, you'll have to find a new campaign manager."

Craig appeared ready to faint. "You...can't mean that."

"I'm sorry," Boyd said gently. "My conscience won't let me continue this farce. Even if you won, the job would destroy you."

Bewilderment, fear and finally anger flickered across Craig's face. Drink sloshing, he lurched toward Boyd's desk. "Maybe this election is just taking too much of your time," Craig said bitterly.

"What's that supposed to mean?"

Gesturing sloppily toward the phone, Craig sneered. "It means you'd rather spend time with *her* than helping your own brother."

Boyd felt his muscles knot. "Leah has nothing to do with this."

Craig snorted unpleasantly. "Sure."

Swallowing a growing anger, Boyd changed the subject. "Where's the senator?"

"Don' know." Leaning against the desk, Craig smirked and twirled his glass. Alcohol soaked into his brain, slurring the words. "Las' I saw, he was heading to the hardware store."

Boyd was instantly on his feet. "Why?"

Shrugging, Craig said, "Maybe he needs a new hammer. Anyway, you won' be so damn anxious to quit when the senator finds out." As Craig tipped his wrist, Boyd snatched the glass away and slammed it forcefully on the desk. Craig protested. "Hey!"

"Why did the senator go to Wainwright Hardware?" Boyd's voice was low and deadly.

Craig reached for his drink. Boyd backhanded the glass with a vicious swipe. Liquor sprayed and the empty glass bounced across the carpet.

Mouth twisting in fury, Craig snarled, "Maybe he wanted to have a li'l talk with your girlfriend." Craig spat out the words like a bad taste. "The senator isn't happy 'bout you taking up with the town trash, and when he finds out you're turning on your own family for that bimbo—"

Quick as a lightning strike, Boyd's hand shot out and clamped on to Craig's collar, half dragging the stunned man over the desk. Craig's pupils instantly contracted into tiny pinpoints. Shock turned to fear when Boyd wrapped his free hand around Craig's throat.

"Don't you ever speak about Leah like that again." Boyd bit off each word with lethal precision.

Frantically, Craig pried at Boyd's fingers. "I—I was kidding, man, just k-kidding." The pressure against his windpipe made Craig rasp and cough. He clawed desperately at Boyd's hands.

Coldly, Boyd watched Craig's face redden. A tiny, choked word echoed as though from a great distance. Curiously, Boyd tried to concentrate on the faint sound.

"Please . . . p-please . . ."

Blinking like an awakening somnambulist, Boyd stared down and saw his own hand curled around his brother's throat.

Good God, what was he doing?

Horrified, Boyd released Craig, who staggered away wheezing. Boyd dropped shakily into his chair, stunned to the core by the force of his own reaction. Subconscious rage had erupted into a fit of uncontrollable violence that absolutely appalled him.

Boyd Cauldwell, who had never knowingly harmed a living creature in his entire life, had lost his coveted self-control, wanting to thrash the brother he'd always protected. For a brief, terrifying moment, Boyd knew he'd been capable of the unthinkable—all because Craig had drunkenly maligned Leah. That was no justification, no excuse for such explosive behavior. But this was Boyd's rational mind speaking, the logical portion, which for a few devastating moments had been completely suppressed by a deeper instinct: a gut-level reaction to defend the woman he loved.

Love.

Boyd was still in love with Leah. The revelation was both startling and frightening.

It was nearly dusk when Leah and Stacey pulled into the dirt driveway leading to the Wainwright house. Although Stacey had chattered nonstop all the way from the hospital, Leah hadn't really been listening and had punctuated the rare pauses in her daughter's monologue with mumbled responses.

Leah's mind buzzed like a nest of hornets, as indiscriminate, stinging thoughts battered her brain cells like a million beating wings. Today's visit with Cybil had been strained and oh-so-cautious. Leah had wanted desperately to ask about the hateful agreement, but Cybil had still seemed weak and Leah hadn't wanted to upset her. Still, she couldn't help but wonder if, ten years ago, her mother had known about the horrid document.

"Boyd's here," Stacey said suddenly, grabbing the dashboard in excitement and pulling herself forward for a better look. "There's his car, Mommy."

Boyd's name captured Leah's wandering attention and she followed her daughter's happy gaze. The familiar dark sedan was parked by the house and Boyd was sitting on the porch, waiting.

As Stacey rolled down her window, waving and squealing, Leah felt conflicting emotions. She wanted to seek solace in Boyd's arms. But she couldn't.

The irrevocable decision had been made.

From the road behind her, Leah heard the scream of skidding tires and in the rearview mirror, she saw a dented pickup truck fishtailing a U-turn. A half dozen rowdy teenagers whistled and catcalled as the truck swerved and the young driver attempted to regain control.

Fortunately, Leah had already pulled safely in front of the house. Boyd was watching the out-of-control vehicle, tensing as though ready to pounce if the situation so required. Finally, the truck lurched back onto the road and sped away, leaving a legacy of beer cans strewn across the driveway.

Leah groaned in frustration. Summer visitors could be a menace on mountain highways and unfortunately it wasn't unusual for a group of drunken kids to end up at the base of a ravine. Most of Tahoe's permanent residents found the seasonal invasion to be mildly annoying, but several instances of vandalism had been attributed to the more raucous visitors.

At any rate, the truck was long gone and Leah returned her attention to the situation at hand. Boyd.

As soon as Leah turned off the ignition, Stacey leaped from the car, clutching her bird book. "Guess what, Boyd? I saw a hummingbird today, just like the one on page thirty. It had a blue throat and its feathers were kind of shimmery."

Boyd smiled. "What kind was it?"

Stacey frowned. "I don't know. It had a real long name."

"We'll check it out later." Boyd skimmed a glance at Leah and added, "After dinner. What sounds good? Steak, pizza or Chinese?"

"Pizza!" Stacey answered without hesitation.

Pushing the car door shut, Leah pulled her keys from her purse. She gave Boyd what she hoped was a cool look. "It's late, Boyd. Some other time."

Stacey looked crushed. "But Mommy—"

"I've already defrosted the pork chops." Avoiding her daughter's bewildered expression, Leah marched up the steps and unlocked the front door. A childish moan of disappointment turned into a happy giggle. Glancing back, Leah saw that Boyd had scooped Stacey over his shoulder and was carrying her up the porch steps.

"Great," he said. "I love pork chops."

Boyd's cheerful tone contradicted the deliberate glint in his eyes. Without so much as a glance toward Leah, he strode into the house and deposited the girl on the stairway. "Off you go, sprout. Go wash up for dinner, then we'll check out your hummingbird."

Stacey was all smiles. "Okay," she agreed happily, then bounded upstairs.

When Boyd turned around, determination was etched in every crease of his rock-hard expression.

Deciding to postpone the inevitable, Leah spun on her heel and went into the kitchen. Boyd didn't follow. In a few moments, Leah heard Stacey's voice, then booming male laughter. As she fried chops and peeled potatoes, Leah found herself almost enjoying the comforting sounds emanating from the living room. It was so...loving.

Still, she reminded herself that it was a temporary situation and a dangerous one, because Stacey was becoming more attached to Boyd with every passing day.

If Leah was withdrawn during dinner, Stacey and Boyd didn't seem to notice. They were both much too engrossed in discussing birds and squirrels and the forest deer population. Allowing her mind to wander, Leah concentrated on the words she would use to convince Boyd that their relationship should be amicably ended. She'd nearly constructed the perfect sentence in her mind when something caught her attention.

"Is it a big boat?" Stacey was asking.

"Big enough to pull a munchkin like you."

Covering her mouth with both pudgy hands, Stacey pulled her shoulders nearly up to her ears and was beset with giggles. "I can wear my new swimsuit. It's really hot."

Boyd's fork froze in midair. "Hot?"

"Uh-huh." Stabbing at her meat, Stacey peeked up and batted her eyes coyly. Boyd had a sudden coughing spasm.

Leah twisted her napkin. "What's going on here?"

"Boyd's taking me water-skiing." A bite of pork chop disappeared into Stacey's mouth and she chewed contentedly, swallowed, then added, "Do you want to come?"

Leah was stunned. All she could think of was the look on Bitsy's face when she'd seen Stacey's birthmark. So far, Boyd hadn't seemed to notice any family resemblance, but the distinctive port-wine stain exposed by the two-piece suit would be like flashing a neon sign announcing parentage. Leah panicked.

Dropping the wadded napkin on her nearly full plate, Leah stood. Fear gave force to her voice. "No water-skiing."

Stacey's fork clattered to the table. "Why? I can swim good and Boyd will take care of me."

Aware that Boyd was watching with increasing interest, Leah nervously gathered the dishes from the table. "Some other time," she said crisply.

Her daughter's eyes filled with tears. "Please, Mommy—"

"No! Don't argue with me, Stacey."

The child stared as though her entire world had been yanked out from under her. Leah could have bitten her own tongue out. She'd never used that tone of voice with Stacey before and her daughter's shattered expression tore at her heart.

"Darling, I'm sorry. There will be other chances to—"

Stacey's chair scraped the wooden floor. With a broken sob, she ran out of the room and up the stairs.

Shoulders slumping, Leah closed her eyes and willed herself not to cry. Not yet, anyway. Clutching the stack of dishes, she went into the kitchen and struggled to compose herself.

In a moment, Boyd followed, setting a pile of plates and glasses on the counter. Leah could feel his eyes on her, watching . . . waiting. Breathing with short, shallow gasps, she twisted the faucet until a torrent of steaming water blasted into the sink.

Boyd quietly studied Leah's jerky movements. A clamp of teeth stilled the telltale quiver of her lower lip. The tension Boyd had perceived in Leah's voice this afternoon hadn't been imagined. If Leah had been agitated over the telephone, now she appeared ready to jump right out of her skin.

Leah seemed absolutely terrified, but of what? Waterskiing? No, that couldn't be it. During their picnic at the cove, Boyd had noticed that although Leah had kept a close eye on Stacey, she hadn't seemed unduly worried about her daughter's water skills.

A glass shattered on the tile floor and Leah cried out in frustration. Whirling, she sagged against the counter and looked helplessly at Boyd. With a choked sound, Leah bent to pick up the broken shards but Boyd stopped her, gently grasping her shoulders and coaxing her upright.

She spoke in choppy syllables. "You had no right."

"No right to do what?"

"To use Stacey that way."

"'Use'—?" Boyd shook his head. "I just thought she'd enjoy a day on the lake, Leah. That's not a felony."

"You should have asked me first."

"I *did* ask you. You were sitting across the table, for crying out loud."

She looked away. "I—I must have been preoccupied."

"Apparently." He released his grip, spearing his hair with his fingers. "You must have a grand opinion of me if you think I'd deliberately use a child as a weapon."

"I'm sorry," she whispered miserably. "It's just that Stacey has become so...fond of you. I don't want her to be hurt or disappointed."

Boyd's eyes narrowed. "I'm fond of her, too, Leah. Why would you think I'd hurt her?"

She hesitated, then shrugged and stumbled to the broom closet. "What do you see when you look at Stacey?"

His skin chilled. "I see a charming little girl."

"A charming little girl who was fathered by another man." Leah boldly met Boyd's gaze. "You and I both know that you can't truly accept the fact. Eventually, Stacey would sense your resentment and feel rejected."

Now it was Boyd who looked away. Leah's words had struck home. He'd tried to pretend, to ignore the brutal fact, but he *was* bothered by it. "I won't lie to you. It does hurt to know...what happened."

With a stiff nod, Leah jerked out a broom and attacked the shattered glass.

Boyd tried to explain. "When I first saw Stacey, all I could think of was where she got that chin, or what color *his* hair was. I found myself staring obsessively at strange men on the street, wondering if maybe..." His voice trailed away helplessly.

Leah tightened her fingers around the broomstick, squeezing until her knuckles were white. "I understand."

"No. No, you don't understand." Irritated, Boyd yanked the broom from her grasp. "*I* don't even understand, but each day my perspective seems to be changing. Now when I look at Stacey, I see Stacey—not Leah's child, not the genetic issue of some unnamed villain, just Stacey."

Boyd saw Leah's lips sag apart, trembling. As she searched his eyes, Boyd recognized a tiny, hopeful glimmer. But her eyelids fluttered shut and when she opened them, Boyd saw only sadness and resignation.

"It doesn't matter anymore," Leah said quietly. "I have to protect my daughter."

"From me?"

"From everyone. You don't know how difficult it's been for Stacey, growing up without a father. She feels abandoned and isolated and that makes her vulnerable to any man who offers the attention she craves. You've been kind to her and you're becoming the center of that fantasy."

Boyd frowned. "Back up for a minute. Are you telling me that you haven't even told Stacey who her father is?"

"I-it hasn't been necessary." Leah had paled three shades.

"Oh, but it *has* been necessary to lie to your own daughter."

"I've never lied to her."

"Are you saying she's never asked?"

Leah's tongue darted out to moisten her lips. "No, I'm not saying that. I've given her as much information as she needed."

Folding his arms, Boyd regarded Leah with an angry narrowed stare. "That's a cop out."

She shot him a sharp look. "You don't know anything about it."

"You're right, I don't. And that's a situation I plan to remedy."

The fear returned to Leah's eyes. "What do you mean?"

"I mean that something is still haunting you. There's a wall between us, built with bricks of deceit and evasion. Only the truth can blow up that wall, and I'm damn sure ready for the demolition." His gaze impaled her. *"Who is Stacey's father?"*

Leah's lips went white. "It's time for you to leave, Boyd."

Ignoring her statement, Boyd leaned casually against the counter. "There are a dozen ways I can find out. Eleven bucks and a phone call will get me a copy of her birth certificate."

A sad smile tugged the corner of Leah's mouth. "Save your money, unless you think the words 'Father unknown' will cast some light on the issue."

"What?" Boyd couldn't believe his ears. "You mean you actually labeled your child illegitimate on her birth certificate? That piece of paper will follow Stacey through her entire life. How could you do such a thing?"

Leah whirled on him. "I didn't have any choice. Like everything else, it had already been taken care of. The hospital got their instructions from a higher source." As if she suddenly realized that she'd said too much, Leah snapped her lips together and stared sullenly at the floor.

Boyd sucked a ragged breath and the hairs on his nape stood at attention. He knew that he'd touched the tip of the proverbial iceberg. For the past ten years, someone had maintained a stranglehold on Leah, someone who was still exerting immense control over her life. That shadowy someone would be powerful, Boyd realized, and probably was not very far away.

And Boyd resolved to uncover the identity of that mysterious someone if it was the last thing he ever did.

A sharp tinkling broke into Boyd's thoughts. Leah had finished sweeping and had dumped the broken glass into the trash. Straightening, she slid him a weary look.

"Please go, Boyd."

Boyd's heart ached at the sound of Leah's tired voice. She'd been through hell the past few weeks and he was only adding to her grief by acting like a raving lunatic. She needed some quiet time, Boyd decided. They both did.

"I'll leave," he said softly, then turned toward the back door, adding, "For now."

Avoiding his gaze, Leah concentrated on scratching at a flaw in the tile counter. "It would probably be best if we didn't see each other again."

Boyd concealed the impact of her words. He had no intention of staying away but at this moment, he was unwilling to argue the point. "Good night, Leah."

Then he spun and walked out of the house.

Suddenly alone, Leah felt the silence engulf her like a heavy shroud. She stood unmoving, listening to Boyd's automobile engine roar to life, then drone into the distance. Upstairs, she knew that Stacey was probably sobbing in the dark, hurt and bewildered, feeling totally forsaken by a hostile world. Leah wanted to be with her daughter, to offer comfort and reassurance. Instead, she found herself staring out the kitchen window, whispering Boyd's name.

Burying her face in her hands, Leah finally cried.

Boyd was like a man possessed.

After spending an entire morning researching old incident reports at the sheriff's office, Boyd drove to the local library. Unloading an armful of folders and notepads, he marched into the periodicals section.

Since the tiny library had no microfiche equipment, Boyd piled neatly-bound newspapers on a scarred wooden table. Seating himself, he took a deep breath. Starting with the first day of that fateful October ten years ago, Boyd began to scan every headline.

There had been a heat wave early in that month, as shown by photographs of laughing children splashing in the lake.

Boyd remembered that Leah had mentioned unusually warm weather and was strangely pleased that he'd validated at least one detail of her story. He carefully read a small article about the annual Oktoberfest, but found no indication of anything sinister occurring during the celebration. In another issue was a picture of celebrating crowds and Boyd repeatedly scanned the scene, searching for a familiar face—Leah's face...and whoever she might be with. But the fading newsprint shared no secrets.

Boyd also noted that the senator had been up for reelection that year and since the newspaper's publisher was a longtime Cauldwell ally, several glowing articles appeared throughout the month along with a supportive editorial. The campaign coverage jogged Boyd's memory. That had been a particularly close election, he recalled, and one the senator had been secretly concerned about winning. Although Fletcher Cauldwell had the undiluted endorsement of the Tahoe region, a controversial agriculture position had eroded support among his valley constituents.

The final vote tally had been extremely close. It was, in his father's political lingo, "a ring-tailed squeaker."

But there was nothing about an assault at the lake. Not that Boyd had really expected a two-column piece on the subject, but he'd hoped to glean some small clue. What kind of clue, he couldn't even guess, but he'd hoped to know it when he saw it.

Still, he found nothing relevant through October or November or December. As he retrieved the January issues, Boyd began to feel idiotic. Since Leah had left in December, before Boyd had returned for Christmas break, it was senseless to continue with this obviously flawed idea. Even as he mentally reprimanded himself, he automatically turned page after page.

Boyd had nearly decided that enough of the day had been wasted when the Wainwright name popped out of a brief article in the business section.

Carefully, Boyd read the single paragraph. It appeared that Louis Wainwright had expanded the hardware store that month, leasing the office next door and demolishing the adjoining wall to double the shop area.

Folding the newspaper, Boyd stared into space. He'd known that the store's sales volume had been increased, of course, but had no idea when it had happened. After Leah had left, it had been years before Boyd could force himself into a place so strongly associated with her.

It was strange, however, that Louis would suddenly display such entrepreneurial ambition while Leah was in the throes of an emotional trauma.

Boyd folded the newspaper in disgust. This was ridiculous. Louis's business expansion had probably been planned for months and Boyd was trying to ferret some scurrilous motivation out of thin air. With a derisive grunt, Boyd returned the newspapers to the librarian and went to his car.

As he drove, Boyd's mind wandered, remembering the trusting and loving and happy child-woman that Leah had once been. She'd had laughing eyes, filled with enthusiasm and zest for life. Her eyes had hardened over the years and were now curtained with pain and suspicion.

Blinking and disoriented, Boyd glanced around and realized that he'd driven to the hospital. Although the trip had been subconsciously navigated, Boyd knew why he was here. He was certain that Cybil Wainwright had answers. And Boyd definitely had a lot of questions.

As he walked through the sterile halls toward Cybil's room, Boyd felt an indefinable pang, an uneasiness. Was he really going to confront a frail woman in her hospital bed? That kind of behavior would be considered crass and insensitive, even for the senator. Cybil's doorway loomed and Boyd felt icy perspiration bead his upper lip.

No. He simply couldn't do it. Not even to relieve the torture of his own private hell.

Turning, Boyd started to leave but a familiar childish laugh stopped him. Drawn, he peeked through the small glass opening in the hospital-room door. Stacey was sitting on her grandmother's bed, holding a book and pointing out something that was apparently amusing. Looking a bit tired, Cybil smiled and lovingly touched her granddaughter's cheek.

And Leah was standing at the window.

Although he couldn't see her face, Leah's profile reflected her wistful gaze outside. She stared at the clouds with an expression of anguish and profound yearning, like a wounded sparrow longing for flight.

The sight hit Boyd like a fist. With a rasping sound, he wheezed air into deflated lungs and stared at Leah as though she were a heavenly specter.

God, how he loved her.

But Boyd had expressed that love with sullen suspicion and inane jealousy and by allowing doubt to overpower reason.

Suddenly, Boyd realized that it simply didn't matter who had fathered Stacey. The child was simply herself, charming and funny and lovable, with her own unique personality.

Boyd's intense fixation had blinded him to the fact that Leah had a right to the privacy of her own soul. Violating that privacy wouldn't help her. If Boyd were to find the man responsible for Leah's grief and if his fury exploded into violence again, would justice then be served? And would such justice be for Leah—or for Boyd himself?

Suddenly, Boyd's legs felt weak and his hands began to shake.

It *had* all been for himself, he realized. Everything he'd done had been motivated by a need to relieve his own feelings of guilt and betrayal. Yet Boyd's own self-delusion had been the cruelest betrayal of all.

Suddenly Leah turned from the window and looked straight at him. He held her gaze, savored it and mentally promised that never again would he be the cause of her pain.

Leah seemed to hear his silent message. Her eyes softened, misted by poignant, aching need.

When Leah saw Boyd, she thought him merely a vision superimposed on the tiny window by her overactive imagination. He seemed different, his expression too reverent for existence on an earthly plane. But then Boyd had slowly closed his eyes and Leah had known that he was real, standing just beyond the door like a guardian angel.

Last night, when she'd sent him away, Leah had felt as if part of her life had ended, like a spiritual death. Lying awake until dawn, replaying Boyd's words over and over in her mind.

Not Leah's child, not the genetic issue of some unnamed villain, just Stacey.

I'll leave... for now.

At the time, fear and weariness had prevented Leah from analyzing those words. Boyd *would* come to her again, and in spite of her brave lies, Leah desperately wanted him to. Trying to send Boyd away was like trying to saw off her own arm. Her logic insisted there could be no happiness in a relationship shrouded by secrets.

But Leah's heart just wasn't listening.

Chapter Eight

Night seeped fretfully over the mountain and an eerie hush permeated the rugged terrain. Even crickets refused to challenge the oppressive silence. Air, thick as a mourning shroud, offered no breeze to stimulate nearby foliage in a comforting rustle. Leah heard only the faint lapping of lake water.

Upstairs, Stacey slept soundly, wrapped in the bliss of sweet innocence while Leah paced in agitation, waiting and wondering if her heart had misled her—again.

Leah had been waiting for Boyd, hoping and praying that he would come, and that for at least a short while, she wouldn't be alone.

Sighing, Leah folded her arms, then glanced down at her attire and moaned. She should change clothes, just in case. Certainly, the blue-and-gray fleece jogging suit she wore wasn't the type of garment most women donned to entice a would-be lover. Leah usually dressed for function rather than style. Tonight, however, she wanted to be alluring and beautiful.

She was on the stairs when something caught her attention.

There was a sound from the yard, a soft crunch of pine needles pressing into earth. Freezing in midstep, Leah paused, ears straining for another tiny clue. When she heard it, her stomach knotted.

It couldn't be Boyd. No droning car engine had heralded his arrival, or anyone else's for that matter. Instead, Leah had heard only faceless footsteps in the dark. Fear surged into her throat and she snapped off the living-room lamp. Tall, narrow windows flanked the front door and Leah stealthily moved toward them. Curtains, secured by rods at the top and bottom, stretched over the glass and Leah carefully hooked the gauzy fabric with her finger, drawing it aside. She saw nothing but shades of gray, unmoving shadows on the moonlit ground.

Then a silhouette loomed on the porch in front of her.

Gasping, she released the curtain and jumped back, flattening herself against the solid wall. The weathered planks creaked beneath a heavy weight, then stopped. For several long moments, Leah heard no sound at all. She began to wonder if her imagination was working overtime.

Her gaze landed on the light switch beside the door. With a deep breath, she whirled around, hitting the switch and simultaneously pulling back the curtain. Light flooded the porch, illuminating the startled person who stood there.

"Boyd," she whispered, nearly laughing with relief. Swinging open the door, she placed her palm on her chest, trying to quiet its frantic rhythm.

Hands jammed tightly into his pockets, Boyd stood immobile for several seconds. Then, rocking forward on the balls of his feet, he stared at his shoes and cleared his throat. "When the living-room light went off, I thought I'd waited too long."

"Waited?" Leah gazed over his shoulder to the empty driveway.

"I left the car at the pull-off down the road."

"Why?"

He slid his hand from his pocket and rubbed the back of his neck. "I, uh, didn't want to disturb you." Then he sighed. "That's not exactly true, Leah. I just lost my nerve. I was afraid you'd slam the door in my face, and I've been prowling around out here trying to gather my courage."

"Oh, Boyd," Stepping back, Leah motioned him in, then closed the door. "I'm so sorry."

That surprised him. "You have nothing to be sorry about—"

"Yes, I do. These past two weeks, I've been a complete emotional wreck, vacillating one way then the other until I was as dizzy as if I'd spent a week spinning in my tire swing. I thought I could come to terms with the past, but I've let it overwhelm me instead."

"You've been through hell, honey." Boyd cupped her cheek with his palm. "I should have helped you, but I've just added to your torment."

She met his gaze. "No. You've done so much for me and for Stacey. You made us feel . . . special."

"You *are* special, Leah," Boyd murmured. "You're both very special." He caressed her cheek with his fingertips, shivering as she turned her face into his palm. With great effort, he lifted his hand and turned away. "I have to say something. It's not easy, so I hope you'll be patient with me."

Boyd's desolate expression nearly broke Leah's heart. She wanted to hold him, kiss away whatever was causing pain, but as she reached out, he shook his head, as though her touch would unravel the final thread of his resolve.

In a halting voice, Boyd said, "I've been obsessed by finding the man who . . . hurt you, to the point that I lost sight of what is really important." Boyd stared at the ceiling. "Do you know what I did today?"

A feeling of dread washed over her. "No."

Boyd took a deep breath, then began to speak in a low monotone, telling Leah of his excursion to the library and the sheriff's office, culminating with his appearance at the hospital. When he'd finished, he seemed drained. "I deceived you, sneaking around behind your back. Even though you'd told me everything you wanted me to know, it wasn't enough."

Leah began to tremble. Boyd had felt that *he* was being deceitful. Oh, God! Guilt twisted through her chest like a dull corkscrew. "Boyd, don't—"

Swinging around, Boyd grasped Leah's shoulders, impaling her with an expression of absolute sincerity. "It doesn't matter any more, Leah, I swear it. If you'll forgive me, I promise never to ask about Stacey's father again."

"T-there's nothing to forgive." The words nearly choked her. "You don't understand—"

"I understand that you're a strong and courageous woman. You've lost your father, nearly lost your mother and come back to a hostile environment filled with sad memories...." His eyes softened to a rich amber hue as he added, "And I hope some good memories as well."

Images strobed through her mind. "Wonderful memories," she whispered. She reached up, hesitated, then lightly traced the deep groove etched from his cheekbone to his jawline. He sucked in a sharp breath and she pulled her hand away.

"Don't stop." He wrapped his hand gently around her wrist, then pressed his lips into her palm. "I love to have you touch me."

Thus encouraged, she explored his face with her fingertips, combing back the silvery streak of hair falling carelessly across his forehead, using the soft pads of her thumbs to stroke and smooth his thick eyebrows.

Boyd closed his eyes and a satisfied moan vibrated in his throat. His hands rested lightly on her waist, and he gave himself to the delight of her delicate exploration.

Leah returned her attention to his hair, gently brushing the thick mahogany strands with her fingers. "So soft," she whispered, more to herself than to Boyd. Her eyes were wide with curiosity and wonder. The tactile sensuality of his hair seemed an odd paradox to the strong face, rugged and rough with masculinity.

The friction of his throat was a sensual contrast, pleasing to the touch. Fascinated, Leah saw a dark thatch peek over the V of his sweater, remembering that as a young man Boyd had deplored his sparsely furred chest. Apparently nature had remedied the problem and Leah touched the fine hairs, testing their texture with her fingertip. They were crisply curled and prickly. His muscles were firm and well defined. One of God's finest sculptures, she mused, molded in muscle and bone instead of cold marble.

She was engrossed in her sensual inspection, unaware that Boyd had gone completely rigid.

"Leah..."

Dreamily, she rubbed her palms across his chest. "Umm?"

Boyd's fists were clenched at his side and his voice had a strange, rasping quality. "I...think...I'd better...go."

Leah's eyes, which had been partially closed, snapped open and her hands stilled, resting lightly against his chest. "Why?"

Uncoiling his fingers, Boyd stiffly laid his hands over Leah's. He tried to smile but the result was more of a strained grimace. "Because in one more minute, all the willpower in the world won't keep me from doing to you what you've been doing to me."

"Oh." Blood rushed to her face and she jerked her hands away, knotting them together as she took a step backward. Boyd looked positively agitated, as though he wanted to unzip his skin and leap out. A furtive glance confirmed the reason for his obvious discomfort.

How humiliating. Leah was inexperienced, but she was certainly educated about the biological facts of human sexuality. A tiny voice in the back of her brain, however, confirmed her inner suspicion. She had indeed known what she was doing to Boyd, and to herself. A liquid warmth was permeating her body, along with a quickening pulse and a feeling of light-headedness.

It wasn't as though she'd never experienced these feelings before. She had. But each time it had been Boyd who had induced them.

A movement broke into Leah's thoughts. Boyd had turned away and was reaching for the doorknob.

"Wait!"

Surprised by the desperation in her command, he gave her a questioning look.

She licked her lips. "Please don't go."

He released his grip on the knob.

"I . . . don't want to be alone." Rubbing her damp palms together, Leah was unable to meet his gaze. This might be wrong, but she couldn't seem to help herself. An exquisite sweetness was surging through her and she had an overwhelming desire to share that experience, to express her love in the only way she could.

Eyes cast downward, she reached out until her fingers brushed his sweater, then she brought them to rest on the throbbing pulse at the base of his throat.

He took a ragged breath. "Are . . . you sure this is what you want?"

She spoke to the floor. "I want you to hold me and care for me. I want to feel . . . like a woman."

Suddenly there were only inches between them and Boyd's body heat radiated outward, warming Leah's chilled skin. One hand was pressed stiffly at his side, as though nailed in place, but he stroked her cheek so delicately with the other it was more sensation than touch.

"You're more woman than I've ever known." His voice had a low, shaky tremor. "You're everything that's soft and feminine, warm and giving and exquisitely desirable."

Raising her gaze, Leah looked into Boyd's eyes. She saw the heat of passion, glowing yet restrained, caged like a dangerous beast lest it wreak havoc on its unsuspecting prey.

For a moment, fear flooded through Leah, a brief panic. Boyd was a formidable man, exuding an aura of raw power pulsing just below the surface. The thought of that awesome strength surging out of control made her feel faint.

Recognizing Leah's apprehension, Boyd gently brushed his lips across her brow. "Whatever you want, Leah, and nothing more. Do you believe that?"

"Yes." And she did. Deep down, Leah knew Boyd would never hurt her, never ignore her wishes. But still, she felt perturbed and confused. "I just don't know what I want," she lamented. "I feel so . . . restless."

Boyd's lips curved in a knowing smile. "I believe there was some mention of being held. Do you want me to hold you, Leah?"

"Yes, please."

Slowly, he took her in his arms, engulfing her in a loving cocoon. Resting her cheek against his chest, she sighed contentedly, enjoying the feel of Boyd's fingers massaging her back. "That's so nice," she murmured, her body humming with pleasure.

"Umm." Boyd buried his face in her hair, lifting the silken strands and allowing them to feather across his cheek. "You smell wonderful, like a spring meadow."

She purred. "You do, too."

"I smell like flowers?"

"No, more like a pine tree."

"Oh." He chuckled softly. "Well, that's appropriate, since the sap is definitely rising."

Smiling, Leah wound her arms around his waist and rubbed like a cat against him. "The hairs tickle my nose." Suddenly, she wondered if his chest was now covered with a crisp mat or merely sprinkled by a light dusting of curly hairs. She slipped her hands under the loose sweater, ignoring his involuntary muscle spasm as she stroked her palms over his skin.

The sensation of her hands traveling beneath his clothes was nearly too much to bear. His back stiffened slightly and a muscle ticked in his jaw.

Feeling his reaction, Leah looked up into his face. "Does this bother you?"

He answered without moving his jaw. "Not at all."

"Then why are you grinding your teeth?"

In spite of his discomfort, he laughed. "I think we need a couple of rules here."

"What kind of rules?"

"Rule number one is—" his eyes gleamed "—whatever you do to me, I get to do to you."

Leah's gaze darted to her hands beneath his sweater. The image of his hands under her clothing, sliding over her bare skin made her shudder with delight.

She cleared her throat. "That sounds, uh, reasonable."

"I'm glad you agree," he said warmly. He brushed his knuckles over her spine, then slowly slid his hand under her sweatshirt. When his fingers grazed her skin, she flinched as though she'd been burned. Boyd pulled back instantly. "Did I hurt you?"

"No." Her vehement head shake emphasized the point. "It's very...pleasant."

That was certainly an understatement, considering her legs had nearly buckled. The slow warmth that had been gently unfurling had suddenly erupted into an uncomfortable, aching heat. When Leah felt Boyd's mouth on her throat, she moaned and rolled her head backward, allowing him greater access. He took advantage of the movement, covering the delicate skin with kisses and tiny, moist tongue touches. As his lips traveled to the corners of her mouth, Boyd paused uncertainly.

But Leah was in no mood for caution. She wanted his lips and mouth, wanted desperately to taste him, to feel the silken stroke of his tongue against her own. Leah could overcome her fear, but knew it would be possible only with Boyd, the man she so deeply loved.

Struggling against the encumbering sweater, she finally extracted her hands and wound them firmly around his neck.

With a deep, shuddering groan, Boyd took her lips in a kiss filled with passion and promise. He tightened his arms, then immediately relaxed, as though unwilling to frighten her with the extent of his desire. But Leah wasn't the least bit frightened. In fact, at that very moment, all she wanted was to feel Boyd's arms around her, to savor the maleness of him and revel in the contrast between her softness and his strength.

When the kiss ended, they stared at each other with mutual expressions of shock and wonder. He continued to caress her bare skin and Leah was aware that her breasts were throbbing with a strange heaviness. They were bare beneath her sweatshirt and they craved his touch.

Hugging Boyd tightly, she rubbed against him, but the sensation wasn't satisfying enough. She knew what she wanted, but was too shy to ask, yet certain that he wouldn't touch her intimately unless he was convinced that she wanted him to.

Blushing furiously, she stammered, "Do you remember the night we... drove to Hansen's Hill?"

The hands on her back stilled. "Oh, yes."

"You, uh, did something that night that was very... stimulating."

"If I recall, we were both rather stimulated that evening," Boyd teased her gently, recalling that the night in question was the one time he'd nearly lost sight of his wait-until-the-wedding credo. "What exactly did you have in mind?"

Leah's face felt hot enough to glow in the dark.

Sensing her embarrassment, Boyd spoke soothingly: "There's nothing you can't say to me, Leah. Physical pleasure between two people who care for each other is natural and beautiful. Shall I touch you here?" He slid his finger around to her stomach. "Or here?"

Leah gasped as he gently cupped her bare breasts. "Yes."

With both hands, Boyd tested their soft weight, then brushed his flattened palms across her sensitive nipples. An electric jolt snapped through her, then turned into a fiery ache as he teased the tiny crown with the fleshy pads of his thumbs.

"Rule number two." Deep within her muddled brain Leah heard Boyd's voice, gently coaxing. "Whatever I do to you, you get to do to me."

That, too, sounded reasonable—and exciting.

Burrowing her hands under the sweater, Leah found Boyd's nipples were as hard as her own and she eagerly practised the caresses that he'd just shown her. She was rewarded by a rumbling groan of pleasure.

"You learn fast." Boyd's expression was twisted in what could have been either terrible pain or exquisite delight. Heavily hooded eyes gleamed with suggestive promise and a slow smile tugged the corner of his mouth. "Are you ready for another lesson?"

"I—I think I can handle that."

"Honey, I guarantee you can handle it." With a quick movement, Boyd pulled off his sweater and tossed the garment aside.

Leah's eyes widened until the blue irises were completely surrounded by white. Stumbling back a step, she wound her arms protectively across her chest and Boyd saw that she seemed to be holding her breath.

Damn it. Too late he realized that he'd gone too fast. Leah hadn't been prepared for the sight of a half-nude man in her foyer.

"You've filled out," she mumbled, eyes darting as though seeking escape. Moistening her lips with the tip of her tongue, she tried a casual laugh. It came out like a choked gurgle. "Have you taken up bodybuilding?"

Self-conscious, Boyd managed a tight smile. "I try to keep in shape."

"Yes...well." She cleared her throat. "You certainly have."

Boyd picked up the sweater and straightened, holding the wadded garment like a shield.

Reaching out, Leah said, "Don't put it on." Then, as though shocked by her own boldness, her gaze skittered away. "Perhaps we...should go upstairs."

Hesitating, Boyd saw trust in her eyes and a strangely desperate expression. His chest contracted. Lord, how he loved her. Of that, Boyd had absolutely no doubt. But he couldn't seem to find the words to share what he felt; and deep down, he knew why he couldn't.

Leah had left him once and he still bore the scars.

Spearing his fingers through his hair, Boyd tried to shake the cobwebs from his mind. "I want you, Leah. You have no idea how much I want you." He felt her body convulse in a violent shiver. "Talk to me, honey. Tell me what you want from me, what you need."

There was a flash of white as she nibbled her lower lip. When she spoke, her voice was soft but steady. "I guess I wanted to recapture what we once had, if only for a few hours. We loved each other so much, but we never shared the ultimate expression of that love. And I've always felt...cheated." She took a deep breath, then quickly continued, as though afraid her courage would fail. "I wanted to share that with you now, because it's all we can ever have."

Boyd looked into her eyes and saw the truth of her words. He too, wanted to share an expression of the sweet love they'd once had; the love he still carried in his heart. He could show her the beauty of physical love, a tenderness that he intuitively knew she'd never experienced. Her experience had been one of terror, her memories clouded by pain. Only through love would Leah experience joy and passion and the awakening of her inner self.

Boyd had that love to give.

Taking Leah's hand, he kissed the palm and gently sucked the fleshy pad beneath her thumb. Wide blue eyes questioned him and he took a step toward the stairs. "I've always felt cheated, too," he whispered.

They held hands, looking so deeply into each other's eyes that they found themselves in Leah's bedroom without realizing that they'd made the trip. Light from the hallway sprayed into the dark room, silhouetting Boyd's muscular frame. The beam narrowed and disappeared as the bedroom door was quietly closed.

A soft click broke the silence as Boyd turned the lock.

Leah had a moment of uncertainty, then Boyd scooped her into his arms and laid her on the soft mattress with such loving tenderness, that all doubt dissipated into the darkness.

"Leah." He made her name sound like a prayer. "You're so beautiful—" The words seemed to clog in his throat, so he simply stretched out beside her and stroked her cheek.

There was no urgency to his lovemaking and he seemed content merely to touch her, massaging her through her clothing, brushing his lips across her face and throat. Soon, he was awash in warmth, flooded with sweet sensations.

A rush of cool air whispered over her as Boyd rolled away to remove his clothes. Before she could protest, he'd returned, wrapping her in his arms and kissing her with increasing fervor. Leah went rigid, suddenly uncomfortable with the intensity of his embrace.

But Boyd was attuned to every nuance of her body language and instantly loosened his grip as his lips coaxed gently—offering all, but demanding nothing.

Relaxing, trusting him completely, Leah allowed hersel
to float into the delicious warmth. She purred like a con
tented kitten. "That feels wonderful."

"Umm ... which is better—this?" He slipped his finger
tips beneath her sweatshirt. "Or this?" he mumbled, ther
his tongue seared a moist trail down her throat.

She gasped. "Both."

"Greedy woman," he murmured, as he slid his finger
tips up to tease her waiting breasts. The heavy fleece shirt
however, was impeding his progress. Levering himself or
one elbow, he smiled down at her. "Shall we dispose of thi
encumbrance?" He emphasized his request by caressing her
nipple with his fingertips.

Leah squirmed restlessly as his touch sent sharp jabs o
current through her body. At the moment, she was too
aroused to be shy and with a deft movement, she pulled of
the offending shirt, tossing it into the darkness.

Moonlight filtered through the open blinds, scattering
silvery beams across her bare skin. She heard Boyd's sharp
intake of breath and quivered with pleasure.

"I've dreamed of seeing you like this for so long." H
spoke with wonder, as though he'd just been given a beau
tiful gift.

"Are you ... pleased?"

"Oh, Lord! Yes, I'm pleased. You're the most desirabl
woman on earth and I'm very, very pleased."

Contented, she allowed the breath to slide out from be
tween her lips. Soft night air brushed her breasts. They wer
exquisitely sensitized, prepared for the sensual touch o
Boyd's tongue. When he lowered his mouth to her body, sh
cried out in sheer pleasure. The gentleness of his lips, th
slick heat of his mouth, was almost too much to bear. He
head rocked against the pillow and her soft moans echoe
through the darkness.

"I want to feel your skin against mine," Boyd whis
pered. "I need to touch you all over."

Half dazed, Leah smiled and sighed, reveling in the glor
of Boyd's pleasure, yet not truly cognizant of what he'
said.

Then she felt a breeze slide across her bare hips and realized that Boyd was removing her jogging pants, pausing only to brush his lips over her bare stomach. Her body pulsed with pleasure as his hands glided over her skin, stroking until Leah tingled with an electric sensation.

Boyd was murmuring softly, sweet nonsensical words sweeping her ear like a delicate touch, arousing her to even greater heights of desire. Their bodies pressed together, knees to knees, chest to chest, lips to lips. Passion slickened their skin, then the moisture vaporized and enveloped them like a humid jungle mist—musky, hot, arousing.

Circling them slowly, Boyd slid his fingers from her abdomen to her thighs, then upward, closer and closer to the most intimate part of her. Tensing, she waited, knowing where the caress would lead but suddenly feeling afraid. When Boyd finally touched her femininity, Leah sucked in a breath and rolled away.

Boyd's voice offered gentle reassurance. "It's all right, honey. I won't do anything you don't want me to do."

Leah blushed furiously and trembled, wondering if she was sexually scarred for life. Intellectually, she knew perfectly well that the most personal part of her anatomy would be involved in the procedure. Psychologically, however—well, that was another matter entirely. Leah had never willingly allowed any man such a liberty. Even her gynecologist was a female.

"Do you want me to stop?" Boyd asked softly.

She squeezed her eyes closed and shook her head. In spite of her reluctance, Leah's blood was on fire, her loins throbbed, and she felt as though her insides had completely melted. No, she certainly didn't want him to stop. She knew in her heart that only Boyd could help her overcome this irrational fear.

Unable to speak, she forced her tight muscles to relax and turned back to Boyd. Leah's eyes met his and she knew that he understood. Lowering his head, Boyd cherished her mouth with his lips, savoring and tasting until she clutched at his shoulders, moaning with need.

Then a fire erupted in her very core. Boyd was loving her with his hand and every shred of her modesty exploded in a burst of fiery need. Crying out, she pulled at him, instinctively lifting her hips. Even the soles of her feet were engulfed in searing flames.

Moving over her, Boyd whispered something but she could only sob in frustration. She dug her heels into the mattress, then froze as she felt him shudder and press himself against her moistness. A choking terror surged through Leah and she stiffened, unable to breathe.

Boyd kissed her throat. "It's all right, my love. I'll never hurt you. No one will ever hurt you again."

He made no move to consummate their lovemaking. Instead, he continued to stroke and caress and whisper loving words of encouragement.

They lay together, their bodies intimately entwined yet not quite joined, until Leah's need once more overcame her deepest fears. She was fully aroused and ready.

Boyd knew it. "Take what you want, Leah."

"I—I don't know how."

He slid his hands under her hips. "Listen to your body, love. Close your eyes and let it tell you what you want to know."

Rolling her head, Leah squeezed her eyelids together and was instantly overcome. She'd been stiffly resisting the desire to move against Boyd, to feel the fullness of him deep inside her. Without conscious thought, her hips thrust upward and engulfed him.

He cried out, calling her name. They clung to each other as he allowed her body to adjust to him, then he began to move slowing, rocking against her.

Then it was Leah who cried out.

Cocooned in Boyd's arms, Leah listened to the reassuring rhythm of his heartbeat and tried to sort out the dichotomy of emotion flowing through her. She didn't regret what had happened between them—how could she possibly regret something so incredibly beautiful? But she also realized that making love with Boyd had been a tremendous mistake.

Now, leaving him would be like tearing off a piece of her soul.

But she had no choice. Cybil would be released from the hospital in a few days and with Sy managing the store, all of Leah's excuses for remaining in Cedar Cove would have been eliminated.

Unfortunately, the necessity of leaving had *not*. Leah loved Boyd too much to risk hurting him. And if she stayed much longer, the truth about what had happened so many years ago would be exposed.

It was only a matter of time. One by one, Leah's secrets were being exhumed. Even Bitsy Cauldwell had guessed the horrible truth after seeing Stacey. Eventually, Boyd would look at the child and see his own brother's face. The realization filled Leah with dread.

Suddenly, a deafening crash echoed from downstairs, quickly followed by the sound of shattering glass.

Boyd bolted upright. "What was that?" Without awaiting an answer, he swung his feet to the floor and stepped into his jeans.

By the time Leah had grabbed her robe from the closet, Boyd had unlocked the bedroom door. As he headed toward the stairs, Leah dashed to Stacey's room, tying her sash as she ran. She pushed open the door, sighing in relief when she saw the small figure curled sideways on the bed. Quietly, Leah pulled the door closed, then tiptoed into the hall.

As she hurried downstairs, a knot of fear formed in her throat. The air was cold and fresh, as though the front door had been left open. But when she got to the entry landing, she saw that the door was still closed and locked. Turning toward the living room, she saw Boyd snap on a lamp. In the soft glow, she noticed that he held something in his hand.

"What's that?" she asked.

"A rock." Extending his hand, he showed her a piece of granite the size of a tennis ball, then gestured toward the living-room window. The sheer drapes danced erratically as the night air pushed through the fabric.

Her eyes widened in comprehension. "Someone threw a rock through the window?"

"So it seems." Boyd was grim. "Whoever it was is gone now. Probably another group of tourists out on a binge of booze and mischief."

"Oh, God." Leah's skin blanched.

Boyd set the rock on a nearby table, then looked at Leah. She was as white as a bed sheet. Alarmed, he went to her, guiding her to the sofa. "What's wrong?"

"Wrong?" Her short laugh was tinged with panic. "What could possibly be wrong? Just because there's some maniac out there prowling around, throwing rocks into the house—"

Boyd interrupted by grabbing her shoulders, shaking her gently. "Calm down, honey. You don't know that anyone's been prowling around. The house is only fifty feet from the highway. Any kid with a good pitching arm could have flung that rock out of a moving truck. Hell, it might even have been an accident."

Leah was silent for several seconds, then rubbed her face. "Of course, you're probably right." But her expression said otherwise.

Boyd regarded Leah and was bewildered by her reaction. He could understand anger and indignation. After all, it *was* rather irritating to be awakened by a carelessly tossed rock. But Leah wasn't simply annoyed. She was terrified.

Suddenly Leah stood, lacing her fingers together. "It's late, Boyd." Her voice was thin and wispy. "You'd better go now."

"Go?" Cocking his head, he stared at her, noting the nervous twitch of her jaw. "I'd rather hoped to stay."

"You can't."

"Why not?" He skimmed a glance at his watch. "It'll be breakfast time in a couple of hours and I was counting on an invitation."

"I'm sorry that I can't accommodate the usual courtesies." Her voice was cool. "I don't want Stacey to find you here."

He considered that. "Do you think it would upset her to discover me in your bed?"

Leah winced, knowing that nothing would make Stacey happier. "I have no intention of finding out." She took a deep breath, leveling a steady stare at Boyd. "None of my male friends have been allowed to see morning from my bed."

With a hissing sound, Boyd sucked in air and felt as though he'd been kicked by a mule. Leah was standing there, rigid and prim, insinuating again that she'd had a series of men rolling across her mattress.

But why? Boyd was no expert, but he knew enough to realize that it had been a very, very long time since Leah had known any man. In fact, Boyd would have believed Leah a virgin had it not been for the tangible evidence to the contrary asleep upstairs.

"Good God, Leah." His eyes narrowed and she flinched. "If you're trying to convince me that you're some kind of femme fatale—"

Her face flaming, she snapped, "I'm not trying to convince you of a damned thing. Believe whatever you want, just go."

Pursing his lips, Boyd decided to try a different tact. "What we just experienced was special and beautiful."

Tears brimmed in her eyes. "Yes."

"Then why do you want me to leave?"

"Stacey's old enough to understand . . . certain things."

"Ah." Boyd regarded Leah shrewdly. That much was probably true, he decided. "And this bravado about having a stable of lovers was all a crock, wasn't it?"

"Yes." Leah sighed and massaged her stiffening neck. "And since it was painfully obvious that I hadn't the slightest idea what I was doing tonight, you must think me rather naive."

"Never." Boyd caressed Leah's cheek with his thumbs. "I just don't understand why you felt it necessary to . . . embellish your past."

Leah looked miserable. "I didn't want you to feel pressured."

"Pardon me?"

"You know—obligated." Frustrated, she tossed up her hands and turned away. "You've always been so responsible, so moral, everyone's knight in shining armor. Just because we spent these hours together, I didn't want you to feel compelled to, uh . . . Oh, rats. I don't know what I mean.''

Suppressing a smile, Boyd stepped behind Leah, winding his arms around her until she lay her head back against his shoulder. He felt her firm, round derriere press warmly into his flesh and fought the stirring in his loins. At this moment, she needed love and reassurance, not a sexual sequel.

Swiping aside her thick mane, Boyd kissed her nape and felt her shudder. ''I *do* take my responsibilities seriously, but I like to think I have free will and a certain amount of self-control. There was no calculated seduction tonight, by either of us.'' He felt Leah stiffen slightly at the comment. ''What we had was two adults who . . . cared deeply for each other and who chose to express that caring in a physical and spiritual way.''

Gently turning Leah to face him, Boyd waited until her gaze met his, then continued. ''I wanted to be as close to you as I could get. What I feel for you wasn't changed by what we shared. It's really the other way around. What we shared was the natural result of what I feel for you.'' Boyd frowned. ''Did that make any sense? Or am I rambling?''

Leah's eyes were misted by a sheen of moisture. ''It . . . made sense.''

''Good.'' Boyd's tone gentle. ''Now, you go on up to bed and I'll see you in the morning. Okay?''

''Okay,'' Leah whispered, then raised her mouth for his kiss and clung to him with her lips. Shaken, she stepped back and managed a tremulous smile. ''Good night.''

Boyd, too, seemed to be experiencing second thoughts about separating, even for a few hours. Finally, he forced his fingers to release Leah, then whirled and began to toss sofa cushions onto the floor.

Leah gaped at him. ''What are you doing?''

''I'm going to get some sleep,'' he said cheerfully. ''And I'd recommend you do the same. I understand your concern about Stacey, but I'm still not going to leave you alone tonight.''

''But—''

With a quick flick of his wrist, Boyd turned off the lamp and stretched lazily on the couch. Even in the dim light, Leah could see his sexy smile. "Care to join me?"

It took all of Leah's willpower to turn away and drag herself upstairs.

Leah sat on her bed and sighed. She'd been foolish tonight, pretending that their lovemaking had been anything other than the most beautiful experience of her life. Perhaps she'd thought her desperate ploy would send Boyd away, but it hadn't. He was much too clever to have fallen for such an obvious deception.

And Leah was secretly glad. She fantasized briefly about how life could be with Boyd—away from Cedar Cove and the Cauldwell conspiracy. At the cabin, Boyd had told Leah that he would come to Sacramento. Obviously he didn't want it to end, either.

Maybe it *could* work. Maybe . . .

Leah's dream faded. She was fooling herself again.

Several people wanted her out of Cedar Cove—including Craig, the senator and even Bitsy. Now it appeared that at least one of them was deadly serious. The rock incident had been more than an adolescent prank. It had been a warning.

Chapter Nine

Stretching, Leah mumbled sleepily, then burrowed into the squishy down pillow. A faint scent wafted up, a musky male flavor that simultaneously consoled and aroused. She rubbed her face against the soft percale and inhaled deeply.

The bedroom walls vibrated. Leah tensed, listening. Soon the entire house began to dance with a steady pounding rhythm. Still half asleep, Leah frowned at the intrusion, moaning in protest. The noise stilled and she floated back to her dreams.

Boyd had loved her last night.

The sweet ache of her body was strangely soothing and Leah felt reborn. She was whole, awakened in flesh and spirit. She felt ... wonderful.

The rapid-fire thuds resumed, shaking the bed like a series of small earthquakes. Bolting upright, Leah rubbed at her eyes and tried to clear her fuzzy mind. What in the world ... ?

Then she remembered that Boyd hadn't left last night. Had Stacey found him asleep on the sofa? Leah looked at the clock and groaned. It was nearly eight, and Stacey rarely slept past seven. How does one explain to a nine-year-old why Mommy has a man in the house at the crack of dawn?

Mentally pondering this meaty question, Leah swung out of bed, grabbed her robe and hurried downstairs. The incessant noise was soon joined by the hum of voices—familiar voices. When Leah reached the living room, she saw that a board had been nailed over the broken window. Or rather, was in the process of being nailed.

Boyd's voice boomed from the yard. "Hey! I thought you were going to be my helper."

The reply was fainter, more distant. "But Rumpelstiltskin is having his breakfast."

"That's fine, sprout. But who's going to keep me supplied with nails?"

Stacey's response was muffled.

Opening the front door, Leah walked to the end of the wide porch, peering around the corner of the house. Boyd was holding a sheet of plywood to the window while he gripped a claw hammer with his free hand. He was staring toward the bird-watching tree, waiting patiently as Stacey scrambled down the ladder. The child grinned happily at Boyd, then ran to pick up a small box lying in the dirt just out of Boyd's reach.

Stacey extracted a nail from the carton, dropped it into Boyd's outstretched palm, then squinted up at the wooden shutter. "Are you almost done?"

"Almost." He positioned the nail, hammered it home and reached out for another.

Stacey dropped one into his palm. "How come it got broken?"

"Well, it could've been bears, but I didn't see any tracks."

"Bears don't break windows," she said with a giggle.

Boyd feigned surprise. "They don't? Hmm."

As Leah covertly watched the two of them, her heart inflated like a balloon. It was good to see them laughing together and she was touched by their casual camaraderie. It was as though they'd been together always, as though they truly were father and child.

How much easier life would be if that were true, Leah mused. Stacey deserved a father like Boyd, someone who would guide her and teach her and love her. Instead, Leah had given her daughter only a faceless silhouette, a mysterious, intangible presence lurking in the shadows of their lives.

Truth, however, could be far worse than ignorance.

Leah believed that Stacey would be crushed to discover that her "real" father was a man both weak and cruel, pathetic and frightening, a man who would deny and disdain his child's very existence.

Still, Leah's mind wandered. Although she would soon be leaving Cedar Cove, a part of her wanted to believe that her problems and her secrets would stay on this troubled mountain. Boyd still cared, Leah was certain of that. If she'd had doubts, last night had effectively dispelled them. In Sacramento, she and Boyd could be happy. Perhaps, someday, they would even be a family.

It would take a miracle, but at this moment, even the supernatural didn't seem too far from the realm of possibility. Last night had certainly been miraculous, Leah mused.

"I'm hungry," Stacey complained, bringing Leah's mind back to the present. Covertly peeking around the corner, Leah saw her daughter impatiently tapping her foot.

"You are, huh?" Boyd gave the board a final whack. "How about if we raid the kitchen and rustle up some pancakes to surprise your mommy?"

Leah smiled.

Hopping excitedly, Stacey clapped her hands together. "Pancakes are Mommy's favorite."

"I know." Bending, Boyd slipped an arm around the child's shoulders, but Leah couldn't hear what he said.

Quietly, Leah slipped into the house and hurried upstairs to dress. Since she was going to be "surprised" with a delightful breakfast, the very least she could do was be presentable.

After slipping into her most flattering summer dress, Leah brushed her long hair until it shone, then tiptoed downstairs as she mentally rehearsed an oh-isn't-this-wonderful speech. Happy voices filtered from the kitchen and Leah paused just beyond the door, enjoying the moment.

The conversation she overheard, however, soon took a somber turn.

Stacey's voice was pensive. "Boyd, do you know my daddy?"

Leah heard a clank, like a heavy pan was being set on the stove. Then there was a pause. Boyd's reply was guarded. "I don't think so, Stacey."

"Oh. Mommy doesn't like to talk about it," she said with a sigh. "Maybe I don't even have a daddy."

Leah swallowed heavily and nearly choked.

After an eternal, silent moment, she heard the scrape of a chair.

"Come here, honey," Boyd said. "That's good. Now, let's talk about this, okay?"

"Okay," Stacey said without much enthusiasm.

"You know that all people have a biological mother and father, don't you?"

"Yeah." The reply was somewhat listless. "I know all about eggs and fertilizer and stuff."

"Yes . . . well." Boyd cleared his throat. "Sometimes, it isn't possible for natural parents to raise their children."

"Why not?"

"There are a lot of reasons. The parents might be too ill to take care of a little baby, or they might want their child to have a better life than they could offer."

Stacey seemed to consider this. "But what happens to the baby?"

"Usually the baby is adopted. That means the adoptive parents will become the baby's *real* mommy and daddy, who will love and care for it." There was a moment of silence, then Boyd spoke again. "Why is your face all screwed up?"

"How can they be *real* parents if it's other people's baby?"

"Remember how worried you were that Rumpelstiltskin's mother wouldn't take care of him?" Stacey's reply was muffled and Boyd continued. "Well, what would you have done if that had happened?"

"I would have made him a bed and fed him from an eyedropper until he was all grown-up and could fly away."

"And would you have loved him?"

"Uh-huh." The child's tone was becoming more animated. "Would I have been his *real* mommy?"

"What do you think?"

"I think yes."

"There you go."

"Do you think that someday I might get a real daddy who will love me and take care of me?"

Boyd's voice softened. "I think any man would be proud to have a beautiful daughter like you."

Leah knotted her fingers against her chest. Deep down, she'd known how desperately Stacey had wanted a father of her own, but because it had been a situation over which Leah had no control, she'd consistently dismissed her child's fears. Boyd had confronted those fears honestly and directly, without allowing Stacey to slide into a state of self-pity.

If only Leah could have been as objective and as wise.

Brushing the dampness from her face, Leah squared her shoulders and went to the kitchen door. As she slowly pushed it open, she saw Boyd and Stacey seated at the table. Suddenly, her daughter leaped from her chair and launched herself into Boyd's lap, flinging her pudgy arms around his neck.

"I love you so much," Stacey sobbed. "Will you be my new daddy? Please?"

Boyd looked as though he'd been shot. "I—uh—"

Tightening her grip, Stacey pleaded, "I'll be good. I'll be the best little girl in the world, honest."

With an expression of complete dismay, Boyd tried to untangle the small arms. "It's not that simple, sprout."

Stumbling back, Leah allowed the door to swing shut, blocking out the heartbreaking scene. Choking back tears, she spun around and ran to the stairs. She cursed her foolishness, her gullibility. She'd taken golden threads of illusion and woven them into a blissfully romantic fantasy, a Cinderella fairy tale, with Boyd as her gallant prince.

So much for happily-ever-after.

Leah's prince had quite obviously been horrified by the thought of becoming Stacey's father.

* * *

"You're looking better every day, Mother."

Cybil smiled warmly. "The doctor is releasing me on Monday."

"That's wonderful." Leah's voice lacked conviction and Cybil's eyes immediately reflected concern. Forcing a more cheerful tone, Leah said, "I guess it's time to finalize our plans."

"Plans, dear?"

"I've spoken to a realtor about putting both the store and the house on the market. It may take a few months to find a buyer, but she's confident that you'll get good prices."

"Oh." Tightening her lips into a thin line, Cybil plucked at the starched bedclothes. "I suppose we'll be leaving for Sacramento soon."

"I'll start packing your things over the weekend. We might be able to start back Tuesday morning." Leah regarded Cybil, noting her sad expression. "Is something wrong?"

Smoothing the sheet across her lap, Cybil took a determined breath. "We have to talk, dear."

Leah didn't like the sound of this. "About what?"

"Simon stopped by last night. He was...very upset." Her thin fingers worried the sheet, twisting it into a tight spiral. "He offered me money—something about a note coming due."

"I'll take care of that," Leah said, a bit too sharply. Blast it. Apparently, Sprague had excluded Cybil from his promised silence.

To Leah's shock, Cybil's eyes flooded with tears. "You found out, didn't you?" A small sound bubbled from the older woman's throat as she tried to continue. Tears streamed over her deeply creased cheeks. "I didn't know, Leah," Cybil finally whispered. "You have to believe that I never would have allowed Louis to accept Fletcher's money and—" A sob choked off the words.

Leah's heart sank. "Exactly what did Sy tell you?"

"He knows only that Fletcher loaned Louis some money and is threatening to call the note."

Cautiously, Leah studied Cybil's face. "Is that all?"

Cybil nodded stiffly. "I should have suspected something when Louis suddenly started building up the store, but I never did pay much mind to your father's business and I was too sick with grief at losing my only baby to even think—" She drew in a ragged breath, then met Leah's eyes with imploring directness. "I swear to God, Leah. Until Fletcher Cauldwell told me about that horrible agreement, I had no idea that Louis had been paid to send you away."

Releasing Cybil's hand, Leah abruptly stood and walked to the window, remembering the senator's unexpected visit the day Boyd had built Stacey's bird platform. Turning, she looked at her mother. "That's why you looked so...so stricken after Cauldwell left, isn't it? He'd told you about the note."

"Yes." Her eyes were dull. "I didn't believe him. I couldn't think that even a man as ambitious as Louis would do such a thing, but Fletcher pulled out a paper." Cybil's voice hardened. "He made me read it, then promised that if I made sure that you went away and never came back, you'd never have to know what your father had done to you."

Leah emitted a sharp cry of anguish, overwhelmed by an almost murderous rage. "He won't get away with this." Her tone was venomous, her expression deadly.

Cybil's eyes widened in fear. "What are you going to do?"

"I don't know, but I'll..." Leah's voice dissipated and her eyes glittered. "Perhaps the newspapers would like a copy of that agreement." Ignoring Cybil's horrified gasp, Leah paced the room. "The voters have a right to know that their glorious senator is a blackmailing scoundrel and that his son is a rapist."

"Leah!"

Whirling, Leah fixed Cybil with an agonized expression. "They have to pay for what they've done, don't you see? They're slimier than pond scum—they deserve to be hurt."

Shaking her head in disbelief, Cybil spread her hands in a pleading gesture. "And does Stacey deserve to be hurt?"

Leah stopped short and gaped at her mother as the soft words echoed in her brain. Then she sat heavily in the chair.

Resting her elbows on her knees, Leah dropped her face into her palms and moaned.

Of course, Cybil was right. Such a stunt would be an embarrassing setback to the Cauldwells' political ambitions, but it would be a devastating emotional blow to Stacey.

And to Boyd.

Leaning back, Leah rotated her head until the kinks in her neck loosened. There was one positive aspect to this disgusting mess. Cybil hadn't been involved in the deception. For that, Leah felt relief and gratitude.

The remainder of the visit, although strained, revolved around details of packing for Cybil's move to Sacramento. Later, Leah returned to the Wainwright house alone, allowing Stacey to spend the afternoon with the Varner children. That would allow time for boxing some of Cybil's clothing for the trip.

Leah had nearly emptied her mother's closet when the phone rang. Grabbing the receiver, she heard only the sound of ragged breathing. "Hello? Is anyone there?"

A voice filtered over the line, muffled and electronically distorted. "I sent you a present last night."

Leah's fingers tightened until her knuckles went white. The rock.

"Who is this?" she whispered.

There was a crackling hiss, followed by a chilling laugh. "This is Santa Claus, and I've got a whole bagful of presents for you, but you may not like the next one."

With her breath coming in shallow gasps, Leah tried to keep the terror out of her voice. "What do you want?"

The distortion caused a wavering, broken, almost robotic sound and it was impossible even to distinguish whether the caller was male or female. "You know what I want."

Desperately, Leah tried to maintain a calm tone. "No. No, I don't."

The voice was muffled but the ominous message was crystal clear. "Go home. And take the brat with you."

* * *

The living room looked like a warehouse, piled with sealed cartons and packing crates. Leah surveyed the chaos, wondering how many of Cybil's possessions could be squeezed into a three-bedroom condominium.

A lightning flash bathed the room in eerie blue. Absently, Leah counted seconds, anticipating the accompanying clap of thunder. When she reached five, she was rewarded by a resounding boom. Years ago she'd learned the trick, and she was able to guess that the lightning had struck several miles away. The increasing intensity of wind-driven rain hammering on the window told Leah that the heart of the summer storm would soon vent its force on Cedar Cove.

Leah wondered briefly if Stacey would awaken, then discarded the thought. It wasn't likely. Her daughter was a comatose sleeper and had been known to snore through earthquakes. No, it was Leah herself who couldn't close her eyes during a thunderstorm. It would be a long night—and a lonely one.

Leah was suddenly bone weary. She'd managed to keep her mind and body occupied with the infinite number of details associated with uprooting thirty years of her mother's life. Now her exhausted body had shut down and Leah fervently wished her aching brain would do the same.

Instead, freed from concentration on mundane tasks, her mind relentlessly focused on the painful matters she'd tried so diligently to avoid—her mother's anguish at leaving, for example. Leah was still haunted by the hollow torment in Cybil's eyes, the fear of being torn from all that was familiar. Leah had finally suggested that the house not immediately be put on the market. That way, Cybil could cling to the hope, however fragile, that once fully recovered, she might return to Cedar Cove.

Other unpleasant thoughts also crowded Leah's mind. Since yesterday's threatening phone call, Leah had been a bundle of raw nerves. When she'd called the sheriff's department, they'd been politely patronizing. The desk sergeant had told Leah that if the "prank calls" continued, a trace could be installed, but even so, it would be a civil matter. After all, no crime had been committed—yet.

Disgusted, Leah leaned into the soft sofa cushions and smoothed her palms over her face. Her hands were cool, soothing away her frustration.

Despite the fact that she suspected the Cauldwells were behind all this, she had no idea who exactly had called her. As a matter of fact, it could have been some unknown third party specifically hired for the task. Leah couldn't prove a damn thing, and one simply didn't go around hurling unsubstantiated allegations at powerful people.

Besides, how could she explain to Boyd why she'd turned on his family without letting the proverbial skeleton rattle out of the closet? Leah had little choice but to follow the sergeant's advice and hope that the anonymous caller would be patient for two more days. By Tuesday, there wouldn't be a Wainwright within a hundred miles of Cedar Cove.

A sharp knock startled Leah. For a moment she thought the vicious wind was banging a tree limb against the house, then she realized that the sound had come from the front door.

Her heart pounded once, then seemed to stop. Instinctively she knew it was Boyd.

Another, more insistent knock pulled Leah to her feet.

With a deep breath, she lifted her chin and pulled the door open. A gust of wind caught the door, yanking it from her hand and slamming it into the entry wall. She stared at the hunched figure on the porch. "Good Lord, you're soaked to the skin."

Boyd sneezed, then mumbled, "Coffee."

"Come in before you drown." As she spoke, she grabbed a handful of wet coat sleeve and hauled him inside, then threw her weight against the door until it finally snapped shut.

Turning, she looked at Boyd. His hair was plastered to his scalp, rivulets of water were racing down his face like tiny rivers, and he'd never looked more handsome. Her pulse quickened at the sight and erotic thoughts filled her head as distant rumbling thunder matched the erratic beat of her heart.

Their eyes met and he smiled. In spite of the muggy warmth of the summer storm, goose bumps marched down

Leah's arms. She ignored them and somehow managed a steady voice. "I didn't expect you."

Looking away, Boyd shrugged out of his wet coat and hung it on a nearby wall rack. "We have to talk."

His serious tone confirmed Leah's fears. She hadn't spoken to Boyd since yesterday morning, when he'd left her without a backward glance after Stacey had begged him to be her daddy.

The memory of her daughter's pale face and Boyd's grim expression stiffened Leah's shoulders. Apparently he felt some obligation to say goodbye in person. She met his gaze. "I'm listening."

Pulling a handkerchief from his pocket, Boyd mopped his face, stalling for time. He couldn't remember when he'd been so damned agitated. A covert glance at Leah's contemplative expression convinced him that she wasn't necessarily pleased by his presence. That didn't make things any easier. He suppressed the urge to turn tail and run as though the devil himself were at his heels.

"How about that coffee first?"

Leah tilted her head, regarding him quietly. For a brief moment, Boyd was afraid she would force the issue, demanding to know why he was here after such a cowardly retreat yesterday morning. But Boyd wasn't ready yet. This was one of the most difficult things he'd ever had to do, and he needed a few more minutes to gather his thoughts.

Finally Leah nodded and went into the kitchen to prepare the coffee.

Relieved, Boyd sank onto the sofa. For two days, he'd been lost in the quagmire of his own muddled mind. When Stacey had thrown her small arms around his neck, something deep inside Boyd had splintered. Her childish, trembling voice still echoed in his mind.

Will you be my daddy? Please?

Her wide eyes had been filled with love and trust. It had torn Boyd apart, because a few hours earlier, in the passion of their lovemaking, Leah's eyes had shone with the same emotions.

Boyd scoured his forehead with his fingertips. After some agonized soul-searching, he'd finally made a decision. Now, if he only had the courage to follow through—

The kitchen door swung open, breaking his thought.

"I hope instant is all right." Leah set a steaming cup on the table, then seated herself in the armchair across from the sofa.

"It's fine, thank you."

Leah balanced her cup on her lap and watched Boyd. As he sipped his coffee, his gaze swept around the room as though he'd just noticed that something was different.

He gestured toward the stacked cartons. "What's all this?"

"Some of Mother's things. She's coming home on Monday."

The cup rattled as Boyd set it on the table. "So you're leaving." It wasn't a question.

"Yes."

A palpable silence followed. This would be their last time together. The realization hit Leah like a fist in her solar plexus. For a moment, Leah panicked. Leaving Boyd would be even more difficult now that she'd experienced the sweetness of his lovemaking. For the rest of her life she would cherish that memory. But after seeing his reaction "the morning after," it was clear that he would never join her in Sacramento.

Lightning flashed, followed quickly by thunder that cracked like a sonic boom, then rumbled away as though a convoy of tanks were rolling through the black clouds. Outside, wind-whipped branches scratched the house and driving rain beat the roof in a pounding, sensual rhythm.

The air was humid, crackling with current and smelling of hot rain.

A familiar warmth unfurled in slow, velvety petals. Like those of a predator onto a scent, Boyd's eyes darkened. Leah felt as paralyzed as a rabbit caught in the headlights of a speeding truck.

As though in a slow-motion filmstrip, they both stood, their eyes still locked in silent yearning. Leah's mental war was brief. Forever was a long time to be loveless. She needed him tonight.

"Leah," Boyd whispered. "There's something I—"

Reaching out, Leah silenced him by placing her finger on his lips. "Later," she said huskily.

A war raged in Boyd's eyes—the bloody inner turmoil of conflicting emotion, conflicting needs. Leah saw it, knew that he was locked in battle with himself and that she was the cause.

Finally he spoke, raggedly: "I'm not here to seduce you with honeyed words and implied promises." His breath caught as Leah's fingers brushed his neck. "But if you keep touching me like that, my honorable intentions will be nothing more than a fond memory."

She moistened her lips with the tip of her tongue and felt him shiver. "What if I want that fond memory?"

Reluctantly, Boyd captured her wrists, cradling her hands against his chest. "We shared something the other night, something so beautiful that it makes my hands shake just to think about it. But it was wrong, Leah."

Boyd might as well have slapped her with a tire iron. The effect wouldn't have been as devastating as those horrible, soft-spoken words.

Extricating her hands, Leah pressed her stiff arms to her sides. "I see," she murmured. "I'm sorry that you...regret what happened."

"'Regret'? My God, Leah, I don't regret one glorious moment of it."

"But you just said—"

"I said it was wrong." Breath shuddered into his lungs. "It was wrong of me to take advantage of your innocence without giving you a promise for the future."

Turning away, Leah felt her heart sink. She'd heard Boyd's philosophy of love before, years go. Boyd was a good and decent man, one of the few who believed that lovemaking was an act that should be cherished between husband and wife. Leah had always felt that the sexual excesses of Boyd's stepmother had influenced his belief that the physical expression of love should be the natural evolution of a lifetime commitment. Even in high school Boyd had disdained the usual adolescent locker-room mentality that considered sex to be a sport, a game where the victorious "scored" and the vanquished were scored upon.

Boyd had refused to compete, always treating Leah with reverence and respect. He must have been emotionally distraught to believe that Leah had betrayed those ideals.

But Leah knew that Boyd had participated in the sex game somewhere along the line. He'd never married, and yet the man who had loved her so expertly, so exquisitely, was definitely no novice.

Boyd seemed to read Leah's thoughts. He stood behind her, so close she could feel his warmth radiate through her back.

"I haven't always followed my conscience," Boyd said quietly. "There were cold years and empty nights. Sometimes I tried to fill that void at the expense of others. *That* is what I regret—not what *we* shared." Gently, he urged her to turn, then coaxed her chin up until she faced him. "In my mind and in my heart, I was always loving the woman with midnight hair and morning eyes. It was you, Leah. Always."

Looking at him through a blur of tears, Leah touched her fingertip to the corner of his mouth. She wanted to memorize the fine textures of his face, its contours and planes, the softness of his hair contrasted by the roughness of his jaw and throat. His eyes closed and he seemed to have stopped breathing. Still absorbed, she explored and caressed.

If it was to be the last time, she had to remember.

Lifting herself on tiptoe, Leah hesitated, then slowly fitted her mouth to his. Their lips clung without moving, assimilating the delicate nuances of flavor and scent.

Just as slowly, the kiss ended. Neither of them moved. Their bodies stood immobile, yet delicately pressed together from knee to chest. Each breath was shared, each pulse point synchronized. Leah's skin tingled with heightened sensitivity and she literally felt the prickle of every goose bump roughing Boyd's flesh.

Boyd's eyes glowed like candle flames, two rims of amber fire around sensually black pupils. Then he groaned, drowning the rumble of distant thunder as their mouths mated with increasing fervor and mounting passion.

With a soft gasp of pleasure, Leah clung to him, winding her arms around his neck as though fearing he might otherwise escape. His response was to shudder from toe to scalp, then tangle his fingers in her hair and delve deeper into her mouth. Stroking and tasting, Boyd's tongue moved provocatively, simulating the slow glide and withdrawal of lovemaking.

At the first sensual assault, Leah moaned and went pliable, allowing him to explore her softness as he wished. Then, awkwardly at first but with increasing skill, she matched his erotic motion.

With a choked sound, Boyd pulled away, his breath rapid and shallow. Closing his eyes, he sifted his fingers through Leah's hair, lifting until the long silken strands floated from his grasp.

"Your hair is so soft," he whispered. "It's like holding a cloud in the palm of my hand. And kissing you is like a taste of liquid fire." Boyd opened his eyes and dragged his hands away as though releasing a jeweled treasure. "You're a demon in my blood, Leah. I'm addicted to you, intoxicated by your touch until I lose sight of reality."

With some effort, Boyd pulled back, allowing a pillow of space as a buffer zone. Leah felt suddenly empty. She saw his somber expression...and she knew. He would tell her now. Boyd would say goodbye and somehow, Leah would have to find the strength to accept what they both knew couldn't be changed.

Boyd's words finally emerged, each selected with apparent care. "The past two days are an enigma. I know I lived them, but the moments are blurred. My own mind has held me captive and I fought like a caged animal, prepared to chew off my own foot to escape the torment."

His desolate expression ripped Leah's heart. "Boyd, don't—please. I—I understand."

Ignoring her plea, he continued in a quiet monotone. "When we made love, something inside me cracked. It was frightening, but I rationalized and tried to ignore the impact, the intensity of my feelings." His gaze settled on thin air and he took a ragged breath. "Then something happened the following morning that forced me to look deep inside myself. I didn't like what I found."

Leah swallowed awkwardly, remembering exactly what had happened on that fateful morning.

Will you be my new daddy, Boyd? Please?

Boyd's expression of abject horror was still indelibly etched in Leah's brain.

"You don't have to tell me this." Curling her fingers until the nails bit into her palms, Leah tried to maintain a calm voice. It wasn't easy. Desperation tightened her throat. She didn't want to hear the harsh words she knew were rolling on his tongue.

"I *want* to tell you, Leah. It's important that you understand—"

She cut him off. "I do." Silently cursing her sharp tone, she forced herself to smile. "No one could have been kinder or more compassionate to me . . . or to my daughter. You must realize that Stacey is, well, exuberant. If she feels something, she expresses it." She laughed tightly. "You mustn't take her too seriously."

Puzzled, Boyd regarded Leah through narrowed eyes. "But I *do* take Stacey seriously."

Leah sighed. "All right. As long as we're playing true confessions, you should know that I heard what she told you."

"You did? Why haven't you said anything before this?"

"Because I could see how . . . upset you were."

Boyd smiled sadly. "Was it that obvious?"

"Yes," she whispered, unable to meet his eyes.

Breakfast on the morning in question had been as pleasant as enduring a root canal, with Stacey staring into her plate while Boyd did little more than ventilate his pancakes with a fork. Then he'd suddenly stood, mumbling some unintelligible excuse as he stumbled out the back door. Those had been the last words Boyd had spoken to Leah.

Until tonight.

"It's true. I *was* upset, damned upset." Whirling, he squeezed the back of his neck, then folded his arms across his chest like a shield. "I mean, my heart melted. Here's this beautiful child, hugging me as though I was her personal savior, telling me she wishes I was her daddy. God, I've never been so touched in my life.''

"S-she's very fond of you, Boyd. It was simply her way of telling you that."

His eyes burned with intensity. "Are you saying that Stacey is in the habit of trying to recruit fathers?"

"No." Leah's gaze darted as though seeking escape. "As far as I know, she's never done that before. But you needn't feel...trapped."

" 'Trapped'?''

"You know, 'like a caged animal'—whatever you felt that made you so unhappy."

"Ah. Shot down by my own words." His eyes twinkled. "However, you misunderstood. The cage was inside me and was one of my own making. You and Stacey offered the key, but I didn't know how to unlock the damn door." Leah blinked at him and he laughed. "Obviously, metaphors aren't my forte. I love it when you scrunch up your nose like that.''

"I aim to please," she muttered irritably. "But I haven't a clue as to what you're talking about."

"Then I'll drop the simile and be blunt. I came to Louis's funeral for one reason and one reason only: because I knew that you'd be there and I wanted to get you out of my mind once and for all."

Leah stiffened.

"For years, the image of you has haunted me. By seeing you again, I thought I'd rid myself of the illusion, the vision of perfection."

"Well." She gulped air and exhaled slowly. "Here I am, warts and all."

Leah felt drained. Boyd had just verbally expressed her own secret thoughts. She, too, had hoped to release the fantasy of her heart. But it hadn't worked. Instead of a childhood memory, she found a man, flesh and blood, muscle and bone. She'd hoped for a healing, but had learned that true love slices too deep. It creates a wound that would neither mend nor scar; it would simply remain open and tender. Always.

Boyd brushed a strand of black hair from Leah's face. "No warts," he said softly. "But it would have been so much easier if there were."

"Life isn't easy," she said, wincing at the pain reflected in her voice.

"No, it isn't. I wanted release. I wanted my heart back. Instead, I found a snub-nosed little girl hiding beside her mother, and I realize that I'd never be free."

Boyd sounded so lost and bewildered, it broke Leah's heart.

"I won't try to hold you, Boyd. I know Stacey's presence is eating away at you, but you've been kind to her and cared for her because you're such a fine man. Children have a gift for recognizing goodness and compassion. That's why Stacey was drawn to you." With a final caress, Leah slid her fingertips over Boyd's cheek. "Thank you for giving us both such wonderful memories. You'll always be in our thoughts." Before her courage failed, she pasted on her most convincing smile and said, "Goodbye, Boyd."

With that, Leah turned and walked quickly toward the stairs, hoping only that she could reach the privacy of her room before the torrent of tears began. She'd gotten two steps when Boyd snagged her belt loop and she lurched to a stop. Mouth open, she gaped over her shoulder at Boyd's thunderous expression.

"What the hell do you mean, 'Goodbye, Boyd'?" he growled.

When he released his grip on her jeans, she faced him. "You came here to say goodbye—and we said it."

Now it was Boyd's turn to gape. "Where did you get that ridiculous notion?"

"From you... From all this talk about guilt and commitment and caged animals, for crying out loud." Closing her eyes, she shook her head in confusion. "Look, I'm going back to Sacramento and you're staying in Cedar Cove. Let's not part with a quarrel."

Grasping her shoulders, Boyd lifted her until only her toes brushed the floor. "Listen to me, you beautiful little fool. I don't know whether I have a speech problem or you have a hearing deficiency, but in any case, our ability to communicate is woefully inadequate.''

"Nevertheless—"

"Be quite and listen," he snapped.

Leah's teeth clicked together and she stared at him sullenly.

"That's better." Boyd seemed somewhat mollified by her compliance. "Now, pay attention. I didn't come here to end our relationship." His eyes drilled into hers. "Didn't I make that clear enough?"

The entire scene was too much for Leah. Chewing her lip, she mulled over Boyd's words.

"Repeat what I just said."

"I heard you, I just—"

"Repeat," he insisted.

Leah sighed. "All right. You didn't come here to end our relationship."

"Very good. Now listen carefully, because there will be a pop quiz on the subject." Capturing her chin with his thumb and forefinger, Boyd forced her to meet his compelling gaze. "Everything I said tonight, everything I went through for the past two days has led me to realize—" He exhaled forcefully. "That is, I want you to know that—" Breaking off with a muttered curse, Boyd released Leah's shoulders and raked his fingers savagely through his damp hair.

Finally, he threw up his hands and fixed her with a look of utter frustration. "Good grief, Leah. I want you to marry me."

Leah uttered a cry of disbelief and the room started to sway.

Chapter Ten

Don't faint on me, now."

Boyd quickly propped Leah's sagging body, gently guiding her to the sofa. Her face was the color of chalky eggshells and she had the dazed, round-eyed look of one who'd witnessed the ascent of a messiah.

Vigorously rubbing her icy hands, Boyd watched her with growing anxiety. "Leah? Honey, are you all right?"

Without blinking, she gazed around the room once, then squinted, trying to focus on Boyd.

"M-m-marry?" she croaked.

"Uh, well yes, that's what I had in mind."

On cue, lightning flashed. The sonic clap was nearly simultaneous as the furious turbulence hovered directly overhead. Absently, Boyd noted that the rain had passed over. The hot wind would evaporate the remaining moisture and by morning, crystal-clean air would be the final remnant of the storm.

But inside Boyd, a storm still raged.

Apparently marriage proposals, like metaphors, weren't high on Boyd's list of marketable skills. Well, he'd only done this once before. In college, when he'd asked Leah to be his wife.

That night, however, she'd cried and thrown her arms around his neck and sobbed "Yes, yes, yes" into his shoulder. Now, she looked as though she'd been shot.

Lifting Leah's cold hands, Boyd warmed them with his mouth, never taking his eyes from her face. Her lower lip sagged, then moved and a small sound emerged.

Boyd leaned closer. "What did you say?"

"Why?" came the thin reply.

"Why what?"

"Why—" the words broke. She tried again. "Why did you say that?"

Bewildered, Boyd sat back and stared. "I said that because I love you and I want to spend the rest of my life with you."

"Oh." Leah's lower lip disappeared under a flash of white teeth. After a brief nibble, her mouth curved into a quivering smile and her eyes brightened beneath a sheen of tears. "Oh-h-h," she said again, more like a breath than a word.

Encouraged by the glow of color returning to her cheeks, Boyd felt his tense muscles begin to uncoil. "Shall I get on my knees and do this by the book?"

Boyd was rewarded by a soft, melodic laugh. It warmed his heart and he knew beyond doubt that this was absolutely right. So much time had been wasted, so many dead years. Yesterday was gone, but there would be so many beautiful tomorrows. And Boyd wanted nothing more than to share those tomorrows with the only woman who'd ever truly touched his heart.

"God, I love you, Leah. I've always loved you." Cupping her face with his palm, Boyd took a shuddering breath. "If you'll give me another chance, I promise never to let you down again. I'll always be there for you . . . always."

"'Always means forever,'" Leah murmured, then slanted a shy glance. "That's what you said that night at the lake."

"I remember." Boyd swallowed a hot lump, then casually dabbed the moisture from his eyes. They had shared solemn vows that night, swearing that they would be together always.

Over the years, that evening had become a focal point of Boyd's reminiscence. The memories had been so painful that he'd tried to trivialize that night, telling himself that the experience had been a maudlin melodrama exaggerated by an overdose of adolescent romanticism.

But the emotions Boyd had expressed then had been real and ran deeper than the fathomless waters of the lake. For nearly a decade, Boyd had suppressed his feelings and nursed a wounded ego. Obstinacy and false pride had nearly destroyed their love. Fate had offered a second chance, and Boyd had gratefully accepted.

Leah, however, had not.

Boyd was painfully aware that she hadn't said that she would marry him. Of course, she hadn't said that she wouldn't, either. In fact, Leah had said almost nothing at all.

She sat rigidly beside him, her gaze locked on his face. There was a deep sadness in her eyes. The expression alarmed and confused Boyd.

Finally, Leah stretched out her hand, touching his face with the same gentle compassion one would use to stroke a wounded animal.

Boyd was suddenly struck by a horrible thought. "Is it that you don't...feel the same way about me? Is there someone else, Leah?"

Leah's hand stilled against Boyd's face. "Don't say that," she whispered. "Don't even think it." Her voice firmed with conviction. "I've never loved another man and I never, ever, will. It's you that I love, Boyd. Only you."

"Then wh—?"

"Shh." The words were silenced as Leah rested two fingers on his lips. "I've dreamed of hearing those words from you, prayed that just once before I die, I'd see love in your eyes again and know it was for me. It's just that..." The sentence evaporated and she gestured helplessly, unwilling to utter the words that would end this beautiful moment.

"We'll work it out, Leah, whatever it is." Emotion cracked his voice. "There's nothing we can't handle as long as we're together."

Averting her gaze, Leah murmured, "A lot has happened during the past ten years, to both of us." She laced her hands into a ball, straightened her shoulders and stared sightlessly into her lap. "There are things you don't know, Boyd—things you may not be able to accept."

"Try me."

"I—I can't."

Folding his arms, Boyd regarded Leah thoughtfully. "All right. You don't have to tell me anything, Leah. I love you, I want to marry you, but I won't invade your privacy."

"You don't understand. I haven't been totally honest with you about . . . the incident."

He nodded. "I know."

Unable to believe what she'd just heard, Leah slowly raised her eyes. "You'd be willing to marry me, even though I haven't told you who fathered my child?"

Boyd didn't hesitate. "Yes."

"And if I said that I would never tell you, would that change your mind?"

"No." Leaning forward, Boyd clasped her knotted hands. "I've thought a lot about this, about us. The past is over and done with. We can't change it, therefore it simply doesn't matter. Only the future is important, Leah. And my future is with you."

"What about Stacey? Could you raise another man's child?"

Boyd sighed. "Two weeks ago, I'd have cringed at the thought. But that was before Stacey wiggled her way into my heart with squeaky little giggles and trusting blue eyes. I can't imagine not watching her grow up into a beautiful woman, just like her mother." With a sheepish smile, Boyd shrugged. "I may lack experience, but I'm tenacious and a very quick learner. My sixth-grade English teacher said so."

Leah felt as though her chest would explode with the force of her love. Moisture seeped from her eyes, sliding over her lashes before she could brush them away. Then Boyd took a deep breath and Leah focused on his words.

"I'll try to be a good father, if you and Stacey will give me that chance." Boyd's tone was as serious as his expression. "If you ever want to tell me what happened ten years ago, 'll listen. Otherwise, I'll never mention it again. It's over, Leah. Nothing could change the way I feel for you.''

"I love you so much," Leah whispered, going into his waiting arms with a choked cry.

It *was* a miracle. For the first time, Leah saw real hope for the future. Not the dreamy fantasies she'd woven over the past two weeks, but a tangible promise backed with love and faith and trust.

Trust.

The word sent a chill down Leah's spine. In spite of Boyd's declaration to the contrary, Leah knew that a lifetime commitment couldn't be built on a foundation of lies and deceit. Only with honesty and truth could they have a chance of happiness.

And Leah desperately wanted that chance.

Lifting her head from Boyd's shoulder, Leah gently moved from his embrace. She trembled in fear, yet she loved Boyd too much to carry her secret into their life together. It would hang over their marriage, a moldy shroud of suspicion and deceit. Eventually, the truth would emerge, and in spite of Boyd's protestations that it didn't matter, Leah knew that it would matter—very much.

She stood, wrung her hands, then slowly walked to the center of the room, gathering her courage.

"Leah?"

Turning, she forced herself to meet his bewildered gaze. "I have to tell you the truth, Boyd," she said. "Then, if you still want me, it would make me the happiest woman on earth to become your wife."

Nervously, Boyd wiped his palms on his slacks. He seemed apprehensive, as though he realized that what Leah was about to say would profoundly impact their future.

Focusing her gaze on a distant wall, Leah spoke in a quiet monotone. "Everything I told you about that October night was true. What I didn't tell you was why I had gone in the first place. I went because..." The empty sentence hung in the air as Leah mentally chose just the right words. "I went because it was with someone very close to you, someone you trusted completely."

A darting glance confirmed that Boyd's eyes had narrowed dangerously. Licking her lips, Leah refocused on the safe, white wall. "As I told you before, there were warning signs that I should have heeded. He was very troubled and drinking heavily. In retrospect, I remember his bitter words, heavy with anger and pain. He...resented you, Boyd."

"Me?" His shoulders snapped square. "What had I done to him?"

"You had been too perfect. He felt insecure, unable to compete."

"Compete for what?" His voice grew deceptively soft. "For you, Leah? Was he in love with you?"

"No." Emphasizing the point, she vigorously shook her head. "He felt nothing for me. It was *you* he loved. He loved you like...like a brother. I didn't realize at the time how torn he was, loving you and resenting you at the same time. He started to drink and—well—I've already told you what happened then."

Digesting this information, Boyd worried a loose thread on the cuff of his sweater. "Are you saying that this.. person attacked you to get even with me in some way?"

"I think so."

With a savage yank, Boyd snapped the thread. He didn't look up. "Is that all you wanted to tell me?"

Leah swallowed. "No. I—I just need to go slowly, that's all. It's...difficult."

Boyd remained silent, waiting for her to continue.

Leah again spoke to the wall. "When I realized I was pregnant, I went to see your father."

"You told me about that," he pointed out.

"Yes, but I left out a few crucial aspects of that visit." Tentatively, she continued. "The senator brought me home. He and Papa got into a terrible row and I ran upstairs. The next morning, I was bundled off to Sacramento. My father never spoke to me again."

A muscle twitched in Boyd's jaw. "I'm sorry, Leah—"

Leah interrupted, determined to spill the entire story before her nerves exploded. "It seems they made an agreement, my father and yours, based on an evil little piece of paper that traded my absence for cold cash.''

"What?" Suddenly, news clippings flashed through Boyd's mind and he recalled the tiny column announcing Louis's business expansion. Angrily, he pushed the thought away. "That's ridiculous. You're reading sinister motives into something that was in all probability just a common business deal, an investment that had been initiated months earlier."

"You have no idea how much I wish that were true," Leah said quietly. "But it isn't."

"What possible reason would the senator have for wanting you out of Cedar Cove?"

"He was trying to protect the man who... hurt me."

"You told him who—?" Boyd sucked in a sharp breath. "I don't believe any of this." Even as he said the words, Boyd knew Leah wasn't lying. He thought of how Fletcher Cauldwell's eyelids beat like hummingbird wings every time Leah's name was mentioned.

"It's true," Leah said dully.

"This just doesn't make sense." Boyd was on his feet, pacing, skewering his hair with his fingers. Abruptly he stopped, impaling Leah with a long, cold stare. "My father has his faults, but he'd never defend the man who'd raped his own son's fiancée."

Trembling, Leah lifted her chin and faced Boyd. "He would if the stakes were high enough."

Something in the quiet tremor of Leah's voice caught Boyd's attention. Icy fingers of fear squeezed his spine. "Tell me the truth. Why did you go to my father for help?"

"Because—" Blinking, Leah pressed her palm against her heart. "Because I was carrying his grandchild."

Boyd looked bewildered, like a youngster facing a lesson too difficult to grasp. "That's impossible. We never... you and I didn't..." His voice trailed off, and he looked up questioningly.

Leah struggled against an onslaught of fresh tears. "Stacey is Craig's child."

Air rushed from Boyd's lungs as though he'd been kicked in the gut. His face twisted, he gasped, unable to catch his breath. Fragmented images ricocheted, splintering against his skull before they could bind into cohesive thought. Boyd grabbed his head with both hands, as though afraid it might suddenly explode.

Finally he straightened, staring coldly at Leah. "You're lying."

She closed her eyes, then opened them and met his empty gaze. "That seems to be the standard Cauldwell response to unpleasant news. I've told you the truth."

It *was* true. Instinctively Boyd knew it. He'd been blind not to have put the pieces together sooner. He remembered the telling looks between his father and brother—their strange, almost paranoid behavior over the past two weeks.

And then there was Stacey herself. How could he have missed it? The wide-slashed mouth, the split-dimpled chin... She was almost a mirror image of Craig's five-year-old daughter.

The senator had seen the resemblance. Boyd remembered how the older man had studied Stacey's face, turning it to profile, as though memorizing each tiny freckle. Hell, everyone in Cedar Cove probably saw it. Everyone but Boyd.

His own brother.

God, what a cruel joke.

"Boyd... I'm so sorry." Leah would have given her life to take back the pain she'd just caused. "I hope you understand why I had to tell you."

Numbly, Boyd looked up.

Leah cringed at his empty expression. The flame of hope that had so recently flared to life, flickered out. Boyd walked slowly toward the foyer and took his coat from the wall rack. Without a backward glance at Leah, he opened the front door and walked out into the night.

A single window glowed gold.

From his vantage point, Boyd sat in the darkened car, staring at the Cauldwell mansion. It was truly a house of ill repute, giving sanctuary to recreants who defiled and defrauded and deceived. Fury bubbled through Boyd's blood like a raging fever.

His own brother, his own father, duplicitous co-conspirators who had, for more than a decade, schemed to conceal a vicious attack. They'd protected themselves and the Cauldwell name even if it meant ruining a life—Leah's life.

They were criminals without conscience.

Pushing open the door, Boyd leaned into the wind. The earth had dried quickly and the few remaining puddles would evaporate by morning. There would be no trace of the storm, of the turmoil that had torn through the silence of his night.

Nothing—except painful memories.

Lightning flashed. Thunder crashed. Then the huge, carved doorway suddenly loomed within reach and Boyd realized that he was on the porch. A bitter taste flooded his mouth. His hands shook. An uncontrollable tremor raced through his body as a deep, burning emotion seared him to the core. The emotion was unfamiliar, frighteningly intense.

Taking deep breaths, Boyd's rational mind fought for control. He listened to the lawyer deep within himself. *Innocent until proven guilty; circumstantial evidence; beyond a reasonable doubt.*

But Boyd had to know—now.

The housekeeper would have retired hours ago, so Boyd used his key and let himself in. The foyer was dark and the stairs wound up into blackness. Ghostly gray shadows spilled over polished marble, distorted by a thin beam of light spraying from beneath the parlor door.

Boyd followed the light, grasped the doorknob, then hesitated. A sound filtered from the room, an expressionless voice, mumbling without conviction. Craig's voice.

With a twist and a slam, Boyd threw the door open.

Startled, Craig looked up. He was standing in the center of the room, holding a sheet of paper. When he saw Boyd, he grinned.

"Man, am I glad to see you!" Craig wiggled the paper in Boyd's direction. "This damn speech is making me crazy Listen to this."

Boyd stood motionless as Craig started to read, pacing and gesturing with renewed enthusiasm. Fists at his sides Boyd heard nothing but an annoying hum as he focused cold eyes on the man in front of him.

"'You, the voters, will determine the future of Placer County,'" Craig intoned, reading from the sheet in his hand. "'It is an awesome responsibility, my friends, and one I know you will use wisely.'" With a grunt of disgust, Craig dropped the speech on the table and looked at Boyd. "It's garbage isn't it? That new guy the senator hired couldn't write a letter to his own mother."

Boyd's fists opened, then clenched again.

"I knew you wouldn't really quit as my campaign manager." Craig took two strides and happily slapped Boyd on the shoulder. "You're the best brother a man could have. I knew you wouldn't let me down."

Through narrowed eyes, Boyd stared at Craig. "Get your hand off me or I'll break it."

Craig's eyes widened as he finally took note of Boyd' grim expression. Slowly he lifted his hand and backed away in obvious bewilderment. Extending his palms, Craig pushed air and said, "Okay, no problem. I'll handle the speech."

With an explicit description of how that could be accomplished, Boyd took a menacing step into the room.

Craig's Adam's apple bounced frantically. "What the hell's the matter with you? You're acting crazy."

"Leah." Boyd's voice was low and deadly.

Craig went white. "W-what about her?"

Baring his teeth in an icy pseudosmile, Boyd said, "You tell me, Craig."

"I...don't know what you're talking about." Hooking a finger in his collar, Craig nervously loosened his tie. He licked his lips, then stumbled to the bar and poured himself a stiff drink.

Boyd noted the sheen of perspiration on Craig's face "You're sweating, Craig. Why is that?"

"It's summer, man." Craig managed a tight laugh. "It's always hot in July."

"Sometimes it's hot in October, too." Boyd's eyes thinned into fiery slits.

Craig gulped his drink, coughed, then wiped the dribbling liquid from his chin. Averting his gaze, Craig stared at the floor, the wall, the ceiling, then spun around and poured another drink. Silence permeated the room like a foul odor. Tension mounted. An eerie electricity that raised the hairs on Boyd's neck.

Slowly, his spine rigid, shoulders squared, Craig turned and faced Boyd. A muscle spasm jerked his arm, then his cheek twitched uncontrollably. Raising his eyes, Craig flinched under the impact of Boyd's unblinking stare, then licked his lips.

Outside, thunder crashed with the force of a grenade and Craig jumped. Boyd took another step forward and Craig threw out his hands, as though trying to stave off some invisible, deadly force. His face cracked like a shattered mirror.

"No!" He screamed. "She's lying! I never touched her."

Boyd's mouth was a tight, white line. "If she's lying, how is it you know exactly what she said?"

His eyes darting like those of a rodent in a trap, Craig backed farther into the room. Sweat beaded across his upper lip and he wiped it away with the back of his hand.

With the speed of a striking snake, Boyd leaped, snatching a fistful of Craig's collar and yanked him to his knees. *"How is it you know?"*

The younger man screamed in fear. "She's always lying about me. Even her own father threw her out." Craig's voice had risen to a crescendo of terror as he clawed at Boyd's hand. "She's just a tramp, that's all. A cheap slut. She wanted me. She threw herself at me but I wouldn't—"

Twisting the wadded cloth, Boyd jerked savagely, dragging Craig to his knees, then suddenly releasing his grip. Craig collapsed on the carpet. In a state of panic, his limbs flailed as he attempted to crawl toward the door, but Boyd's foot landed on his back, pinning him in place. Sobbing and struggling, Craig flopped like a beached carp.

Using the toe of his shoe, Boyd flipped him over. With a strangled cry, Craig threw his arms across his face and screamed for help.

Boyd stared in disgust. "You miserable bastard. I ought to kill you." Reaching down, Boyd hauled the younger man to his feet.

"What'n holy hell is going on down here?" Fletcher Cauldwell stepped into the parlor, tying the sash of his silk robe. As the senator's gaze swept the scene, his expression hardened. He fixed Craig with a glacial stare. "Quit your damn bellyaching before you wake up the whole house." Cauldwell turned his attention to Boyd. "Let go of your brother, son. He's turning blue."

Boyd opened his fist. Craig dropped with a thud, gasping and clutching at his throat.

Rolling away, Craig scurried on his hands and knees, then clutched at the senator's leg. "H-He's crazy. He tried to kill me."

"Shut up," Cauldwell said casually. "If that's what he wanted, you'd already be dead. Now wipe the drool off your chin and act like a man."

Boyd felt as if he'd been chiseled from stone. He couldn't seem to move. The senator was watching him closely, weighing the situation as though assessing a political opponent.

Finally, Cauldwell's jowls vibrated with the force of a decisive nod. He met Boyd's gaze. "So you know."

At least one person realized the lies were over, Boyd thought grimly. "No thanks to my loving family."

"There's two sides to every debate, boy." Ambling over to the coffee table, Cauldwell opened a silver box and extracted a fat cigar. "How'd you find out?"

"Leah told me."

Startled, Cauldwell raised one bushy eyebrow. "Exactly what did she say? Never mind. I think I know."

"I'm sure you do," Boyd said through clamped teeth.

"Now, don't you go getting on your high horse. You're seeing what you want to see, not what's in front of your nose."

"What's that supposed to mean?"

Cauldwell bit into the unlit cigar. "I can't blame you for being taken in by Leah's sweet face, but the fact is that she's not what she seems. Hell, yes, I know she went and got herself in a heap of trouble, but instead of owning up to it, she tried to blame the whole thing on Craig here." A flame leaped from Cauldwell's hand and he lit the cigar. Boyd watched the smoke waft up in lazy circles and felt as though he'd been kicked by an elephant.

The senator's eyes were clear and steady. He hadn't blinked once. If his father was telling the truth, that meant that Leah had lied.

Boyd couldn't take this. It was all too much.

Scouring his eyelids until they stung, Boyd listened to his parent's droning voice and felt as though his life was draining away.

"Craig was weak then like he is now and he didn't have the sense to say no. Leah's no different than any other woman—except your mama, God rest her—so when Leah found herself in trouble, she tried to say Craig forced her."

With some effort, Boyd kept his voice steady and his fists at his side. "What makes you think he didn't?"

The senator emitted a grunt of disgust and gestured toward Craig, who was cowering by the doorway. "Look at him. He wouldn't wrestle down a three-legged kitten for fear it might scratch him." Puffing the cigar, Cauldwell shook his head. "No, she was lying, all right . . . trying to sully the Cauldwell name to save her own hide."

"So you bought her a one-way ticket out of town by bribing her father."

Surprised, Cauldwell managed a casual shrug. "Louis needed money. It worked out for everyone."

"Everyone except Leah."

"I won't say I didn't feel a twinge of pity for Leah, but she brought it on herself. In truth, I wasn't sure that Craig had even been involved until I saw that little girl," the senator mused, more to himself than anyone else. "Always figured Craig was too much a coward to risk playing house with his brother's girlfriend."

"*Coward?*" Suddenly, Craig came to life, straightening to his full height. He faced the senator with a malevolent expression. "You don't know a damn thing about me, do you? It's always been Boyd this and Boyd that, like I didn't even exist. Well, I showed you, old man." Craig's voice dripped venom. "And I showed the bitch, too."

Before Craig got two steps out the parlor door, Boyd emitted a guttural cry and hit him with a flying tackle. They rolled on the floor and Boyd heard a woman's panicked scream.

Straddling Craig, Boyd struggled to pin his brother's flailing hands, but Craig doubled his fist, unleashing a blow that knocked Boyd backward with surprising force. As Boyd tried to clear his head, he was vaguely aware of Bitsy standing on the stairway, wringing her hands and crying.

Before Boyd got to his feet, Craig had reached the front door. Suddenly, Bitsy shouted, "No," then ran down the stairs and grabbed her husband's arm. With a savage stroke, Craig flung Bitsy across the room, then disappeared out the front door.

The senator hurried over to the sobbing woman, helping her up and murmuring soothing words. Bitsy's eyes were wild. Pulling away, she ran to Boyd and clutched at him as though she were possessed.

"Stop him," she begged. "He's dangerous when he gets like this. You've got to do something!"

Boyd felt as if his head were filled with feathers. He tried to focus on Bitsy, but her face was a blur of red lips and black-rimmed eyes. Boyd stared down stupidly as she beat on his chest in frustration.

The senator's voice filtered into Boyd's consciousness. "When he gets like what? What'n hell's going on with that boy?"

Bitsy's fists fell away from Boyd's chest and she spun to face the senator. "You wouldn't know, would you? You've never spent the time to find out." She panted like a winded animal. "Craig is your *son*, for heaven's sake, but you don't know anything about him. And the saddest part is that you don't even care."

Then, with a broken sob, Bitsy whirled away and ran outside.

The senator stood, gaping.

Boyd steadied himself by leaning against the nearest wall.

"Great balls of fire," Cauldwell said shakily. "Damned if I know what the devil's got into them two." He took a deep breath, then mumbled something about needing a drink and tottered into his study.

After a moment, Boyd pushed himself upright. Hot wind rushed through the entry and Boyd shut the front door, then followed his father. The senator downed one brandy in a single swallow and poured another with trembling hands. Turning, he met Boyd's hard stare.

The two men regarded each other. Except for the thin whistle of wind gusting outside, the room was silent. Thrusting thick fingers through his wispy hair, Cauldwell took another gulp of brandy.

Boyd spoke first. "Leah was telling the truth," he said quietly. "You know that now."

Shaking his head, Cauldwell mumbled, "No."

"Yes." Boyd felt ill. His father had been deluding himself, unable to accept that his own son could have done anything so vile. The senator suddenly looked old, and in spite of his girth, he seemed frail. His skin hung in colorless folds, as though the bones inside were melting away.

Shoulders rounded, the senator stared into his glass and mumbled, "He's my son, my blood."

Boyd closed his eyes, shutting out the painful sight. There was nothing to say; nothing that could ease the terrible emerging truth. It was a truth neither Boyd nor his father wanted to acknowledge out loud. Eventually, perhaps... But not now, not yet.

However, Boyd couldn't still the warning voice in his own mind: Craig was sick—dangerously sick.

When Cauldwell looked up, Boyd saw his father's torment. "I'm sorry," the senator whispered.

"I know."

A loud noise startled them both as the front door slammed open. Spinning, Boyd ran toward the foyer just as Bitsy collapsed on the marble floor.

Hunching over, Boyd grasped Bitsy's shoulders. Her head lolled backward.

"My God, child," muttered Cauldwell from somewhere behind Boyd.

Bitsy's face was streaked with tears and running mascara. An ugly purple lump puffed her cheekbone. Blood trickled from the corner of her mouth, staining her pink bathrobe with scarlet gashes. She hiccuped hysterically, clawing at Boyd's arms.

"Easy now," Boyd said soothingly. "You're safe."

"G-got to find him." Bitsy choked on the words.

Kneeling beside the trembling woman, the senator took her hand and patted it reassuringly. "Don't you worry about a thing. Craig's a bit ticked off, but he'll get over it and everything will be just fine."

She shook her head violently. "You don't understand—" Bitsy looked up at Boyd with imploring eyes. "Craig's gone mad. I—I'm afraid he's going to kill someone!"

Chapter Eleven

Leah stood by her bedroom window and watched forked tongues of lightning lick the horizon. Tree-covered peaks were silhouetted by a blinding burst, then faded into shadowy blackness. The display was a visual commentary on Leah's return to Cedar Cove—explosions of bright white hope, followed by plunging darkness.

From her second-story vantage point, Leah could see the lake shimmering through thick forest foliage. Reflected lightning spears danced across the smooth water like a laser ballet.

Ordinarily, Leah would have enjoyed the performance, but now the extravagant display gave her no pleasure. The light in Boyd's eyes had died tonight, like the distant hills fading into night.

She never should have told him.

Her eyes burned from crying. The tears were gone now, shed for Boyd's pain, not for her own. Silently she cursed herself. She'd greedily grasped for happiness and in its quest, had struck Boyd a mortal blow. He'd offered his heart and Leah had given him . . .

Dead eyes.

With a soft, tormented cry, Leah turned from the window. Regret and recrimination wouldn't repair the damage. Maybe Leah could recant everything. Yes, that was it. She would convince Boyd that it was all a lie because—

Leah pressed her knuckle into her mouth and bit down. Because why? Rubbing her temples, Leah tried to concentrate, finally accepting that the cause was lost. There simply *could be* no reason to have lied about such a thing.

Besides, Boyd's horrified expression was indelibly etched in Leah's mind. He'd mumbled something about Stacey's mouth—Leah hadn't heard him clearly, but knew he'd been mentally fitting pieces of the puzzle together. Boyd *knew* that Craig had fathered Leah's child. There would be no escape from the truth. Not for Boyd. Not for Leah.

God, she was tired. Her muscles shook with fatigue and she was mentally exhausted. Perhaps a few hours of sleep would offer her solace and escape, however temporary.

As though on automatic pilot, she went through her nightly routine. First, she went down the hall to check on Stacey, smiling as she tucked in a small pink foot and smoothed the rumpled bedclothes. Stacey grunted, flounced onto her back and began to snore loudly.

Leah watched the slumbering child and felt a sense of wonder as acute as the day Stacey had been born. Her daughter was a miracle, one that never ceased to bring Leah a deep sense of serenity. No matter what was wrong with the world, no matter what tragedies life held in store, Leah had been blessed.

Leah could only pray that someday Boyd, too, would experience such a miracle of love.

Returning to her room, Leah automatically reached for the hairbrush. After the first stroke, her hair crackled and stood out as though she'd stuck her toe into a light socket. The storm, she mused, then set the brush down and went to bed.

Bitsy was hysterical.

Grasping her upper arms, Boyd tried to shake her into

some semblance of coherence. "Where's Craig?" he demanded. "Where did he go?"

"I—I—" She hiccuped, then seemed to choke on her own words.

"Don't rattle her head off." Fletcher Cauldwell placed a firm hand on Boyd's arm, then softened his voice as he spoke to Bitsy. "Now there, you just sit down over here and tell us all about it."

Bitsy sobbed, wiped at her wet face, then allowed Cauldwell to guide her to the massive leather couch. The senator picked up her hand. "What's all this about someone getting killed?"

All Bitsy could do was nod stiffly and stutter.

Cauldwell frowned, then angled a glance over his shoulder. "Boyd, bring that brandy glass."

Boyd turned glazed eyes in the proper direction and somehow managed to retrieve the requested object. He watched his father gently place the glass rim between Bitsy's trembling lips, tilting it until the amber liquid barely touched her tongue. Her eyes widened and she coughed, but Boyd saw a touch of color spread across her cheeks.

With a deep shuddering breath, Bitsy spoke. "H-he's having another one of his spells, b-but this one's bad...real bad."

The senator frowned. "What spells?"

She shook her head. "When he drinks too much, he gets mean. It's like two people living in one skin."

Touching the bluish swelling on Bitsy's face, Cauldwell spoke, his voice cracking. "Did...Craig do this to you?"

Bitsy winced, averting her gaze.

Cauldwell looked like a broken man. "Craig knows better. No man ever raises his hand to a woman. Even when I caught his mama with—" A ragged gasp cut off his words. "Even then, I never hurt her. Never did."

Boyd closed his eyes, remembering their childhood and the occasions when Craig had acted strangely. "I should have seen it."

"Seen what?" Cauldwell demanded.

Grimly, Boyd shared the secret stories of the past. He withheld nothing, telling of Craig's unprovoked tantrums and even recalling his brother's attempt to torch the school gym.

When Boyd had finished, Bitsy sniffed and nodded.

The senator had gone white. "Can't be. I never saw any of this, never knew...."

The words dissipated and Boyd saw moisture in his father's eyes. It was a chilling sight. In thirty-one years, Boyd had never seen the senator express such emotion.

Shoulders stooped, Cauldwell shuffled aimlessly across the room. "You should have told me."

"Yes," Boyd agreed quietly. Both men knew that Cauldwell had been at best, an absent father; and at worst, a negligent one. It would serve no purpose to restate that now. Boyd had accepted responsibility for raising his brother, shielding Craig from the consequence of his own behavior. At the time, Boyd had told himself he was defending a weaker sibling; in truth, he'd done his brother no favor at all. Boyd had ignored Craig's obvious cries for help.

Tonight had exposed the tragedy of that ignorance.

Now, seeing the terror in Bitsy's eyes, Boyd felt a stab of fear. In a quiet, firm voice Boyd said, "Tell me everything that Craig said to you tonight."

Bitsy looked confused. "It didn't make any sense. He was rambling... mumbling something over and over." She chewed her lip. "He mentioned leaves."

"Leaves?"

"Yes... something about hating leaves." Her face twisted in concentration, then her eyes widened. "That's it.... He kept saying 'Leaves no good. Ruined everything.'"

Boyd's blood froze. "Bitsy, think very carefully. Did Craig say 'leaves'... or did he say 'Leah'?"

Bitsy's expression of stark horror answered Boyd's question.

With a low moan, Leah buried her face in the pillow and tried to stave off impending consciousness. She didn't want to wake up, but something had flipped her brain switch on

nd her mind was insistent. Tugging the blanket over her
ead, she burrowed deeper, then coughed.

Keeping her eyes closed, she listened, hearing only the
amiliar wind sounds. Again she coughed and, as she tried
o take a deep breath, the air seemed to sear her lungs. She
vas suffocating.

Heart pounding, Leah threw back the blanket and was
ocked by another spasm. She forced her eyes open. They
urned and she rubbed them. Then she noticed a pungent
dor, thick and acrid. Ignoring the sting, she opened her
yes and stared into the darkness. The room was hazy, va-
orous. And smoke rolled from the crack under her door.

Fire.

The word slid smoothly through her mind, then returned
vith the impact of a jackhammer. *Fire! The house was on
ire.*

Oh, God. Stacey!

Leah opened her mouth to scream but could only choke
n the thick, seeping smoke. In her panic, her legs tangled
n the bedclothes and she plummeted to the floor. Wheez-
ng, she sucked cleaner air and realized that the heaviest
moke was above her.

Shimmying on her belly, Leah moved toward the door.
Tears blurred her sight as her eyes tried to cleanse them-
elves of the stinging smoke. Panic turned her stomach and
a metallic bile flooded her mouth.

When she reached the door, Leah pulled herself to her
nees and placed her palms against the wood. It was cool to
he touch.

What did that mean? It meant something, Leah knew and
earched her dazed brain for an answer. Finally it came to
er—it meant that the door was safe to open. Instantly she
wisted the knob and was met by a thick gray wall. Leah
collapsed, choking and hacking, trying to clear her lungs.

"Mommy!"

Stacey's terrified wail penetrated Leah's mind. She tried
o call back, to tell her that Mommy was coming, but her
hroat had convulsed shut. Crawling, Leah followed instinct and the sound of her daughter's voice.

"Mommy, I'm scared. Where are you? *Mommy!*"

The smoke was billowing up the stairway, rolling over Leah and down the hallway toward Stacey's room. Focusing on the door that separated her from her daughter, Leah painfully dragged herself along the rough carpet, her mind screaming what her throat couldn't utter.

I'm coming, baby! Mommy's coming!

Every moment passed like an hour, every crawling stroke was a slow-motion nightmare. Desperately, Leah stared at the doorway. It faded as her oxygen-starved brain began to shut down.

Leah fought the loss of consciousness. She had to save Stacey, had to keep going.

Crawling blindly, her fingers finally bumped smooth wood. Reaching up, she felt frantically for the knob, then the door was suddenly open and Leah collapsed into Stacey's room. Smoke poured in beside her.

"Mom-m-my!" Her daughter's shrill scream cut through Leah's foggy mind.

"Door," Leah croaked. "Close ... door."

Leah heard a slam. The smoke went from billowing clouds to wispy streamers. With Herculean effort, Leah managed to choke out the word "Window."

The room started to spin. Totally disoriented, Leah didn't know which way was up. She heard the grating sound of the window being opened, then felt small hands tugging at her shoulders. In a moment, fresh sweet air filled her throat and she gulped greedily. Breath after breath cleaned her choked lungs and Leah's mind began to clear, screaming that they had to get out.

Now!

Leaning out the window, Leah felt her heart sink. Because the house had been built on a slope, solid ground was some thirty feet below—an impossible drop. Extending the upper part of her body as far out as possible, Leah scanned the east side of the house. She saw no flames, but the wind was whipping from the north, driving black smoke south into the forest.

Once she'd calculated where the fire was, Leah's mind churned with lightning speed, sifting through and discarding options. Cybil's bedroom was across the hall, also on the

outh side and was positioned over the kitchen. The front
oor would be away from the main fire. Maybe there was a
hance....

Leah's gaze darted around the room, searching for
omething—anything that could increase their odds of sur-
ival. Noticing the dresser, Leah yanked open the top drawer
nd dug frantically through her daughter's clothes. She
ound a large cotton scarf.

"Turn around. I'm going to tie this on you, like a mask."

Tears ran down Stacey's face. The child sobbed in fear,
ut instantly obeyed. As soon as the task had been accom-
lished, Leah hauled a blanket off the bed, wrapping it
irmly around them both. Stacey clutched at Leah.

"Listen carefully, darling. We're going to crawl down-
tairs and out the front door."

Over the improvised mask, Stacey's eyes were wide with
error and Leah was afraid the child was too frightened to
nderstand.

"Stacey!" Forcing an authoritative tone, Leah captured
er daughter's attention. "No matter what happens, keep
he blanket over you, stay low on the floor, and *get out of
he house*. Do you understand?"

She managed a jerky nod.

Wrapping an arm around the trembling child, Leah
auled the blanket over their heads, then pulled Stacey to
he floor. They crawled to the bedroom door.

"Take a deep breath," Leah said grimly. Then she twisted
he knob and they dragged themselves into the smoke-filled
allway.

Painfully inching across the carpet, Leah was disoriented
y the thick pall. She stretched out a hand, using it as a blind
nan would use a cane, trying to feel her way toward the
tairs. She felt a blast of heat on the left side of her body.
ifting the blanket slightly, Leah saw a orange glow flick-
ring from beneath the door to Cybil's room.

The stairs would be to the right.

Leah made a directional correction, and after what
eemed like an eternity, her outstretched hand patted air,
hen dropped to the first step.

But their journey had taken too long. Smoke had seeped under the blanket and Stacey was coughing spasmodically. Leah wasn't. In fact, she suddenly realized that she wasn't coughing because she wasn't breathing.

Opening her mouth, she tried to inhale. Nothing happened. There was a raspy wheezing and she realized that the noise was coming from herself. But the sound was fading, becoming fainter and fainter.

From a million miles away, Leah heard Stacey crying.

I'm coming, baby. Mommy's coming.

It was Leah's final thought before everything went black.

There was a soothing hum. Something cool brushed Leah's face. Her neck was limp and she felt as if her head were hanging backward over the mattress. But she was bouncing.

Earthquake.

Somewhere in Leah's mind, the fuzzy thought emerged. The ground was moving and her head was dangling over the bed. How strange.

She heard a low moan. Who was moaning? Maybe it was the wind.

What was pressing against her face? It annoyed her, and she whipped her head back and forth, trying to escape. There was a hissing sound and air blew into her mouth. She gulped it, only to be racked by a convulsive coughing spasm. Her back pressed into something hard and Leah vaguely realized that she was lying on the ground.

Why was she on the ground? Why was she sleeping outside?

An image floated through her mind—memories of campfires and Girl Scouts and laughter. She relaxed, smiling.

The campfire expanded, flames licking higher and higher. Something exploded in her brain. *Fire!*

Oxygen cleared her head. The house had been on fire.... There had been smoke—vile, suffocating smoke.... Stacey... Stacey....

Struggling, Leah ripped the breathing mask from her face nd screamed, "Stacey!"

A familiar voice soothed her, strong hands held her houlders and a gentle touch brushed her face. All Leah ould think of was Stacey, and she fought against the im-osed restraint, calling her daughter's name again and gain.

Finally, Leah's eyelids flew open. A shiny yellow mass oomed over her and she croaked at it. Above the reflective icker was a smudged face with friendly eyes.

"You're fine, Miss Wainwright, just fine. Breathe deep, ow. That's good."

"S-Stacey." Leah wasn't certain if the word had gotten all ie way out of her throat, but the fireman smiled and nod-ed.

"Your daughter's just fine. Breathe deep, miss."

Blinking, Leah obeyed, then twisted her head. The house vas a ball of cherry fire leaping horizontally, as strong winds ushed the blaze toward the forest. A dozen yellow-garbed ien were positioned there, using massive hoses to spray the dvancing flames.

Garish red-and-blue lights strobed from the myriad mergency vehicles crowded in the yard. It was surrealistic, ke a movie scene. But this was real. Frighteningly real.

"Leah. Oh, God, Leah." The choked male voice was fa-iliar.

Turning, Leah looked up into Boyd's smoke-stained face. lis fingers trembled against her brow, smoothing the hair rom her sticky forehead.

"You," she whispered.

Before Boyd could respond, Stacey's shrill voice pierced he air. "Momm-m-my!"

Leah's heart leaped. Twisting from Boyd's grip, she hirled toward the sound. There stood Fletcher Cauldwell olding her daughter, who'd wrapped her arms around his hick neck and was hanging on for dear life. The senator had he vacant gaze of a shell-shocked soldier.

Leah opened her arms and Stacey cried out, squirming for elease. Cauldwell set the child gently on the ground and she ashed into Leah's embrace.

"I—I was so scared. You wouldn't get up and yo wouldn't move and—" she sobbed. "I thought you'd die like Grandpa."

"No, no, darling." Leah's words were muffled, distorte by the plastic oxygen mask. Frustrated, she levered herse to one elbow, ripped the mask away, then covered he daughter's face with kisses. "Oh, baby, are you all right?

"Uh-huh." Stacey gulped and wiped the back of her han across her wet face. The gesture resulted in a sooty blac streak from nose to jaw. "Grandma's house is all burne down."

"I—I know, sweetheart." Cupping the small grimy fac in her palms, Leah kissed Stacey's forehead, then with small cry, hugged the child fiercely. "All that matters is tha you're safe. I love you so much—so very, very much."

"I love you, too, Mommy," Stacey mumbled into Leah' shoulder, then straightened, regarding her mother with se rious wide eyes. "But Grandma will be so sad." A fres flood of tears splashed over the small stained cheeks.

Boyd's voice was strong and reassuring. "Don't worr about a thing, sprout. Your grandma will get a fine ne house."

"Really?" Stacey sniffed, then looked at the senator fo confirmation.

Cauldwell cleared his throat. "I'll take care of every thing. Don't you be worrying. You've got Cauldwell blood child, and Cauldwells take care of their own." Squattin beside Boyd, he opened his arms to the young girl. "You mama needs some rest now."

"Don't touch her!" Something snapped inside Leah "We don't need your help. This is your fault, all of it!"

Cauldwell's jaw sagged and Leah saw the truth of he words reflected in his eyes. Heaving himself to his feet, th senator stumbled backward then stared guiltily at th ground.

Holding her daughter, Leah speared Boyd with her fury "Get away from us," she hissed. "I never want to see an of you again." There was no doubt that Leah had encom passed the entire Cauldwell clan in those tight words.

Leah looked at Boyd and felt a sharp stab. *Dead eyes.*

But he was part of this. He was a Cauldwell.

"Ma'am?"

With some effort, Leah focused on the owner of the unfamiliar masculine voice. She saw a round-faced young man wearing a khaki uniform and a wide-brimmed hat.

"I'm Deputy Berry, Placer County sheriff's department. Are you up to a few questions, Miss Wainwright?"

Nodding jerkily, Leah tightened her grip on Stacey's rigid body.

The deputy flipped open a small notebook. "Did either of you see or hear anything unusual before the fire broke out?"

"No . . . we were both asleep," Leah replied dully.

"Our records show that you've reported earlier incidents of harassment." Berry frowned at his notes. "Have you received any further threats?"

Leah felt rather than saw Boyd stiffen beside her. He spoke in a cold, deadly voice. "What threats?"

Ignoring Boyd's question, Leah focused on the deputy's kind eyes. "No, not since the day before yesterday."

"What damn threats?" Boyd growled, capturing Berry's attention.

"We received a complaint that a rock had been thrown through the window of the Wainwright home," the deputy said, reading from his notes. "The following day, Miss Wainwright received an anonymous telephone call in which the caller took credit for the rock incident and issued vague threats of further such occurrences."

With a choked obscenity, Boyd grasped Leah's shoulders, turning her toward him. His face was twisted in pain. "Why didn't you tell me?"

For a brief moment, Leah wanted to fall into Boyd's arms, to lean into his strength. But she wouldn't. Her daughter could have been killed tonight and Leah had no doubt that whoever was responsible carried the Cauldwell name.

Stiffening, she tightened her jaw and met Boyd's tormented gaze with one of cold anger. "Because you're part of it."

He flinched, slowly releasing his grip. His hands droppe
limply away. "You can't believe that."

The officer listened to the exchange with growing inter
est. "Under the circumstances, we've called for a full arso
investigation. Meanwhile, I'd like a list of anyone wh
might have a motive to harass your family."

Leah's icy gaze swept from Boyd to the senator. Berr
followed Leah's stare with interest.

At that moment, the south wall of the house collapsed i
a fiery roar. There was pandemonium in the yard as yellow
coated fire fighters jockeyed for defensive positions. The
the entire roof disintegrated, crashing to the ground whil
glowing embers sprayed like red rain.

With a choked cry, Leah curled herself around he
daughter, protecting her from the flaming debris. Leah'
surging terror snapped the final thread of her rationality.

"They're trying to kill my baby," she shrieked. "Don't le
them hurt her.... Oh God, don't let them—" Her word
were torn by a racking sob.

"Who? Who's trying to hurt her?" asked the confuse
deputy.

Leah could only sob frantically, desperately clutchin
Stacey as her brain whirled out of control.

It was a Cauldwell conspiracy, Leah's tormented min
said. They were all in on it—a family of bullies and black
mailers and rapists and...and...

Boyd.

No, not Boyd. Never Boyd.

"We'll check into it, Miss Wainwright," Berry said qu
etly.

With some effort, Leah pulled her mind back from th
razor's edge. Oh, God. What had she said?

"N-No." Leah mumbled.

The officer had stood and was saying something to Boyd
Leah grabbed at the khaki-colored slacks. "I didn't mea
it....Please, Boyd didn't—"

"Shh, honey, you didn't say anything." Boyd bent down
smoothing Leah's hair. "It's all right. Craig will never hur
you again, I promise." Straightening, he said something t
the sheriff, then the two men walked away. Leah saw th

senator's shoulders slump heavily as he turned and followed.

Reaching out, Leah gestured helplessly, but strange hands were pulling Stacey from her grasp, then lifting Leah. She struggled.

"It's all right, miss." A white-coated man smiled down. "We're going to take you and your little girl to the hospital now."

Leah licked her lips. They were cracked and as dry as parched pine needles. As the gurney was lifted into a waiting ambulance, Leah saw that Stacey had already climbed inside and was waiting.

"That was a close call," the young medic said. "You're going to be fine, but I hate to think what might have happened if he hadn't shown up when he did and pulled you out."

" 'He'?" Leah was completely confused. Someone had pulled them out. "Who—?" The question shattered as a vague memory rolled through her brain.

The blanket . . . choking smoke . . . a fading blackness.

Then strong hands had lifted her, and Leah remembered the sound of a deep, reassuring voice.

It had been Boyd's voice.

After watching the ambulance until flashing red lights disappeared into the night, Boyd shoved his hands into his pockets. If Leah's house had been deliberately torched, there was no doubt in Boyd's mind that Craig had done it. The thought of what had nearly happened to Leah and to Stacey made Boyd's skin crawl.

And the cold hatred in Leah's eyes had made Boyd's blood run cold.

But he didn't blame her. He blamed himself.

For years, Leah had been abused and tormented by Cauldwells while Boyd, blissfully ignorant, had turned a blind eye. There had been clues, subtle hints that Boyd had blithely disregarded. And it had been Leah who had suffered for it.

The deputy's voice broke into Boyd's thoughts. "Where's your son now, Senator?"

Cauldwell absently rubbed his sagging jaw. "I don't know. Not far, probably."

The older man had just given an emotional statement of everything that had happened over the past two weeks. The senator had withheld nothing, even admitted that he'd threatened to call the loan unless Leah lived up to the terms of Louis's agreement.

Voice breaking, Cauldwell had told not only of Craig's erratic behavior earlier tonight, but of the incident ten years ago that had instigated this nightmare of pain.

Boyd knew that confession had cost his father dearly. Still, he felt no pity. As Boyd heard the full extent of what Leah had been through, he experienced only a deep, burning fury.

And shame.

"We'll send a squad car to the mansion in case he comes back," the deputy said crisply, then reached through the window of his car and pulled out a palm-size microphone. "Meanwhile, I'll broadcast his description and last known position. He won't get far."

The senator nodded bleakly and his chin drooped into the fleshy folds of his neck.

"That won't be necessary," Boyd interjected quietly. "I know where he is."

The deputy's finger lifted from the transmitter. Leveling Boyd with an authoritative stare, he barked, "Where?"

Boyd was unmoved by the officer's peremptory tone. "I'll bring him in."

"This is a matter for the sheriff's department. You could be detained for withholding evidence."

"I said I'll bring him in." Boyd met the deputy's gaze, then said softly, "He's my brother."

Eyes narrowed, Berry seemed to be weighing his options. Finally he sighed, and with a clipped nod, tossed the radio mike back through the squad-car window. "You've got two hours," he muttered, then turned and folded his arms, as though giving Boyd a head start.

Spinning on his heel, Boyd strode away. As he slid into the driver's side of his car, the passenger door opened and Fletcher Cauldwell dropped into the seat.

Boyd hesitated, then twisted the key and the engine roared to life. When Boyd hit the accelerator, the big sedan spit gravel and spun onto the highway.

The senator stared out the window, watching the forest whiz by, a smear of black and gray shadows. Boyd turned sharply to the left, steering the car up a winding dirt road.

Cauldwell recognized the route. "The old Massie place? That's nothing but a broken-down hut."

Boyd tightened his grip, swerving around a fallen log. "We used to play there as kids. For Craig, it was a sanctuary—someplace to hide when he couldn't face things."

After several silent moments, Cauldwell said, "I didn't know that, either."

"There's a lot you didn't know." Jerking the wheel more sharply than necessary, Boyd avoided a large rock. He slanted a sideways glance and saw his father's head sag. Angry at himself for being deliberately cruel, Boyd added, "I guess we've both made our share of mistakes."

"I...thought I was protecting my own." Cauldwell swallowed hard and seemed to want to say something else.

Whatever it was, Boyd didn't want to hear it. The twitch of his jaw apparently conveyed that message, because the senator sighed and looked away.

Boyd slowed the car, simultaneously turning off the headlights as they eased into a small clearing. The years hadn't been kind to the old cabin. Rotting boards dangled precariously, exposing lopsided gaps in the deteriorating structure. The splintered porch sagged dangerously, as though the weight of a field mouse would reduce it to rubble.

Although the building appeared on the verge of collapse, Boyd knew that the structural beams were still relatively sound.

Parking about fifty feet from the cabin, Boyd quietly stepped out.

"Craig's car isn't here," the senator announced, glancing around.

Boyd had already noted that. "He could have hiked."

"Not from the Wainwright house."

That was true enough. Leah's house was three miles away. The Cauldwell mansion, however was three-quarters of a mile due west, uphill and through a thick forest, well within walking distance. As children, they'd made the trek regularly and because the old logging road they'd just driven in on was unmapped, few people knew of the cabin's existence. It had been the brothers' secret hideaway.

Maybe Boyd had been wrong. Perhaps Craig wasn't here, after all.

When Boyd reached the crumbling porch, he carefully avoided the steps, swinging himself up to the reinforced planks on the perimeter. Silently, he gestured a warning to the senator, who nodded grimly and followed Boyd's movements precisely.

More than half of the roof was gone. Swift wind had swept a portion of the thunderclouds away and a shaft of thin moonlight filtered into the dank interior. In the far corner of the single room, Boyd saw a huddled shadow. The shadow moved and emitted a muffled moan.

Boyd picked his way over the cluttered floor, ignoring the crunch of dried leaves and twigs under his feet.

Craig sat in the farthest corner, arms wrapped around his legs, knees folded beneath his chin. Alerted by the sounds, Craig slowly raised his head. His eyes were dull. "I . . . hurt Bitsy."

Boyd's chest tightened. "Yes."

Dazed, Craig shook his head. "I've never hurt her before. . . . I love her."

"Why'd you do it, son?" The senator's voice reflected his anguish. "Why'd you set that fire?"

Squinting into the darkness, Craig tried to focus on his father. "Fire? What fire?"

Boyd clenched his fists, torn between love and fury. "The lies won't work anymore. You've hurt Leah for the last time. It's over."

Craig looked bewildered, then a spark of lucidity lit his eyes. He shook his head. "I just wanted her to go away, that's all."

Trembling, Boyd willed his hands to stay firmly glued to his side. If he lost control ... The thought was too horrible to contemplate.

Intuitively, Cauldwell stepped between the brothers, hunkering down to Craig's level. "I'm going to ask you some hard questions, Craig, and I want straight answers, understand?"

Dully, Craig nodded.

"Did you pitch a rock through Leah's front window?"

His eyes widened and he nodded again.

"And you made that telephone call, threatening her?"

Craig's face crumbled. "Yeah."

Cauldwell closed his eyes, took a deep breath, then said, "Did you burn down her house?"

Craig blinked.

"Answer me!" Cauldwell growled.

"Burn—?" Craig's eyes widened in horror. "No!"

Suddenly Craig bolted to his feet, flattening himself against the frayed timbers as his eyes darted wildly. "You've got to believe me! I didn't do it!"

"You're lying." Boyd took a menacing step forward and Craig cringed. "Just like you lied about the night you took Leah to the lake."

Covering his face with his palms, Craig sagged against the wall. When he looked up, his eyes were clear and filled with sadness. "Yeah, I talked Leah into going to the lake with me. I wanted her to like me. We laughed and joked and everything was great. She ... was nice to me." Craig's voice suddenly hardened. "But then she started talking about you—always perfect, always wonderful, Boyd, the magnificent. You had everything ... and you had Leah, too."

Boyd turned away from the hateful words, the horrifying image of Craig and Leah. Only his father's firm hand kept Boyd from rushing at him in the darkness.

"I knew that if I could make Leah love me, everyone would know that I was as good as you," Craig said blandly. "Only nothing worked out right. She didn't want me and I ... I got so mad ..." The words trickled into air.

"My God," the senator whispered.

A palpable silence followed, disturbed only by the thin whistle of a dying wind blowing through the open timbers of the cabin.

Boyd suddenly couldn't breathe. His stomach churned and twisted in sick rebellion. Spinning, he stumbled to an open gash in the splintered wall and sucked in fresh air. His entire world had catapulted from its axis. For a decade, Boyd had constructed an emotional barrier, a protective, anesthetizing shield. All these years, Boyd had thought himself to be controlled, in command of his life. Instead, he had been blind, seeing only what he'd wanted to see, ignoring that which might cause grief. He'd been without pain, but so was a corpse.

Now he had to confront the unendurable and Boyd felt that barrier collapse like a rotting cabin.

Craig was whimpering pathetically. "It's not my fault, is it? Everyone's against me, just like they always are. You won't let anyone hurt me, will you Boyd? You've never let anyone hurt me."

A numb tingling traveled down Boyd's spine. Craig was right. Ever since they'd been children, Boyd had never let anyone hurt Craig. Boyd had, in fact, always excused and taken the blame for his brother's behavior.

But by constantly defending Craig instead of encouraging him to overcome his weaknesses, Boyd had effectively relieved Craig of responsibility for his own actions. That, along with Boyd's misguided loyalty and the senator's harsh, judgmental discipline, had contributed to the pathetic individual Craig had become.

From the far side of the room, Boyd heard his father speak quietly to Craig. "It's time to go back, son."

There was a pause, then Craig's choked reply. "Y-You never called me that before."

Angling a glance over his shoulder, Boyd saw his father's expression metamorphose from disbelief to shock, and finally, to realization. It was true. That affectionate term had been reserved for Boyd alone.

As he jabbed his fat fingers under his busy brows, Cauldwell's body shuddered. He sniffed audibly, then looked up, placing a firm hand on Craig's shoulder. The senator hesitated, then hauled Craig into an emotional bear hug. It was a behavior Boyd had never before witnessed between his brother and his father.

Finally, Cauldwell sputtered, stepped back and began guiding Craig toward the sagging cabin door. "We'll pick up your car in the morning," he mumbled.

Moonlight illuminated Craig's bewildered expression. "My car's at the house."

Fletcher halted. "How'd you get here?"

"Down the hill."

"No, I mean how'd you get here from the Wainwrights'?"

"Wainwright?" Craig's vapid gaze fell on Boyd. "I ... don't remember."

The senator sent Boyd a telling look, then escorted his dazed younger son to the car. When Craig had been safely tucked into the back seat, Cauldwell saw the anger in Boyd's eyes. "What he's done to Leah was wrong, but your brother hasn't been ... in his right mind."

"Maybe." Boyd's mouth flattened and his eyes burned. "What's your excuse?"

The older man's jaw sagged, and fear sparked in his tiny eyes. Craig hadn't been the only Cauldwell to cause Leah grief.

And Boyd knew it.

Chapter Twelve

Stacey screamed in terror.

Leah bolted upright, disoriented, wild eyes searching. She saw unfamiliar surroundings—a strange painting on bland walls, a nondescript dresser, an impersonal chair. And the bed in which Leah now found herself.

"Momm-m-my!"

Leaping up, Leah followed the panicked cry to an open door and found her daughter in the adjoining room. The child sat rigidly in a too-large bed, fists pushed against her mouth, eyes expanded until they looked like blue-yoked eggs.

"What is it, baby?" Leah ran to the bed and Stacey dived into her mother's arms. "Oh, sweetheart, you're safe now," Leah crooned. "It's all right. Everything's all right."

At the sound of Leah's voice, Stacey's body began to soften and shake with deep sobs. Rocking her daughter, Leah soothed and reassured, allowing her to vent her tears. Finally, the child shuddered violently, hiccuped, then blinked owlishly up at Leah.

"I—I didn't know where you were," Stacey cried, then sniffed loudly.

Leah gently wiped away her daughter's tears. "I'm right here, darling."

"W-Where are we?" Stacey looked around the small room with dazed eyes.

"We're at a hotel. You were pretty sleepy when we got here, so you probably don't remember."

Accepting this information without further question, the child sagged against Leah, burrowing into her mother's warmth, silently seeking comfort. Leah gave it, continuing to murmur softly until the small body began to relax.

"I—I dreamed that Grandma's house burned down." Stacey looked up with hopeful, wet eyes.

Leah swallowed. "It wasn't a dream, darling."

Stacey's eyes dulled and she nodded weakly. "We went to the hospital in an ambulance, didn't we?"

"Yes. Do you remember how the doctor listened to your chest and gave you oxygen through a little plastic mask?"

"Uh-huh."

"And the nurse gave you a lollipop, but you fell asleep in the waiting room and it got stuck on the couch?"

Stacey frowned and shook her head.

"Well, after the doctors checked us over to make sure we were all right, we got into a big car.... Do you remember that?"

"No."

Leah wasn't surprised. Exhausted by the ordeal, Stacey had been either sound asleep or in a stupor throughout most of the long night. Leah hadn't been thinking well, either. A strange man in a chauffeur's uniform had approached Leah in the hospital and informed her that Senator Cauldwell's limousine was waiting. Hearing the Cauldwell name at that point had nearly turned Leah into a fangs-bared she-wolf. She'd turned on the startled man, snarling that she wanted nothing from the great senator unless he would be so kind as to drop dead in her presence.

Fortunately, the driver knew something that Leah didn't—that Cedar Cove taxicabs weren't available at three in the morning. Patiently, the chauffeur had waited until

Leah had exhausted the yellow pages and, for her daughter's sake, ungraciously accepted the ride.

When they'd arrived at the hotel, Leah's indignation was
doubled by discovering that two adjoining rooms had been
reserved for several days—and paid for in advance. By the
senator.

Utterly determined not to accept a single penny of
Cauldwell's guilty blood money, Leah had made a complete fool of herself. She'd informed the stunned desk clerk
that the senator's payment was to be returned immediately
and that she would pay for the rooms herself.

Except, of course, she had no money. Her purse was
somewhere in the charred remains of her mother's home—
as was her checkbook, her identification, her credit cards,
ad infinitum.

Leah had only felt this dependent, this helpless, at one
other time in her entire life: on the day she'd been bundled
out of town like so much dirty laundry.

If it hadn't been for Stacey, Leah probably would have
slept on the street rather than accept Cauldwell charity. But
her daughter needed a warm bed, good food and a place
where she could feel safe.

So here they were.

But Leah was already making plans to repay the senator
every last dime. She would owe him nothing. Ever.

"Mommy?"

"Umm?" Mentally shaking herself, Leah refocused her
attention to the situation at hand. "What is it, darling?"

"Do we live here now?"

"No, but we're going to stay here until Grandma is well
enough to go back to Sacramento with us."

"How long will that take?"

"A couple of days, perhaps."

"Oh." Stacey chewed her lip, seeming preoccupied.

"Don't you want to stay here?"

"I don't care," she said with a shrug.

Stacey's eyes glazed in a faraway look, and Leah knew
that the child was remembering that awful night. The fire
itself had been only part of the terror.

Suddenly Stacey blurted, "Don't you like Boyd anymore?"

Invisible fists closed around Leah's throat. "Why do you ask?"

"Because you were awful mad at him. You yelled and everything." Disapproval tinged her tone. "You always said it wasn't nice to yell at people."

Oh, this would be sticky, Leah thought miserably. "I...I know, darling. I lost control of myself and I shouldn't have done that."

Stacey considered this, then threw Leah a major curve. "What kind of blood do I have?"

Closing her eyes, Leah felt the room spin around her. So she *had* heard. Oh, good heavens! How could she handle this without lying—and without telling the truth?

As Leah tried to compose herself and mentally regroup, Stacey lobbed the final blow. "If I have Cauldwell blood, does that mean that Boyd's my daddy?"

"No." Leah's eyelids were squeezed so tightly that her cheeks ached. "Boyd isn't your father."

A confused silence followed. Leah had always known that someday Stacey would have to be told the truth. It was just that the "someday" had always seemed fuzzy, unfocused, like a distant horizon that could never be clearly viewed.

Suddenly, "someday" was now.

The decision made, Leah tested her voice. "Sometimes people can physically become parents while they're still children themselves. That's what happened with me and the man who is your father. We were very young and—"

"You wanted different things out of life," Stacey chimed, her enthusiasm renewed by the familiar story. "But you wanted me and loved me more than anything in the whole world."

"That's right, darling." Leah managed a tight smile. "Your real father—"

"You mean my 'logical' father," Stacey said, interrupting.

Leah blinked numbly.

"Boyd told me all about it. Everybody has logical fathers and mothers, but that doesn't make them real parents." Stacey explained all this with great patience, as though the parent-child roles had been suddenly reversed. "Real parents are the people who raise you and take care of you and love you for your whole life. I don't have a real father yet, but Boyd says that someday I will."

That said, the child looked up expectantly.

Leah drew a deep breath and murmured, "Boyd is right. I always planned to tell you who your *bio*logical father is when you were grown-up enough to understand." Seeing Stacey's chest puff indignantly, Leah hastily added. "You're a big girl now, and so intelligent that I think you're old enough to know."

"I'm very smart. Boyd says so."

"Yes...yes, you are." Leah hugged Stacey, then held her at arms's length, meeting the child's serious gaze. "You *do* have Cauldwell blood, Stacey, just like you have Wainwright blood. Your biological father is Craig Cauldwell."

Stacey continued to stare blandly at Leah, as though the news had no real impact. "Do I know him?" she finally asked.

"No, you've never met him."

"Does Boyd know him?"

"Yes." It was more a whisper than a word. "C-Craig is Boyd's younger brother."

Digesting this information, Stacey seemed thoughtful, but not particularly concerned. Finally, she stared up with solemn eyes. "Can we have breakfast now? I'm really hungry."

Simon Sprague hurried across the hospital room and grasped the handle of Cybil's battered overnight case. "I'll just be putting this in the car," he said.

Cybil rewarded him with a grateful smile. "Your help has been a such blessing. I don't know what we would have done these past two days without you, Simon."

Blushing until his scalp glowed pink, Sprague stammered a reply that was muffled by his bristling mustache, and he backed toward the door. Clutching the luggage, he paused, slanting a questioning glance toward Leah.

"Go ahead and pull the car around front, Sy," Leah said. "We'll be down in a few minutes."

A snappy head bob indicated that the message was understood and Sprague disappeared into the sterile hallway.

Leah smiled. "You know, Mother, I do believe Sy has a crush on you."

Cybil's eyes rounded in shock. "Why, that's ridiculous! He's just been a wonderful friend, that's all." Folding her arms, Cybil indicated that as far as she was concerned, the subject was definitely closed.

Sighing, Leah returned her attention to the task at hand, gazing about the room. Stacey sat quietly by the window, holding the doll that Leah had purchased for her the day before. Leah had hoped that the toy would lift the child's drooping spirits, but it hadn't helped much; she'd been somber and withdrawn since the fire.

At first Leah had feared that Stacey was deeply troubled by learning about her relationship to the Cauldwell family. But it had soon become apparent that once her curiosity was satisfied, the child had shrugged off the information as interesting, but not particularly shattering.

Still, Stacey was listless and abnormally quiet.

Leah had told herself that it was natural for a child to be traumatized by such a terrifying experience. But deep inside were gnawing doubts about the real cause of her daughter's distress.

Stacey kept asking for Boyd.

Leah hadn't seen or heard from Boyd since that horrible night. And no wonder. Although Leah's recollection was fuzzy, she was afraid she'd hurled hurtful words and bitter accusations at him. Even if she hadn't, there was still the matter of Boyd's learning that Craig was Stacey's father. Leah knew that the revelation had jolted Boyd to his very core.

"Leah?"

Pulling her mind from the unpleasant memories, Leah focused on Cybil. "Yes?"

"Shouldn't we stay at the hotel for a few more days dear?" Cybil chewed her lip nervously. "I mean, there's so much to do, with the insurance and all."

"I've already called the agent, and Sy has promised to supervise the reconstruction of the house." Leah managed a tight smile. "We'll be in Sacramento by dinnertime, so you can just relax and get your strength back."

"Still, it doesn't seem fair to have Simon do so much. He's got the store to take care of, too." Staring into her lap, Cybil made a production of brushing imaginary lint from her traveling suit. "He might need help."

Leah took a deep breath, then sat on the bed next to her mother. She squeezed Cybil's thin shoulders. "I know you don't want to leave, but the doctor says you'll need several weeks of rest and care. By the time the new house is ready you will be, too. Okay?"

Nodding, Cybil managed a brave smile, which flattened as her gaze swept past Leah and settled on the doorway. Leah swiveled around and stared into Fletcher Cauldwell's grim face.

She stiffened.

The senator puffed nervously. In his hand was a book-size box, neatly tied with a bright red ribbon. He cleared his throat and tried to smile, but his lips simply twisted into a strained grimace.

Stacey broke the tense silence. "I remember you. You're Boyd's senator." Dropping the hapless doll, she leaped from her chair and dashed across the room. Cauldwell squatted, opening his arms as the child squirmed into his embrace. "Is Boyd coming, too?" The excitement in Stacey's voice tore at Leah.

The slow, negative shake of Cauldwell's head sent a dagger through Leah's heart.

"No, child," the senator said. "Boyd's not coming."

"Oh." Dejected, Stacey backed away, then quietly returned to her chair. Leah saw a light spark in her daughter's eyes and could almost hear her little brain gears turning. "Mister Senator, do you know my 'logical' father? He's a Cauldwell, just like you and Boyd."

Leah froze. The senator's bloodshot face paled to a sickly pink. He slid Leah a pleading look and sweat beaded over his bushy brows.

Finally, Leah snapped out of her stupor. "Craig Cauldwell is the senator's son," she explained to Stacey, spearing Cauldwell with an icy expression. Even though the senator's own words had exposed the secret, Leah half expected Cauldwell to deny it.

Instead, his face relaxed, as though a great weight had suddenly been lifted. And to Leah's astonishment, his eyes took on an uncharacteristic warmth as he looked at Stacey.

The senator's words stunned Leah even more. "I'm your grandfather."

"Really?" Stacey's eyes widened and she looked at Leah for confirmation. Suddenly shy, the child lowered her gaze, then she peeked coyly at Cauldwell and murmured, "I'm glad."

"So am I, Stacey. So am I." Cauldwell's eyes reddened and Leah saw him discreetly dab the moisture before he slowly stood. Turning toward Leah, he cleared his throat forcefully. "I guess you know about what the investigation showed."

"Yes." Leah looked away guiltily. She'd been positive that Craig had started the fire and had repeatedly made statements to that effect during the official investigation. When the report had been completed, Leah had been horrified to discover that those allegations had been proven false.

According to the fire marshall, lightning had apparently struck Stacey's bird-watching tree, setting it ablaze while wind-whipped embers had ignited the clapboard walls and roof. No arson, no malice—an act of God.

"I, uh, wanted to thank you for not pressing harassment charges against Craig." Cauldwell pulled out a handkerchief and mopped at his face. "He's . . . getting help. It'll be a long-term process, but they say the prognosis is good."

At least something positive would result from this mess, Leah thought sadly.

"Where is Boyd?" Stacey asked.

Cauldwell's expression rumpled like wadded paper. "I . . . don't know. The cabin is empty. All his things are gone. He closed up the office, told his partner to find a new contract lawyer then just . . . disappeared."

"What?" Leah stood, unable to believe what she'd just heard. Then she moaned and covered her face with her hands. "This is all my fault."

"None of it's your fault," Cauldwell said firmly. "Not one damn bit of it." His jaw drooped. "Boyd won't ever forgive what I did to you. Can't say as I blame him."

The old man's shattered expression tore at Leah. "He just needs some time," she assured him.

"Maybe." His tone held little hope. "I came to apologize for all the grief I've caused. I thought I was doing right—protecting my boy. But I was wrong, Leah, dead wrong." Cauldwell sniffed, then blew his nose. Tucking the handkerchief back into his pocket, he met Leah's gaze. "Being sorry doesn't change the price of potatoes, but . . . I wanted you to know. That's all."

To Leah's surprise, she discovered that although she would never approve of the senator's actions, she was actually beginning to understand them. However misguided, the poor man had acted out of love for his son. Leah wondered how far she herself would go to defend Stacey.

Cauldwell, first hesitating, then ambled across the room and offered the ribboned box to Cybil. Startled, Cybil stared at the gift before accepting with a murmured thank-you.

The senator nodded, then turned to Leah. "Could I speak to you for a moment?" He gestured toward the hallway.

Leah hesitated, then shrugged and followed Cauldwell outside.

Nervously tugging his lapels, the senator stared at the polished hospital floor. "There's something you ought to know about that agreement between me and your daddy."

Leah tensed, waiting.

"Louis didn't do it just for the money." Cauldwell wiped at his forehead. "Fact is, I had to raise the stakes considerably before he'd, uh, cooperate."

Holding her breath, Leah steadied herself against the wall. "Exactly what are you trying to say?"

"The only way I could get Louis to send you away was to..." The senator's voice trailed off and he made a production of clearing his throat. "Was to tell him that I'd see you ruined if you stayed. I said I'd made sure the town treated you like a...tramp and your child would be an outcast." He couldn't meet Leah's stunned gaze. "Louis knew I could do it."

"You're telling me that my father tried to protect me?" Leah shook her head. Nothing made sense. "But...he took your money?"

Cauldwell shrugged. "Louis wasn't a fool."

Closing her eyes, Leah sagged against the wall. "Why did you tell me this?"

"I...just thought you ought to know. That's all."

Cauldwell's voice was strained, and in a moment, Leah heard shuffling footsteps fade into the distance. When she opened her eyes, the senator was gone.

She felt a sense of vindication and relief. Louis hadn't been a saint, but in his heart he'd done what he thought was best. Leah could live with that.

Returning to the room, Leah saw that Cybil hadn't unwrapped the senator's gift. She looked up at Leah and managed a wan smile.

Plucking at the loosely tied bow, Cybil lifted the lid, then peered into the box and frowned. "What in the world...?"

Curious, Leah looked over her mother's shoulder. The box contained jagged paper fragments. Gingerly picking through the pieces, Leah's eyes widened in recognition.

The senator's gift was the shredded remains of the original signed agreement and the outstanding loan papers.

The nightmare was finally over.

The August sun seared Sacramento's streets, beating down mercilessly until it seemed even the huge river splitting the city would evaporate into steam.

Dragging through the muggy heat, Leah climbed the steps to her condo and muttered a silent blessing for the air-conditioned comfort lurking beyond the front door. A blast of cool air greeted her.

"Mommy's home," Stacey chimed happily, scampering from her place in front of the television to receive her anticipated hug.

"Dinner's almost ready, dear." Cybil peered from the compact kitchen area. "Goodness, you look wilted. You just march upstairs and take a nice cold shower."

Leah chuckled at Cybil's stern, parental tone. Her mother had recovered nicely over the past month and now seemed to enjoy her role as family matriarch.

During their first weeks in Sacramento, Cybil and Stacey had both been listless and depressed. Leah had immersed herself in work, feeling both relief and regret for the mental diversion it provided her. For those few pressure-filled hours each day, Leah could divest herself of the aching loneliness that haunted her nights. Still, she felt guilty, because her mother and her child had no such respite.

Then last week, Leah had returned from work to find both Cybil and Stacey suddenly happy as larks, sporting ear-to-ear grins. Leah had been confused about their abrupt turnaround, but was too pleased by the change to question its cause. There had been other incidents of odd behavior, too. When Leah had caught the two of them whispering conspiratorially, they'd leaped apart like guilty adolescents.

Yes, something weird was going on. But whatever it was, Leah hoped it would continue.

"Leah?" Cybil tapped her foot impatiently.

"Umm? Oh... I'm sorry. I guess I was daydreaming." Leah refocused her attention. "Anyway, as pleased as I am to see you so chipper, we had a deal. No housework until the doctor gives you a clean bill of health."

Cybil flicked away Leah's concerns with a careless gesture. "I went to the clinic today. Doctor Evenheim says I'm fit as a fiddle."

"Why didn't you tell me you had an appointment? I would have driven you—"

"I got a ride from... a friend."

"A friend? Ah, you mean Mrs. Gothard from the next building?"

Leah noticed that Cybil and Stacey exchanged a meaningful look, then her mother sniffed the air and mumbled, "The rolls are ready."

Stacey giggled.

Leah frowned. "What's going on around here?"

"I haven't got time to stand around chatting. Stacey, will you please set the table?"

"Okay." Immediately, the child dashed to the china hutch and began pulling out plates—humming, no less.

How strange. For some reason, table setting was a task Stacey had always abhorred. The same child who would whine for half an hour about a three-minute chore was now performing that chore cheerfully, and without the threat of dire consequences.

"Upstairs with you," Cybil told Leah impatiently, shooing her away with hand motions. "And change into that pretty pink sundress. It'll make you feel ever so much fresher."

"After ten hours in a business suit and panty hose, I'd prefer a pair of shorts and my rattiest T-shirt."

"Nonsense!" Cybil made a soft, clucking sound with her tongue and indicated that the subject was closed by retreating into the kitchen.

Blinking in confusion, Leah looked at her daughter. "What was that all about?"

"I don't know." Stacey attempted to shrug innocently, but was suddenly beset with childish laughter. Finally she blurted, "I got to help Grandma," and shot into the kitchen.

Sighing, Leah trudged upstairs and peeled off her sticky clothing. Stepping into the shower, she twisted the knob to "cold" and gasped as the icy water blasted her skin like chilled needles. After Leah caught her breath, she scoured herself from head to toe, using nearly a half-bottle of shampoo to lather her long, thick hair.

Finally, Leah felt refreshed and clean. Ignoring the towels, she allowed her body to drip-dry as she twisted her wet hair into a knot. When she opened the bathroom door, Leah saw that her pink sundress had been neatly laid across her bed.

Obviously, the handiwork of a two-legged elf.

Chewing her lip, Leah stared at the garment. The light-weight cotton fabric and spaghetti straps were summery enough. The garment, however, with its fitted waist and snug bodice wasn't nearly as appealing as a comfortable, cavernous T-shirt and baggy shorts.

Still, it was painfully apparent that Stacey and Cybil had some kind of surprise planned for the evening. The realization was a bit disappointing. Last week, Cybil had shocked Leah by dragging her off to Mrs. Gothard's plastic-ware party. Her mother, it seemed, had decided that Leah needed to get out more and since Leah had always had an excuse not to go, Cybil had turned to more devious methods.

Tonight, Cybil had probably reciprocated by inviting the same group over for another thingamajig bash. Swell and double swell. Just what Leah needed.

Still, she didn't want to embarrass Cybil. Her mother's heart was in the right place, and whatever horrors had been planned for tonight, it was probably too late to cancel them.

Sighing, Leah reached for the dress.

By the time she was clothed and had brushed her hair from soppy wet to merely damp, Cybil had filled the dining-room table with steak and salad, rolls and corn on the cob.

Leah was impressed. She was also suddenly ravenous.

"Eat up, dear," Cybil urged Leah, then smiled at Stacey, who was attacking an ear of corn with enough enthusiasm to have smeared butter from cheek to pudgy cheek.

Leah didn't need a second invitation. "Oh, the steak is perfect. It just melts. Umm."

Cybil beamed, then cleared her throat. "Simon telephoned this afternoon."

"Oh?" Glancing over a forkful of salad, Leah asked, "Are there any problems at the store?"

"No. In fact, everything's going quite well." Cybil toyed with her meal. "Simon told me that the architect Fletcher hired has completed the plans. They're preparing to lay the foundation next week."

Something in the tone of Cybil's voice raised caution lights in Leah's brain. Slowly, she laid down her fork and waited.

Nervously shredding a roll into thick crumbs, Cybil avoided Leah's eyes. "Simon thinks I should review the plans before they start construction."

Leah watched Cybil shift uncomfortably. "All right," she said finally. "I'll drive you up on Saturday—"

"That won't be necessary, dear. Simon will be coming down this weekend, and I can go up with him."

"Oh." Leah refolded her napkin, gathering her thoughts. "When will you be back?"

Cybil's lips pursed as she stared into her plate. "Fletcher has offered me the use of the cabin until the house is finished."

Leah felt ill. Pushing her plate away, she twisted the napkin and fought the emotional rush. The cabin. Boyd's cabin.

That meant that Boyd still hadn't returned to Cedar Cove. He really was gone . . . lost to Leah forever.

And now her mother would leave, too. Subconsciously, Leah had known that Cybil would return to the mountains. It was her home, and as much as her mother loved her and Stacey, Leah also knew that she would never be truly happy in Sacramento.

Looking across the table, Cybil seemed to read Leah's thoughts. "I'll be back often," she said. "Simon has said that he'll drive me into the city every weekend if I want, and Fletcher has even offered me carte blanche to use his private plane."

"The senator has become a regular philanthropist," Leah remarked harshly, then winced at Cybil's disapproving expression. "I'm sorry. I know that he's gone out of his way to help and that he's been good to you."

"Yes, he has. And the poor man has certainly had enough problems of his own. You should be more charitable, Leah."

Nodding, Leah felt embarrassed and properly chastised. Fletcher Cauldwell had been through his own private hell these past weeks. Although the senator had issued a press release in which Craig's withdrawal from the election "for personal reasons" had been cited, speculation and rumors had run rampant.

Cauldwell's enemies had enjoyed a field day. There had been a glut of tabloid pieces, various shades of yellow journalism in which charges from nepotism to influence peddling had been bandied about. Unfortunately, many of the accusations had been true. The senator's political career was in serious trouble.

Fletcher Cauldwell had lost everything that had value to him—his reputation, his power and both of his sons.

Yes, Leah should be more charitable, but she had this immense hole in her heart. It was easier to blame the senator for losing Boyd than it was to face the fact that it had been Leah herself who had driven him away.

Leah never should have told Boyd about Craig. And none of this would have happened if—

Cybil's voice interrupted Leah's thought. "Gracious, look at the time."

Blinking, Leah looked up to see Stacey rapidly scooping plates from the table, then piling them on the kitchen counter. "What—?"

"Are you ready to go, Stacey?" Cybil asked, stacking the final plate in the dishwasher and ignoring Leah completely.

The child nodded happily.

Leah was totally lost. "What's going on?"

"Umm? Mrs. Gothard's niece is visiting so we decided to take the girls to the movies."

Ah. Now Leah understood the sundress's hidden meaning. She smiled. "That sounds like fun. I'll just get my purse—"

Two horrified voices simultaneously chimed "No!"

"Excuse me?"

Cybil recovered first. "We, uh, thought you'd enjoy a nice quiet evening at home, dear."

"Yeah," Stacey agreed. "Quiet."

The doorbell rang and Cybil looked massively relieved as she ducked back into the kitchen. Stacey let out a whoop of delight and screamed, "I'll get it."

This was too much.

"Tell Mrs. Gothard to come in," Leah called out, then strode into the kitchen, and hands on her hips, squared to face Cybil. "Now what's this all about, Mother?"

"I—I don't know what you mean, dear." Cybil started past Leah, who promptly sidestepped to block her escape.

Before Leah could respond, she was startled by Stacey's gleeful chortle and muffled cry that sounded like "Oh boy!" Cybil took advantage of the distraction and slipped out of the kitchen. In a moment, Leah heard another voice, softer and deeper—a masculine voice.

Every nerve ending in her body stood at attention.

Had Stacey said, "Oh, boy"—or "Oh, Boyd"?

It couldn't be!

Whirling, Leah stumbled to the kitchen door, then gasped and steadied herself against the wall. It was.

"Hello, Leah," Boyd greeted quietly, straightening from hugging Stacey.

The child stepped back, turned to Leah and grinned brightly. "Boyd's here."

"Yes," Leah whispered. "Yes, he is."

Their eyes met and held. The palpable silence spoke volumes.

At that moment, neither Boyd or Leah would have noticed a herd of elephants marching through the living room, so when Leah finally got control of her senses, she wasn't surprised to realize that Cybil and Stacey had disappeared.

"You...look lovely," Boyd said and promptly stuffed his hands into his pockets. He looked nervous, as though unsure of his welcome.

"T-thank you."

Leah, too, was unsure. The night of the fire, Leah had told Boyd that she never wanted to see him again. Not a day had gone by that Leah hadn't regretted those despicable lies.

She tried to tell Boyd that, but the words stuck in her throat. "I—I—I'm . . . glad to see you."

"Are you, Leah?" Boyd asked hopefully.

Struck dumb, she could only nod.

Encouraged, Boyd extracted his hands and took a tentative step toward Leah. "That's good," he said. "I was afraid..." His voice trailed away, as though he simply couldn't put his fear into words.

"So was I," Leah whispered. "Afraid I'd never see you again, never have the chance to tell you—" Biting off the words, her teeth scored her lower lip.

"Tell me what, Leah?" Boyd's voice was tense, pleading. "What did you want me to know?"

"The night of the fire..." She swallowed and tried again. "I—I didn't mean any of the things I said to you."

"Oh." Obviously disappointed, Boyd managed a stiff smile. "I understood what you were going through."

"I never wanted you to be hurt, Boyd. It's important to me that you know that." She took a ragged breath. "You'll never know how much I've regretted ... what I told you."

"About Craig?"

She nodded tensely.

"Don't regret it, honey. I don't."

"But you were so ... so devastated." Leah twisted her hands. "After you disappeared, I realized that I'd destroyed your life."

"What?" Boyd's eyes expanded. "Destroyed my life? Oh God, Leah, you *are* my life. I love you."

With two giant strides, Boyd reached Leah as she sagged under the shock of his words. As he embraced her, she melted against his chest, rubbing her cheek into his strength and murmuring a prayer of thanks. Boyd still loved her.

Clutching him desperately, Leah covered his neck and his face with warm kisses, alternately laughing and sobbing with happiness.

Finally, she looked up and saw Boyd's soft smile, his moist eyes. As he spoke, his lips quivered. "Does this mean you're happy to see me?"

Sniffing, Leah wiped her eyes. "Deliriously happy."

"You have no idea how much of a relief that is. Last week I told Cybil—" Boyd froze as Leah's head snapped up. "Oops."

"So that is what's been going on," Leah crowed. "I should have suspected you were behind the sudden mood swing."

Boyd shrugged sheepishly.

Well, things were certainly falling into place—Cybil's insistence that Leah wear her most flattering dress, the hushed conversations, Stacey's glow of excitement. She angled a glance upward. "How long have the three of you been planning to bushwhack me?"

"That's rather harsh." Boyd managed to look stung. "I'd prefer to regard our, uh, preparations as a surprise party."

"Oh?" She cocked an eyebrow. "And when are the guests expected?"

His smile was slow and sexy.

"That's what I thought." She tried for a stern expression but couldn't manage anything but a silly smirk. "Would I be correct to assume that Stacey and Mother have gone to a very long movie?"

"A double feature."

"Ah."

They stared at each other, grinning stupidly until Boyd couldn't stand it. Grabbing Leah's waist, he hoisted her into the air, laughing and spinning until she begged for mercy. Finally, they collapsed breathlessly onto the sofa.

When Boyd caught his breath, he pulled Leah across his lap and whispered, "God, how I've missed you."

"I've missed you, too." Twisting, Leah looked up solemnly. "I've been so worried about you, Boyd. Where have you been?"

His expression sobered. "I've been here in Sacramento."

"For how long?"

"Since the day after the fire. There were...arrangements to be made."

Leah instinctively knew those "arrangements" had centered on finding psychological help for Craig. She also knew how it must have hurt Boyd to have to make them. "That must have been difficult for you."

"It had to be done." Boyd's jaw tightened in determination, even as he eyes betrayed his pain.

"But your law practice— Why did you give it up?"

"It wasn't really what I wanted to do with my life." Boyd scratched at the knee of his slacks. "I have found a more suitable job, though."

"Oh?" Leah perked up. "Where? Doing what?"

With a shy grin, Boyd said, "You're talking to the newest member of the public defender's office."

Joy rushed through her. That was so perfect for Boyd—something he'd always wanted. Defending the weak, the unprotected was simply a part of Boyd's nature. Now it could be his career. Leah was touched to tears, but Boyd saw only the gathering moisture and was instantly alarmed.

"I know it's a cut in salary and prestige," he said quickly, "But there are opportunities to advance."

"None of that matters, as long as this is what you want."

"It's more than that. It's what I need." He took a shuddering breath. "I had a lot of things to sort out. It was as if I'd been groping in the dark for years, and when someone finally flipped on a light, I was temporarily blind." Pausing, Boyd agonized over each word. "My family had caused you such grief...and I'd done nothing to stop it. I felt guilt and shame and pain so deep I thought it would kill me. I thought you...hated me. And the worst part is that I didn't blame you."

"Oh, Boyd, I never hated—"

"Shh. I know that, honey. It's just not in your nature to hate, but I was so racked up inside. Then I realized that I really owned nothing in Cedar Cove, not even my own soul." He rubbed his eyes and sighed. "My life had been carefully orchestrated to conform with my father's wishes. I lived where he wanted me to live, I worked in a profession he chose for me... Hell, I even ended up with a law partner handpicked for me."

"You've never knuckled under to your father." Leah shook her head to emphasize disbelief. "He wanted you to go into politics, didn't he?"

"I've been on two county commissions and have ended up as campaign manager for all of the senator's political allies."

"Well...you moved out of the mansion. I'm sure the senator didn't like that."

"Two miles down the road to a cabin the senator owned isn't exactly rubbing his nose in my independence." Boyd sighed. "Face it, Leah. My father used different methods to manipulate me, but I was as much a puppet as Craig was."

Leah considered this. Fletcher Cauldwell *was* smooth. He had a reputation as a political chameleon who could sell snowshoes to an aborigine, then sweet-talk environmentalists into supporting offshore oil drilling. But Leah had always believed Boyd to be immune to his father's duplicitous maneuvers.

Boyd smiled sadly. "I guess realizing what he'd done to you was the galvanizing force. All these years, I'd ignored the kind of man my father was. Suddenly, I wasn't willing to do that anymore." His voice hardened. "Once he'd spewed his poison on you, there was no forgetting, no forgiving."

Leah's heart tightened at the finality in Boyd's voice. "He's your father, Boyd. You can't just ignore that."

"Watch me," Boyd said grimly.

"I know how difficult it is to accept . . . flaws in someone you love. But you can't withhold forgiveness. It'll tear you up inside." Leah felt the sting of tears. "Someday he'll be gone, just like my father is gone. Then it'll be too late and you'll regret it for the rest of your life."

Compassion softened Boyd's expression, and Leah saw that he realized that she was speaking from bitter experience. With a groan, he pulled her into his arms, stroking and comforting her.

"Promise me," Leah whispered. "Promise me that you'll think about what I've said."

"I promise." Boyd took a deep breath and his entire body tensed. "But one good promise deserves another, don't you think?"

Curious, Leah lifted her head from his chest. A tiny muscle in Boyd's jaw twitched fitfully and he suddenly seemed to be wound tightly enough to spring into orbit. "What kind of promise?"

He cleared his throat. "Oh—love, honor 'till death do us part'—the usual."

Leah licked her lips. "D-do you mean what I think you mean?"

"I think so—that is, if what you think what I mean is really what I mean—"

"Yes."

"Pardon me?"

"I said yes."

"Does that 'yes' mean what I think it means?"

Leah laughed and threw her arms around Boyd's neck, hugging him fiercely. "It means that I want to marry you, Boyd Cauldwell, and if that's not what you meant, then you're in big trouble, because Stacey and I will camp on your doorstep until you cave in."

Boyd's eyes glowed. "Then I guess I'd better save myself the embarrassment of a miniature picket line and agree to your outrageous demands."

"A wise decision."

Leah stood and grabbed Boyd's hand, dragging him to his feet. He blinked in confusion. "Where are we going?"

Leah smiled. "Didn't you say something about a *double* feature."

Boyd's lips twitched. "Hmm, I believe I did."

"They won't be back for hours," Leah murmured.

"How *will* we pass the time?" Boyd mused.

Leah pursed her lips, feigning concentration. "Scrabble?"

"Too cerebral."

"Monopoly?"

"Too materialistic."

"Aggravation?"

"Too aggravating."

She shrugged. "Well, I'm just totally out of ideas."

Boyd's eyes gleamed with mischief and he scooped Leah into his arms. "You may be out of ideas," he said huskily, "but I'm not."

Leah feigned shock. "What about waiting for marriage?"

"Marriage is a lifetime commitment, and my heart has been committed since the day I met you." Boyd's voice shook with emotion. "I love you, Leah. And I always will."

"Always means forever," Leah whispered.

"Forever isn't long enough," Boyd murmured. "But it's a beginning."

Epilogue

I know you'd rather be naked, but this is ridiculous."

As Leah struggled with the baby's squirming legs, a chortle of delight emanated from the pink crib across the nursery. Smiling, Leah called out to the bouncing occupant. "Hold onto your diaper, Celia. I'll be through with your brother in two minutes."

"Mother-r-r!"

"I'm in the twins' room, Stacey."

Appearing in the doorway with huge pink curlers dangling from her head, Stacey wore the wild-eyed expression of a seventh-grader preparing for her first coed dance.

"My hair is totally tweaked," Stacey wailed. "I might a well spend my life in a convent."

Finally gluing the diaper tab into position, Leah squeezed her son's round tummy and slanted a glance at Stacey. "Give me a minute and we'll see what we can do."

"But I only have *three hours*."

"My, that does create a crisis, doesn't it?" Stifling a smile, Leah handed the freshly powdered baby to Stacey

"Would you put Christopher into the playpen while I finish up?"

"But Mom—"

"Honey, I promise we'll turn you into a raving beauty in plenty of time for the dance."

Christopher eyed a colorful curler hanging over Stacey's ear. Then, shrieking as loudly as his six-month-old lungs would allow, the baby grabbed the fascinating object and tried to haul it into his mouth.

"Ouch! Let go, Crissy!" Stacey pried at the fat fingers. Cris chortled happily. Wisps of soft brown hair peeked from his pudgy fist and Stacey moaned, "Great! Now I'm bald."

Leah chuckled, then lifted Celia from her crib. "I think he left enough to work with, sweetheart."

But Stacey's annoyance had already dissipated. "Honestly, you're such a pill, Crissy." Eyes twinkling, Stacey put her lips to the baby's fat cheek and made a raspberry sound that tickled the child immensely. Christopher giggled and kicked, arching his little back as his sister attacked his round tummy with mock growls and teasing kisses.

Even after Stacey had taken the baby into the living room, the loving banter continued. Leah listened and smiled. Stacey adored the twins, and Leah was proud of her oldest daughter. She was a wonderful big sister and some day, she too would be a loving and wonderful mother.

As though reminding Leah of her own small presence, Celia whacked with stiff arms, fretting softly.

"There, there," Leah crooned, lifting the freshly diapered baby. "Mommy knows you don't like to be ignored."

Strange, how her children differed from each other. Even the twins were diametric opposites in temperament as well as appearance. Celia was quiet and intense—like Daddy. Christopher was outgoing and exuberant—also like Daddy. That, of course, was what made Daddy such a fascinating man.

And Leah was the luckiest woman in the world. The past three years had been a fulfillment of a miracle and not a day went by when she didn't fall on her knees in gratitude for her wonderful family.

The sound of the front door slamming caught Leah's attention. He was home.

"Daddy!" Stacey hollered from the living room and Leah heard the sound of running feet.

Carrying Celia, Leah hurried down the hall. As usual, she felt her heart leap at the sight of him. "Hello, darling," she said, gliding into Boyd's arm. "I've missed you."

Embracing both his wife and his baby daughter, Boyd murmured, "Nine hours is a long time between kisses." Then he remedied the situation, mating his lips with Leah's, holding the sweet moment until a sharp pain pierced his right ear.

Wincing, Boyd lifted his head and stared into Celia's serious little face. The baby was intently twisting Boyd's ear as though trying to unscrew it from his head.

When Boyd peeled her fingers away, the small face puckered. "Come here, squirt," he said, scooping her from Leah's arms. At that moment, Stacey reasserted her presence.

"Mother," she demanded impatiently. "What about my hair?"

"All right, darling." Leah's eyes twinkled.

Boyd glanced in Stacey's direction, then grinned. "There's nothing wrong with your hair that pulling those funny pink things out wouldn't cure."

Folding her arms, Stacey issued a long-suffering sigh. "Honestly, Daddy. You just don't have a clue about high fashion."

"High fashion? For a twelve-year-old?"

"Almost thirteen," Stacey corrected.

"And preparing for her first dance," Leah added significantly.

"Ah," Boyd said, as though that explained everything. Then he squinted at Stacey, capturing her chin between his thumb and forefinger. "What's that blue gook on your eyelids?"

"Eye shadow. All the girls wear it."

Boyd blinked, then frowned at Leah.

She shrugged, obviously amused. "It's a special occasion."

"I don't like it," he said sullenly. "It makes her look ... old."

"I'm growing up, Daddy. You'll just have to make the best of it." Cheerfully, Stacey hoisted herself on tiptoe and kissed Boyd's cheek, then dashed toward the hallway, calling over her shoulder to Leah, "Hurry, Mom!"

Leah looked up at Boyd, then burst into laughter.

"What's so funny?" Boyd shifted the squirming baby to the crook of his elbow and stared morosely at the empty hallway.

"You are," Leah replied. "The look on your face when you spotted that eyeshadow—I thought you were going to cry."

"I just don't think makeup is appropriate, that's all."

"Really?" Teasingly, Leah touched Boyd's nose. "Funny, that's what you said when I bought Stacey her first bra."

Embarrassed by the reminder, Boyd made a production of depositing Celia in the playpen. "That was an honest mistake."

"Insisting that the bumps on her chest were baby fat?" Leah was enjoying this immensely. "Admit it, my love. You can't handle the fact that your little girl is on her way to becoming a woman."

Boyd flinched. It was true. Stacey *was* becoming a lovely young lady, and the realization was frightening to Boyd. He and Stacey had become so close. Boyd loved her almost as desperately as he loved Leah. To think that in a few short years, his beloved daughter would be grown and gone.... Well, Leah was right. Boyd was having difficulty handling the thought.

Sighing, Boyd sat in his favorite recliner and stared at the Sacramento skyline, musing the way his life had changed. Cedar Cove seemed a million miles away. Oh, they still visited Cybil several times a year, but it wasn't home anymore. Perhaps it never really had been home—not for Leah, certainly; and not for Boyd.

A familiar squawking sound broke Boyd's reminiscence, then a loud fluttering. Boyd glanced up at one of several wrought-iron cages decorating the living room. Stacey's finches were exceptionally active this afternoon and their excitement had apparently roused the more sedate love-birds. Boyd smiled, proud of his daughter's continued interest in ornithology. Stacey was such a clever child, and exceptionally bright.

His daughter.

In Boyd's heart, Stacey had been his "real" daughter for years. The adoption had merely been a legal formality.

"Darling?" Leah's voice startled Boyd.

He glanced toward the hallway. "Has the hair crisis been resolved?"

"I think so." Leah slid into Boyd's lap, wrapping her arms around his neck. "You looked so pensive just now. What were you thinking about?"

"How lucky I am." Boyd stroked Leah's cheek lovingly. "I wish everyone in the world could be as happy as we are."

"Well, I know of two people who are going to give that a try." Leah smiled smugly. "Mother called today."

Grinning, Boyd looked into Leah's happy face. "It's about time. Have they set a date?"

"The third of April. Mother and Simon would like us to stand up for them. Is that all right with you?"

"It's absolutely great." Boyd hugged her tightly. "Marriage is a wonderful institution, and I, for one, can vouch for that."

"Umm." Leah's forehead furrowed and her mind seemed far away. "I . . . received another call this afternoon."

Stiffening, Boyd knew from Leah's tenuous tone who had made that call. "The senator."

For a moment, Leah chewed her lip, then said, "Craig has been released from the hospital for weekend visits."

"That's . . . fine. I'm glad he's doing so well."

"Craig wants to see you, Boyd, and the doctors believe he's up to that now."

Boyd averted his gaze, staring out the window. Through Leah's encouragement, Boyd and the senator had finally reestablished a relationship. It was a bit strained, but at least they were on speaking terms. Craig, however, was a different matter. The one time Boyd had visited his brother, Craig had gone to pieces, screaming that he'd never seen Boyd in his life.

Guilt, the psychiatrist had explained. Craig had actually erased all memory of even having a brother. Although both Boyd and Leah had done everything possible to help Bitsy and her children through this trying time, Boyd had never again tried to see Craig. The pain was too deep.

"Boyd?" Leah was watching him closely. "He's your brother, and he needs you."

Squeezing his eyelids together, Boyd took a ragged breath. Working things out with Craig would be the final hurdle, Boyd decided. Only then would the past be totally behind them. A voice Boyd recognized as his own said, "All right."

Leah exhaled slowly and she relaxed against Boyd's chest. "Have I mentioned lately what a very special man you are?"

Before Boyd could respond, Stacey swept through the room in a cloud of peach-colored chiffon. Her hair had been swept into a cascade of silky curls, and Boyd wasn't certain for a moment that this lovely creature could possibly belong to him.

She pirouetted twice, then struck a sophisticated pose. "Dah-h-lings," she purred, forcing a husky tone. "How do I look?" She batted her mascaraed lashes.

Boyd stared numbly.

"You look lovely, sweetheart," Leah said quickly, then stood and emphasized the point with a hug.

Stacey's familiar giggle was a definite contradiction to her new image. Opening her arms to display her party dress, she said, "Well, Daddy, do you like the new me?"

"I'm not sure." Boyd swallowed. "What happened to my sprout?"

Pressing her palms over her mouth, Stacey chuckled happily, then bounced into Boyd's lap. He groaned under the impact, then tickled her ribs until she squealed. "That's more like it," Boyd responded. "I'll let you grow up, but you've got to give me a little more time to get used to it. Okay?"

"Okay." Her expression turned serious and she threw her arms around Boyd's neck. "I love you so much, Daddy."

"I know, baby." Boyd's voice choked with emotion. "I love you, too."

Leah watched and felt the familiar lump in her throat. Life just didn't get any better than this.

*   *   *   *   *

Silhouette Special Edition

COMING NEXT MONTH

#565 MISS ROBINSON CRUSOE—Tracy Sinclair
Rescued from a deserted island off the coast of Africa, Bliss Goodwin reluctantly became Hollywood's most sought-after story. But only producer Hunter Lord would gain full rights to it...and Bliss, too!

#566 RENEGADE—Christine Flynn
In Aubrey, Oklahoma, everyone knew everyone, and everyone knew fast-living Cain Whitlow was no good. So what was a model citizen like sweet Ellie Bennett doing with this renegade?

#567 UNFINISHED BUSINESS—Carole Halston
Back together after a decade apart, Tess Davenport and Peter Roussell discovered that their brief, stormy marriage had left too many loose ends—including their unquenchable love.

#568 COME GENTLE THE DAWN—Lindsay McKenna
After her partner was killed in a suspicious explosion, Brie Williams suddenly found herself working side by side with undercover agent Linc Tanner, and the sparks really started to fly!

#569 TENDER TRAP—Lisa Jackson
Rancher Colton McLean thought Cassie Aldridge had tried to rope him into marriage with the oldest trick in the book. Could the disappearance of a prize McLean stallion be another one of Cassie's traps?

#570 DENIM AND DIAMONDS—Debbie Macomber
Letty Ellison had left her rustic Wyoming roots and lover Chase Brown for Hollywood's glitter. But now that her child's future was at stake, it was time to come home—where she'd left her heart.

AVAILABLE NOW: